·SUGARLAND·

ALSO BY PHILLIP FINCH

The Reckoning
In a Place Dark and Secret
Trespass

PHILLIP FINCH

SUGARLAND

St. Martin's Press New York

SUGARLAND. Copyright © 1991 by Phillip Finch. All rights reserved. Printed in the United States of America. No part of this book may be used or reproduced in any manner whatsoever without written permission except in the case of brief quotations embodied in critical articles or reviews. For information, address St. Martin's Press, 175 Fifth Avenue, New York, N.Y. 10010.

Editor: Jared Kieling
Copy-edited by Peter Weissman
Design by Judith Stagnitto

Library of Congress Cataloging-in-Publication Data

Finch, Phillip.
        Sugarland / Phillip Finch.
              p.   cm.
        ISBN 0-312-06474-8
        I. Title
    PS3556.I456S8   1991
    813'.54—dc20   91-21816
                                                    CIP

First Edition: October 1991

10 9 8 7 6 5 4 3 2 1

To Dahlia and Angela
True Filipinas

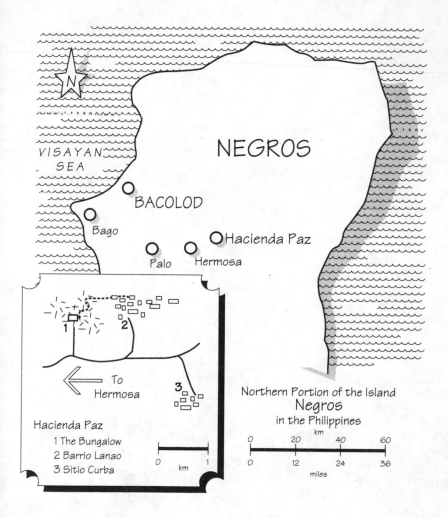

VISAYAN
SEA

NEGROS

○ BACOLOD

○ Bago

○ Hacienda Paz

○ Palo ○ Hermosa

1

2

← To
Hermosa

3

Hacienda Paz
1 The Bungalow
2 Barrio Lanao
3 Sitio Curba

0   km   1

Northern Portion of the Island
Negros
in the Philippines

km
0   20   40   60

0   12   24   36
miles

·1·

The first I saw Vangie was in a snapshot that her cousin held out for me. She sat on a low stone wall and smiled without showing teeth. Slim fingers pulled at the hem of her dress. Beside her a man perched on the wall with his arm around her shoulders, grinning loosely, his shirt unbuttoned halfway to the waist.

She was about twenty-five, the man maybe thirty. Her eyes were dark and wary, and they seemed to belong to someone much older. Those eyes, I knew she had secrets and they were not small.

"This is the last photograph of Lito, one week before he died," said Preciosa Sanchez. The plush vowels, rounded consonants of a Filipino accent.

"How do I know this is him?" I said.

"This is my brother, this is Lito."

"You tell me so. 'This is my brother, a week before he died.' But I don't really know it. I don't know any of it for sure."

"I wouldn't lie to you. Why would I do that, show you a picture of somebody else and tell you it was my dear brother?"

"You'd be surprised, what people will lie about."

"I'm swearing to you, I swear before God, this is my brother Lito."

"This was taken in the Philippines?"

"Yes. Our province. Negros Occidental."

She said it with Spanish pronunciation, made it sound elegant.

"How long was he planning to stay?"

"One month only."

"And he was there how long?"

"Two weeks and two days."

"Then he was killed."

"Yes, he was killed. Of course he was killed. He was burned to death in a hut. Why are you asking questions? You have a death certificate."

"Fifty thousand dollars is still a lot of money," I said.

"The policy is for twenty-five thousand."

"Accidental death, double indemnity."

"Oh. Yes. But why are you asking questions?"

"He takes out a term life policy for twenty-five thousand, a month and a half later you say he's died in a fire, you think nobody's going to ask questions? You must be dreaming."

"It was Lito's idea, the insurance."

"That's very possible."

"I was against it. I thought it was bad luck."

"Not so bad for you. Sole beneficiary, you stand to get fifty thousand. Unless the dead come back and want a piece of the action."

"Don't talk that way," she said, and she crossed herself quickly. She had a pretty face gone fleshy.

"I could use another photo," I said. "Something that shows his face a little better."

She didn't move.

"You don't have to give it to me," I said. "But the sooner this gets wrapped up, sooner you get the money."

"I don't care about the money," she said, but she got up and went to a writing desk, opened a drawer, and began thumbing through a stack of snapshots. I could see papers bound in bunches and crammed into shoe boxes.

Calls herself Precy, the apartment manager had told me. Works at Magnin's on Union Square, takes the bus to work. Divorced. Two kids, six and eight.

"What's this place?" I said. In the snapshot: a long, low building with a facade of broken stucco.

She looked over her shoulder and said, "That is a schoolhouse."

"Who's the woman with him?"

"Our cousin in the barrio. Vangie." *Vahngie*, was how she said it. "She works in Bacolod, she's a teacher. A beautiful girl, huh?"

She turned back to the stack, riffled through for a few more seconds, and then gave a little yelp.

"I know the one," she said. "Wait a minute, huh?" She closed the drawer and went into a bedroom.

I walked over and opened the desk. The first slim bunch was Magnin paycheck stubs for Preciosa S. Allen. The next, her utility bills and rent receipts. I slipped the rubber band off a shoe box. Inside were charge slips and billing statements, at least eight different accounts. A dunning notice from Bank of America, for Carlito Sanchez at a P.O. box in Oakland, forwarded to this address. An overdue notice, Wells Fargo MasterCard, for Carlos Santillo at the POB. From Bank of California, for Carmelo Sandia, the POB. From Hibernia Bank for Carlos. From Bank of America for Carmelo. From B of A, from Wells Fargo, from Bank of California, for Carlos.

When she came in I had the desk closed. She looked at me standing in front of it.

"Here," she said, "you see."

It was an expired passport, *Republika Pilipinas*. The name said Carlito Cabahug Sanchez, with a birthdate in May 1959. The face belonged to the man on the stone wall.

"You see," she said again.

She watched it into the pocket of my blazer.

"Why do you want pictures?"

"If you have to find a man, it helps to know what he looks like."

"Lito is easy to find. He's in the grave. I have his death certificate. Didn't you see it?"

"There was a copy in the file. Who's Carlos Santillo?"

"I don't know," she said quietly. She didn't seem startled to hear the name, just sad.

"How about Carmelo Sandia?"

"I don't know." Even more quietly.

"You have good-looking children." A framed portrait stood on the desktop, two boys in parochial-school uniforms.

"Thank you. American and Filipino, it's a good mix. Everybody says so."

"That's how you got over here, you married an American?"

"I loved him," she said, and I believed her.

"You could lose your kids," I said. "Insurance fraud is serious. You go to jail, you'll lose those kids. Even for fifty thousand, it wouldn't be worth it. But he won't let you keep the fifty anyway. Maybe he promised you twenty." She looked down. "He promised you at least twenty, didn't he? Come on—he's not even giving you twenty thousand?"

She was silent, staring at the carpet.

"This wasn't your idea," I said. "I can tell. You're no thief. You don't lie worth a damn." She kept looking down. "He's using you. I think he's been using you for a long time. How long have you been taking heat for him, helping him out when he screws up? Since you were kids, I bet."

"Go away," she said.

"You're going to ruin your life for him."

"You think you know so much," she said, "you don't know anything."

"I know he's alive, and I know you're going to jail if you don't change your mind."

• 4 •

"It's too bad," she said. "You don't look like a son of a bitch."

"I'm not," I said. "But I hate to be lied to. Honest to God, I do."

I parked in the slot with J. HART stenciled on it and rode the elevator up to the thirtieth floor. At my desk I made a few calls, and after a few more came back, I was ready to bring the file across the room to the District Manager of Investigations.

His name was Gilsa. He had hired me two months before. When I went in, the case was up on his screen and he was peering at it through rimless half-lenses. Pat Collins was there, too. Collins had been to the Philippines on cases like this.

"Sanchez came over in 'eighty-one on a tourist visa," I said, "married an American woman in her fifties, got his green card, left her three weeks later. The guy's been a hard-core pain in the ass from the start. He's nicked us at least twice before. For ten thousand under the name of Carlos Santillo, that was back in 'eighty-four, and for twenty last year, when he called himself Carmelo Sandia."

"Who were his beneficiaries, those two?"

"They named Carlito Sanchez."

"I love it," Collins said. "Eliminate the middleman."

"What kind of agent writes these policies?" Gilsa said. "A creep like this asks for coverage, the bells and red lights ought to go off."

"All three by direct mail," I said. "He got the right credit cards, he showed up on mailing lists."

"Jesus in a jumpsuit. No wonder we take it up the butt."

"We aren't the only ones. He loaded up on bank cards in all three names and topped 'em out. Amex is real anxious to have a word with him, too."

"How anxious?" Gilsa said.

"About seventy-five hundred worth."

Collins clicked his tongue and Gilsa gave a little sneer that said, This is what happens in a world where life insurance is sold like tulip bulbs and any little brown man can finagle a Gold Card.

"Did I mention the Turbo LeBaron?" I said. "They had a rebate offer, remember? Two thousand back on selected models. Lito selected one for himself a few months ago, he used a thousand for the down payment and put a thousand in the bank. Chrysler Credit never heard from him again. Probably sold it to a chop artist."

"Or put it on a boat for Manila," Collins said. "It'd go for big money over there, and nobody asks for a title."

"They like Detroit iron?"

"Eat it up like ice cream. That's one place where Made in the U.S.A. still carries weight."

"They'll learn," I said.

Gilsa had the paper file open now, studying the death certificate. Elaborate engraving, seal stamped on gold foil, it looked like a relic of a distant age. Behind him San Francisco Bay yawned from Sausalito to the Coliseum.

"A fair piece of work," he said, and he passed the certificate over to Collins, who gave it a long glance and said, "I've seen worse, I've seen better."

In the business it's called a Nigerian Death Kit, though that's not really fair. Lagos, Nigeria, is just one place in the world where you can buy good forged evidence of your own demise. Manila is another.

This is the scam. You're a Third World immigrant to the U.S.; you take out a life policy with an American insurance company. Sometime later you go home for a visit, buy a Death Kit, and send it to your stateside beneficiary, who uses it as the basis for a claim. If you keep it small, and if you're patient enough to season the policy for a few years before you try it, probably nobody will notice. Even if a computer does kick out the case for investigation, you and the truth are ensconced in the heart of darkness, in a land where fax machines fear to tread; way, way, beyond the pale.

"Could he be back here?" Gilsa said.

"I doubt it. Last time he used his green card to enter the country was over a year ago."

"How do you know that?" Gilsa looked at me over his glasses.

"They log it in, you know, every time a green-card holder comes through a port of entry. I got his number from one of the banks—he used it for I.D. when he opened his first checking account, back in 'eighty-three. INS ran the Soundex on it."

"That's pretty good, Jack," Collins said. "You have friends at Immigration, do you a favor like that?"

"It only takes one."

"So he's over there someplace," Gilsa said.

"Probably in his home province."

"Sitting in the sun, drinking piñas."

"Oh, the ladies over there," Collins said, "if he has any jizz in him at all, he's not just sitting and drinking."

"Can we get to the sister?" Gilsa said.

"I'd say she's a reluctant accomplice, but I don't think she'll roll over. Family loyalty."

"Spare me."

"I don't say we stop trying. But I doubt that she'll turn, that's my best guess."

"Tits like mangoes," Collins said. "Like ripe mangoes, only not too ripe. If you're a honeydew man you're out of luck, but you can go crazy with the mangoes they got over there. All it takes is money. I don't mean a whole lot, either."

I heard him and thought of the young woman on the stone wall, how she had tugged at her skirt to keep her knees from showing.

"You know this place, Pat, the province, what's-it-called?" Gilsa said.

Collins looked at the certificate.

"Negros Occidental," he said. He didn't say it the way Precy had. "It's an island, Negros, the island has two or three provinces."

"In the central part of the archipelago, about the size of Connecticut, population three million," I said. I had looked it up. "Two provinces, Occidental and Oriental."

"Right," Collins said. "They grow sugar, they have guerrillas in the hills, they have sugar planters with big haciendas, their own private armies, fucking warlords."

"Ever been there?" Gilsa said to him.

"The provincial capital, Bacolod, I may have changed planes there once. I'll be honest with you, over there, I spent most of my time in Manila. It's the only place in the whole country where anything works, and that's only part of the time."

"Sanchez grew up in a barrio," I said. To search for someone, start with family and friends. "Same as the place of death."

"A barrio," Collins said, "you're probably talking about a few dozen huts sitting at the edge of the jungle. Some dump where the bus goes once a month if the road isn't washed out."

"Wonderful," Gilsa said.

The insurer has the burden of proof: this is your ultimate advantage. Most states allow a period of investigation, time for the company to bluster at the beneficiary, but in the end we have prove that you're not dead, and as long as you stay home, we have to prove it on your territory.

"Do we have anybody over there?" I said.

"We have a local on retainer," Gilsa said.

"He works cheap," Collins said, "and you get exactly what you pay for."

Gilsa looked at Collins and said, "I can't be sure, I ought to clear it, but I'd pack my bags if I were you."

Collins held up cupped hands and said, "Mangoes!"

"You can probably use this," I said. I put the passport in front of him.

He took it and opened it and said, "Jack, very nice. Very nice indeed. You're a splendid addition to the firm."

"Something else you ought to know. An item on the bank cards, about a week before he left, sixteen hundred dollars at a gun shop in Reno. I asked myself, what can you buy at a gun shop in Reno that you can't get here?"

After a second Gilsa said: "Assault rifles. We've got a law, Nevada doesn't."

"It came to mind."

"That would make sense," Collins said. "Any gun worth a damn is illegal in the Philippines, and everybody wants one. You can triple your money if it's the right stuff, Ingrams, Sterlings, Uzis. Hide 'em in the Chrysler, the panels. Yeah, get a couple of those goodies into the country, you could do all right."

"I just thought you ought to know," I said. "If he's into that kind of hardware."

" 'Preciate it," he said. "I'll manage."

It was a Friday afternoon, about quarter to four. Gilsa looked at his watch and said that he'd buy us a beer.

"A winner," Collins said, and he left to clear his desk. Gilsa asked me to stay a minute.

"You did a nice job," he said when we were alone. "I mean it. A real first-class effort."

"Things fell into place. It happens, sometimes."

"I want you to push her." Precy. "If she drops the claim, we can save the trip. Otherwise, Collins has to go. It gets expensive."

"I'll try her tomorrow."

"Collins," he said, "Collins has the experience. He's been there before. That's why he's going."

"I know that."

"I don't want you upset if he takes the case."

"I'm not going to get too attached," I said, "one day on a case."

"Well, it was one first-class day."

We went down together, the three of us, to a bar that hunched in the shadows of glass-and-steel towers. Inside it was dim and almost empty. Gilsa bought a round, then I did, and the place began to fill up around us. When we got into our third schooners, Gilsa and Collins started talking about Death Kits, and Gilsa said the best he'd seen was for a Botswanan who was supposed to have died in an explosion at a fireworks factory. The beneficiary, his American fiancée, submitted evidence that included a death certificate, coroner's report and police report, eyewitness affidavits, newspaper clippings, an obituary, billings from the mortuary and the cemetery, and photos of the remains, which supposedly had been recovered from the embers.

"They may have been," Gilsa said, "but they didn't belong to the insured."

"You found him," I said.

"We didn't have to. See, it was a real explosion, and those were real newspaper clips, and one of 'em mentioned that it was an illegal factory, unlicensed. That was all we needed to disallow the claim."

"Just that?"

" '. . . if death occurs while navigating an aerial craft, or while engaged in any illegal or illicit activity, or as a result of war or an act of war,' " Collins said. "It's in the standard accident policy, you can look it up."

"But he got away," I said.

"Not for long," Gilsa said. "A few months later, the fiancée runs into him at a gas-and-go in Compton. He hasn't bothered to tell her he's back. He also hasn't bothered to tell her he's gotten married. She calls us. 'I have reason to believe that Kwangi is not actually deceased, and I wish to inquire as to whether you gentlemen desire any assistance in putting his ass in jail.' "

We laughed hard, we swapped a few more war stories, and we left together, feeling high and strong and smart. I was finishing two months with the company, but I had eighteen years on the SFPD before that. Collins had been with the company for twenty-three years, adjustment and investigation. Gilsa was pulling a twenty-year detectives' pension from the City of Los Angeles and had twenty more with the company. I remember the way we walked out onto the street that evening, secure in all we had seen and learned; believing that there was no lie we had not heard, no hunger or malice or misery or outrage we had not witnessed; slyly swaggering; certain that we were beyond surprise.

I had a date at seven, enough time to buy a bottle of wine and drive up Russian Hill. Carole was her name. She did in-house training for a brokerage company. First time I met her, two months before, she had told me that she was on final approach for a vice-presidency. She had already bought a condo flat with a view of Coit Tower.

She poured my wine and took dinner out of deli boxes; dilled chicken, arugala salad, couscous. Spritzy jazz on the stereo. In the living room, on a second bottle of wine, she hooked one leg of her suede slacks over the arm of a chrome rocker, took the knot out of her hair and let it fall down the back of the chair.

"God what a week," she said, and she told Coit Tower all about it.

When she was finished, she slid the last of the wine down her throat. She got up.

"Give me about ten," she said. Minutes, she meant.

She went to the bedroom. I waited. The walls and ceilings were stark white, the floors ersatz oak parquet. The furnishings ran in the vein of Italian leather, dhurry rugs, butcher-block tables. I think two or three songs came and went on the stereo; that kind of music, it's hard to tell. I stood, started down the hall, went back and turned off the amp and took the wineglasses to the sink.

When I came into the bedroom she was at the bureau, her back turned to me, in high heels and a bustier. She was bent forward, as if studying the dust on the top of the dresser.

I walked up behind her and reached around to touch her stomach.

"Warm hands, cold heart," she said without moving.

I looked over her shoulder. She had opened her makeup case, she had removed the mirror and was raking out four lines of the white stuff on it.

"Now just hold on a second," she said. "Let's get a little zip-a-dee-doo-dah in us first."

She put her face down to the mirror, and one of the lines disappeared. She stepped aside to let me take the next.

"Yours," she said.

This was something new for us.

"Don't you know?" I said. "This is passé. Really. I think I read it in *Newsweek*. Nobody does it anymore."

"The truly fine things in life never go out of style," she said.

She waited.

"Oh come on," she said. "Don't tell me I've been balling Cotton Mather all this time."

She waited.

"You've never done this," she said. "Have you? I don't believe it. Forty-one years old, you're a virgin."

"I used to put people in jail for this."

"Shame on you."

She waited.

"Sweetie," she said, "you're not a cop anymore. You can relax."

I didn't have anything else to say, and I didn't know what else to do. I bent and took the line.

* * *

The fog was in, heavy, when I got home. I had half a duplex in the far western reaches of the city, a block from the ocean, where the fog is almost always heavy. It chokes the morning light and leaves a film of salt scum on windowpanes. The neighborhood is subdued, as a neighborhood will be when the sky hangs so low you can touch it. Cars mutter along the street, kids shuttle glumly in and out of school buses, the wind hisses as it shoves sand under the front door. I had lived in the duplex for more than ten years, since my divorce; why so long, I can't say, except that I rented it on a rare sunny afternoon and never hated it enough to leave.

I opened the door and threw on all the lights. Flipped through my mail and found nothing addressed by human hand. Pawed through drawers and closets until I came up with a pasteboard box, some bubble padding, a roll of sealing tape.

At lunch hour that day I'd bought an ornament, dried flowers within stained glass and crystal. It had seemed a proper gift for a twenty-year-old woman. I had a card, too, a cartoon cat. To a purrfect daughter.

I sat and opened it in front of me.

Dearest Markie, I wrote in the card, and stopped. It sounded childish. Martha was her name. I didn't know what she used these days.

Happy Birthday. How I wish I could be with you.

But you'll have to take my word for it, I thought.

You are forever in my heart—you know that.

Or do you?

Your loving father.

I closed the card and held the ornament up to the light. It was pretty and pointless, a shot-in-the-dark gift. I thought of her and saw a girl ten years old, baby-plump, credulous. That daughter, I knew how to please. It came to me that she was preserved in my mind probably far better than in her own; my memory of her had little competition, for I could count the days we had spent together since I left her mother.

Little Markie, I thought, and found myself saying it out loud. It chilled me some, to hear my own voice that way, almost as if a stranger had spoken into my ear.

The killer hours between midnight and dawn.

I put the ornament aside; no reason to remind her how little we knew each other. I wrote a check for two hundred fifty, slipped it into the card, sealed it, put a stamp on the envelope, addressed it. Her mother's home, Boston.

Her birthday was Wednesday. The card would be on time if it went in the morning. I took it outside and waded slowly through the fog, and put it in the mailbox on the corner.

When I got back I bolted the door and turned out the lights behind me on the way to the bedroom. The last one was the lamp at my bed. I left it on as I slid between the sheets. I had hung my blazer on a chair beside the nightstand; now I reached into a pocket and found the snapshot and held it.

I looked at it a long time, taking in details.

The school looked hot and weary. A palm tree's ragged shadow slashed through the words PAARALANG ELEMENTARIA, several letters of which were missing but still visible in outline. A cracked sidewalk at the foot of the wall. A dusty playground behind it.

Vangie. Her dress was a blue print, no style or vintage that I could name. Plain, loose, unrevealing. Even if she hadn't pulled it, the hem would have covered her knees. Her calves were lean and long. Her shoes were low pumps, and they were clean. There was grace in the set of her head, in the cant of her shoulders and legs, but she was not at ease.

Her smile was unconvincing. She didn't like the camera. Or maybe it was the company. Lito's shirt clung, his black slacks were tight almost to obscenity. Gold glinted around his neck. He grinned with glee. Her own smile was somber.

She wore no jewelry. Thin makeup, or none at all. Long lashes, elevated cheeks, a delicate chin. The kind of face that must inspire those Mexican songs about love and passion and blood. *A beautiful girl, huh?* But those eyes, disturbing, disturbed, as if some dark memory had roosted within her at the instant of the shutter's click.

· 2 ·

Precy Sanchez closed the door when she saw it was me. She wouldn't open it again. When she heard my voice on the phone, she hung up and didn't answer it anymore.

Collins was supposed to leave on Wednesday. Early Monday morning I parked across the street from her apartment, but she must have gone out the back when she left for work. The switchboard at Magnin's put me through—she worked in accounting, they said—but when I spoke to her, the line went dead, and when I tried again they wouldn't connect me.

At four-thirty I went down to Union Square, stood outside Magnin's and watched the front door. The sidewalk got busy. I lost sight of the door more than once, and when I spotted her she was already standing in line at a bus stop.

The bus chuffed in as I worked my way across the grain of the crowd.

"Precy," I said. I touched her elbow.

"Go away," she said. She yanked her arm free and turned away from me.

"We are going all the way on this one," I said to the back of her head. "No free pass this time. We're going to pull him down, and when he falls, you fall too."

"Leave me alone."

"I didn't have to tell you this, but I think you're a nice lady, and I'd hate to see you suffer for something that isn't your idea."

Everybody but Precy was watching me. She stepped onto the bus, clutching her purse to her stomach, eyes straight ahead.

"Will you listen to me?" I said.

She took another step up and dropped some coins into the fare box.

"You're throwing your life away. Your children—you have no right."

She gave me one glance, harder and colder than any of the stares I was getting. Then she moved along, and some others pushed past me, and all I could see of her was straight black hair far down the aisle.

"How does it feel to get shot?" the psychotherapist said.

The question didn't irk me so much as the way he tossed it out, his carefully casual tone. As if he had earned the right to banter about my hurt.

His name was Ted. His wardrobe seemed to consist of wool flannel shirts and corduroys. On him, they were an affectation.

"I don't know to answer that," I said. "I mean, it would vary with the circumstances. An air-gun pellet in the glutes, a head shot with a deer rifle, there's a big difference. The only thing I can tell you is how *I* felt when *I* got shot."

"All right then," he said with a silly smirk. "Why don't we go with that?"

Only Gilsa and my lawyer knew how I was spending Tuesdays and Thursdays at eleven A.M.; I'd had to tell Gilsa, to get the time. My lawyer said I was entitled to disability, given the way I left the force, and he had sent me to the psychotherapist in the same spirit that he'd have sent me to a sympathetic orthopod if we were trying to establish whiplash.

He's on our side, my lawyer would remind me.

"You want to know. Okay. You hear guys say they got shot, all they felt was a little sting, then a couple of minutes later they looked down and saw blood. That didn't happen to me. I knew exactly what was happening. There were two bastards standing in a hallway, no more than ten feet in front of me. I saw one of them bring the gun up, but I couldn't move fast enough.

"I got this taste, awful, metallic. If you can imagine a mouthful of aluminum foil. I stood there, and I was watching. I was watching the gun and I was watching myself too, like I was curious to see what I would do. What I did was, I turned to the wall, like I'd give the bullet room to get by. All this happened a lot faster than I can tell it. I could see the pistol real well. I knew it was about a .38 caliber, and I remember wondering if he loaded .38 Specials or .357 magnum. It could have been either one."

"You noticed the caliber?"

"Absolutely. If somebody points a gun at you, that's the most important thing in the world right then, what he's got in his hand, what's under the hammer. This was a Colt Python, nickle-plated, four-inch barrel. You spend enough time around guns, you notice these things. The Python is chambered for the .357 magnum but it'll handle .38 Specials, too. So I saw it and I wondered, is it the magnum or the .38 Special?"

"Does it matter?"

"Yeah. Oh yeah, it matters. And after it hit me, I knew it couldn't be the .38. Only the magnum would hit that hard."

"Like what?"

"Like somebody smashed me in the ribs with a baseball bat. It knocked me down, I couldn't get up, I couldn't do anything. I heard the other one say, 'Oh shit man, oh shit,' and I thought it was pretty funny, because that's exactly what I was thinking. 'Oh shit, it was the magnum, oh shit.' "

"You weren't wearing a bulletproof vest?"

"Soft body armor—I was. And it had insert panels to handle the magnums, but only on the front and back. When I turned, the bullet caught me in the side, where there's a couple of inches between panels. I knew, the way I hurt, the burning, it must have gone right through the fabric.

"The one with the gun came over to me. I thought he might shoot me again. I couldn't move, I couldn't do a thing, I couldn't even breathe. Getting hit that way, it knocks your air out. So I was laying there, and he was standing over me, and I was wondering if he'd shoot me again. The floor smelled like the men's room in a bus station. I remember thinking that if he pulled that trigger, nobody was going to care. I mean really, nobody. That was the worst moment of my life, laying there in this cruddy hallway, trying to breathe the pisshole air, waiting for the next shot, knowing I was just alone, alone, alone."

"But he didn't kill you."

"He took my service revolver, and they both ran. I got my breath back, partway, but it still wasn't right. My chest hurt, it really hurt. I put my hand down there and I could feel the blood. I didn't want to look.

"Some people came out and said they'd called an ambulance. I thought it wouldn't be too long, I could hold on. Somebody put a pillow under my head. My chest burned like hell. I could hear the siren way off. More people came out. The way they were standing around me, staring down at me, one woman was crying, it was like I was in a coffin already. I didn't like that."

"You were still conscious."

"Uh-huh. I kept telling myself, 'You can't die as long as you stay awake.' But I was getting real weak. I felt my shirt, it was like somebody'd splashed me with a bucket. I wondered how much could be left inside. The siren sounded farther away. The people seemed small, and sort of vignetted, like I was looking at them through the wrong end of a telescope. I told myself, 'You lazy bastard, you're just letting it happen.' But there was nothing I could do. I thought, what a lousy way to go, in a hallway that smells like piss, with these assholes geeking me. Then it all fuzzed out."

"You believed you were dying."

"Oh, I knew. I knew. At that moment. I knew I was a dead man."

Gilsa brought me in after I got back from lunch. Precy had named a lawyer to represent her in all matters concerning the claim. She declined to meet investigators. She demanded full and immediate payment of benefits.

"We can't talk to her," Gilsa said. "But we can still keep track of her."

I went out. Down the hall, by the reception desk, I noticed Collins waiting at the elevator. He looked and saw me. He leered and made a motion with both hands, like turning shower knobs.

He mouthed the word: "Mangoes."

"You were good at your job," the psychotherapist said.

"I thought so. I *was*."

"You made detective after eight years."

"Seven and a cup of coffee."

"You liked the job. It gave you satisfaction."

"It wasn't just any job. I felt like I was making a little bit of difference."

"You were in the prime of your career. You had the knowledge and experience of a veteran, while still retaining a young man's energy. That's a magic time."

"It is pretty good when that happens," I said.

"And then you were shot."

"Life's a bitch."

"Is it a joke to you?" he said.

"That's right. It's a damn joke. Sure. Better than sitting around, wishing you could get back something that you'll never have again. I was doing all right, I got shot—it happens. I quit the job. It happens. I got myself another job. It happens. If you're waiting for me to feel sorry for myself, I've got news for you, you better find another dog to hunt with. Because I won't do it. I refuse."

I squared my shoulders and sat back in the chair.

"Anyway," I said, "I don't feel like I've stopped being a cop. Not in the important way."

"What is that?" he said.

"Who you are. Your outlook on life. Cops are highly moral people. Go ahead and smile, I don't mind, that's the usual reaction. But it's true. Cops have a highly developed sense of right and wrong. Almost like a priest. For priests and cops it's written down. The priest has Canon Law, the cop has criminal code. It's in the books. Cops do not go for any of this situational ethics bullshit. For a cop it's right or wrong."

"You feel this way about yourself?"

"Yes I do," I said. "I'm not saying all cops. I'm not saying you put on a badge, you immediately turn into something else. But real cops. Yes."

"You still feel you're a real cop?"

"Why not? This job, it's the same story. Some asshole does something wrong, he tries to hide it. You work and work to get at it because you know it's there somewhere, the truth. If he was smart, or lucky, you dig like hell and you don't get anywhere, and that's when it gets bad. You feel like he's laughing at you, the son of a bitch. It eats at you."

"You take this personally." He seemed amused.

I said, "Shit, is there any other way?"

* * *

The manager of Precy's apartment just shook his head. "There's nobody to keep an eye on. She left last night."

"Left," I said, "like gone for the night."

"Moved away. Somebody drove up with a U-Haul, seemed about twenty Filipinos jumped out, they carried everything into the truck. And I mean fast. They were finished inside of an hour."

"You sure they weren't burglars?"

"She knocked on the door, gave me the key."

"Her security deposit—don't tell me you cut her a check right there."

"No. The management company has to do that. She gave me an address to send it."

He read the address from a folded slip of paper that he took out of his shirt. It was her lawyer's office.

"But I don't think she's there," he said. "You want to find her, you better be ready to swim or fly. Because you aren't driving and you sure as hell ain't walking."

"Where?"

"I'm not saying for sure. But she was standing in the living room, writing out this address. The kids are with her and the older boy has got a pout on something fierce. I asked him why he was so upset, he said, 'Mama told me, they don't have MTV in the province.'"

"You haven't been as forthcoming as I would've liked," said Ted the psychotherapist. His voice dropped. "I know what you need. I know why you're here." He sounded wheedling and conspiratorial. "I want to help. But you must help me, too."

"It's hard to be enthusiastic about proving how screwed-up I am."

"Hardly. You have had a trauma. I'm trying to substantiate it."

"Any way you want to put it."

"After you recovered—I should say, after the wound healed—you returned to work. For how long?"

"About six weeks."

"Did it go well?"

"If it'd gone well I wouldn't be sitting here, would I?"

"Clearly there were residual effects from the shooting."

"I am not afraid," I said.

"No one has used that word."

"The word has been used, believe me."

"You left the force after eighteen years, only two years short of your pension. You took a job that is very similar to the one you left, but without the element of physical hazard. You don't carry a gun, and you aren't likely to be shot at."

"Once is enough. Do you have a problem with that?"

"I'd say you have nothing to prove."

"Exactly right. I don't want to end up looking like some damn punchboard."

"That sounds reasonable to me."

"I am not afraid. That is not the reason I don't want to be a cop anymore."

"I accept that."

"You say you do. But you don't. Not really."

A ponderous silence.

"I've been going over my notes," he said, as if to change the subject. "One thing struck me. The shooting. You didn't mention drawing your gun."

"I didn't draw it."

"You didn't have time?"

"Get real. If I had time to turn and face the wall—remember?—I had time to draw my gun."

"Why didn't you?"

"I don't know," I said. My voice was flat. I was trying hard to keep it that way. "Not a night goes by, I don't ask myself that question."

"And what do you think is the answer?"

"I couldn't say. I had my gun out of the holster plenty

of times in eighteen years. But never in a situation where I knew I'd have to use it. Then the one time it happened, I didn't do it. I didn't even try. It wouldn't be so bad if I knew why. If I had something to fight. But I have no answer. I have no idea how I'd act if the situation ever came up again."

The silence again. His corduroys made riffling noises as he crossed and uncrossed his legs.

I said, *"That's* why I don't want to be a cop anymore."

I spent a day and a half doing a background check on a new executive hire. When I closed the folio, I still had a couple of hours left in the afternoon. I called the gun shop in Reno. I was wondering what Lito Sanchez had bought with the credit card.

The store manager said he was too busy for me, so I phoned the bank that had issued the card, told them I was tracking one of their skips, and gave them a few minutes to nudge the shop. I was about to try the manager again when he called me. Whatever you need, he said.

He put me through to a clerk, who explained that the store used a computerized point-of-sale register system for inventory and accounting; the charge slip number would be keyed to a sales record that was stored somewhere on a data cartridge. It took the clerk some minutes to find the cart, maybe twenty seconds more to query the data base. I heard a keyboard clicking.

"All right," he said. "We're looking at two Detonics Combat Master Mark Fours, new in box, list price seven hundred fifty-five, we gave him a ten percent discount. That's a honey of a pistol, you know it? Beveled magazine well, polished feed ramp, and the Mark Four has the adjustable rear sights. It's a real sweetheart."

"A .45 auto?"

"You got it. I'm also showing a thousand rounds of .45 ammunition and six spare clips."

A semiautomatic pistol, available over the counter in California. I wondered why he had bought them in Reno.

"You want the other one?" he said.

"What do you mean?"

"It shows a second page. Separate transaction, same customer."

"Please."

The keys clicked a few more times. The next noise in the receiver was a soft grunt.

"Well," he said. "Are you ready for sixty units of Zavastas?"

"You lost me," I said.

"Yugoslavian AK-47's. AKM's, if you want to get technical. The Yugos make terrific AK's."

"I thought we stopped importing military rifles," I said.

"It's a little complicated."

"These are semiautomatic rifles," I said.

"These are automatic weapons. That's what the code says."

"We stopped importing those in 'eighty-six. And if he's buying automatic, there must've been a background check, a waiting period. He'd have had to pay two hundred bucks each, the transfer fee."

"It's a little complicated."

I said, "What does a Yugoslavian AK run?"

"We got six fifty apiece for these."

"Almost forty thousand dollars."

"Thirty-nine thousand. Ninety cases of ball ammunition, caliber seven-six-two by thirty-nine. That's Chinese manufacture, packed in stripper clips, retails at a hundred and five a thousand, a great deal, we've been moving every bit of that we can get in. And three hundred spare magazines."

"That has to run it up near fifty-five thousand."

"You're close."

"I know he didn't put that on plastic."

"Cash. That's what it says."

"Come on. A guy walking around with fifty-five thousand dollars in cash?"

"This is Reno. It happens."

"And I guess he just threw sixty assault rifles and a few tons of bullets into the back of his station wagon."

"The ammunition, we got shipping instructions, our warehouse to some place in Oakland." He gave me the address. The waterfront: docks. "The rifles, I told you, it's a little more complicated. The rifles were in the limbo side of a bonded warehouse in Long Beach. They never went through customs. They were never actually in the country. If you want to get technical."

"You just happen to have sixty AK's sitting on a dock."

"We do a lot of import wholesaling, direct sales to police departments, SWAT teams. He was just lucky that these hadn't passed customs. Otherwise the red tape would be a bitch."

"They went out of the country? You're sure?"

"No background check, no transfer tax, that's all he could do, ship 'em back out. But, see, that's where it worked out so good. If those guns had actually gotten into the country, he'd have had a hard time getting 'em out again. Export licenses, all the paperwork. But since they never cleared customs, all he had to do was put 'em on a boat."

"Convenient."

"The Lord works in mysterious ways."

"Does it say where they went?"

"Can't help you there. We don't keep track of other people's toys."

Gilsa was gone, but his secretary had a number for Collins in Bacolod. She placed the call for me. I went into Gilsa's office, picked up his phone, heard the snap of distant connections introduce a low hum and rattling ring.

"Green Fields Hotel," said a woman's voice, faint.

"I want Pat Collins," I said loudly. I had to say it again, louder.

"Mr. Collins, American," she said.

"That's right."

"Mr. Collins is not in, sir."

"He left already?"

"Oh, sir, Mr. Collins is not in during all of last night."

"What time is it there?"

"Here it is seven o'clock in the morning, sir."

I left a message for him to call me, gave my home number, shouting it over the hum.

Then I drove home. The fog was a solid bank pushing across the water, maybe a mile out. It hit as the sun fell. I lit a Presto log in the fireplace and waited for Collins to call, but he never did. More than once I thought of him halfway across the world, in a green hot place.

Gilsa's call woke me sometime that night.

"Sorry. I had to do it," he said. He didn't sound sleepy, but there was something in his voice. "Take a few seconds. Get yourself collected."

"I'm collected."

"Can you leave for the Philippines in about twelve hours?" he said. "I realize it's short notice. If you have obligations, just tell me. I'll understand."

"No. No obligations. But I don't have a passport."

"We can handle that."

I sat up and let it percolate for a couple of seconds.

"What about Collins?" I said.

He said, "Collins is dead."

· 3 ·

Before lunch he had a passport for me with a commercial visa for the Philippines. My flight left at three, and we chased the sun through the longest evening of my life. Sixteen hours later we were in Manila. It was night, ten P.M., mist on the Plexiglas. A stewardess came to my seat as the engines spun down. She told me I was being met at the gate.

The concourse was empty except for an American about my age. He was sallow, paunchy, unkempt. His polo shirt was rumpled, and several limp curls stuck wetly to his forehead. Later I would recognize the type, wilted denizens of bar and brothel. Someone would explain: Why bother looking sharp when any slob with dollars can satisfy any taste at any time—where's the incentive?

"I think you're looking for me," I said.

He shook my hand. Hugh Dalzell, he said, from the embassy. My mind was loggy, and I had to think about it before I realized that he meant ours.

"We've been in contact with your people," he said. "Just want to make sure you're well looked after. The thing's a damn shame."

"Any news?"

Killed in Bacolod, Gilsa had told me, shot through the head. It was all he knew.

"Why don't we wait? Somebody from the police'll be at the hotel tonight. We only know what they tell us. They'll bring us both up to speed."

We walked down the concourse. Instantly I began to sweat. They should turn on the air-conditioning, I said, and Dalzell said, It is on, just wait.

There were long lines at Immigration, but he went to an

office along the side and came out with a Filipino whose white uniform shirt had captain's insignia and the emblem of the customs police. The captain took my passport to one of the stations, stamped it without looking, brought it back and gave it to me, and asked if I had baggage. I told him, only what I was carrying—a bag and a briefcase—and he led us briskly out of Immigration, around a row of customs inspectors, into the foyer.

"Thank you, Manny," Dalzell said, and the captain waved us off like a mother sending her kids to school.

"I'm impressed," I said as we started to the front doors.

"That's easy. Spread around a little baksheesh, it does wonders. Twenty pesos is the minimum rate for somebody in uniform. A traffic cop gets twenty when he catches you running a stop sign. It goes up from there."

"Twenty pesos, he doesn't write you a ticket?"

"That's right."

"That's only a dollar."

"A little less. A buck still goes a long way here, if you know what to do with it."

We opened the doors and stepped outside, into a wall of heat and people. The air was heavy with a smell of ripe garbage and smog and fried fish. The people were cab drivers and hotel touts, vendors of cigarettes and jasmine garlands; motley hustlers, boys and men hardly larger than boys, scrambling and shouting, elbowing one another to carry my luggage, promising the cheapest fare, the cleanest room, the most beautiful women.

"Watch your wallet," Dalzell said, "don't let go of your stuff," and we had nearly pushed through before I noticed a rectangle of cardboard hoisted above the crowd on a pair of matchstick wrists. MISTER HART U.S.A., it said. I went over to it.

He stood on the fringes as he held the sign, patient, but with a drooping mouth beneath a pencil-line moustache: a Filipino in his sixties, scrawny, in a straw fedora and an old sharkskin suit that had wet crescents under the arms.

He didn't notice me. I had approached from his side, and he was turned toward the door, with a thicket of bodies in front of him. He stood once on his toes, trying to see above the crowd, and when he settled back on his heels a moment later, the ends of his mouth dropped deeper.

"Are you looking for Jack Hart?" I said.

"Yes! Absolutely!" he said, turning. "That is you?"

"That's me."

"I am Bembo Rojas," he said, sounding proud about it. I took his hand when he offered it. I could feel the bones under his skin. "Bembo Rojas. I am your resident operative in the Philippines."

"Right," I said. Works cheap, and you get what you pay for.

"I telephoned our office in San Francisco. They informed me that you were in route. How was your flight?"

"I'm here."

"Yes. Excellent. I must talk to you. The death of our colleague—we must talk. You have reservations at the Silahis, I believe. My car is nearby, a short distance only."

"I have a ride," I said, and he looked at Dalzell beside me.

"Ah. Then if you could spare me a few minutes tonight at your hotel."

"The police," Dalzell said to me.

"When is that?"

"Appointments don't mean much here, but I'd say not too late. It's embarrassing, an American businessman getting murdered, and they're working overtime to salvage a little face. I'd take advantage while you can. *Ningas cogon.*"

"Ah. You speak our language," Bembo said. The lift had gone out of his voice.

"What's that?" I asked Dalzell. "What you said?"

"*Ningas cogon,*" Bembo said. "A brushfire in the cogon grass."

"That's right," Dalzell said. "Hot as hell for about a

minute and a half, then it burns itself out. It's the national attitude. Big ideas, zero follow-through. That's why I say, get 'em while they're hot."

"A few minutes tonight," Bembo said, directly to me. So skinny, the sharkskin hung on him. The collar of his shirt was frayed. "A few minutes only, boss."

"It's all right with me," I said. "Come by the hotel."

"Very good," he said. "Excellent. And by the way, the long distance to San Francisco—I was forced to bill it to my personal telephone. An individual there refused to accept the charges."

"We'll talk about it."

"Actually, it is the telephone of my cousin. I sometimes use his. The toll was five hundred twenty-two pesos."

"We'll figure it out later," I said.

"Thank you. Excellent. Absolutely."

We left him where he stood. Dalzell's car was parked along the taxi ramp, a blue Dodge with diplomatic plates. He turned on the air-conditioning and turned into traffic that flowed sluggishly for a few blocks and clotted in a flaking district of shops and beer gardens and massage parlors. Pedestrians clogged the sidewalks and wended through traffic.

It might almost have been America. Newark, maybe. Parts of Cleveland, or Detroit, or Brooklyn: most big cities have thronged backwaters where money never seems to stretch for potholes and faded paint. A 7-Eleven on the corner, Stevie Wonder on a boom box, Coca-Cola signs above a café, a Marlboro placard on the side of a bus. One quick hit, I could believe I was home.

But only one, and only if it was very quick. The street-lights were sparse and too dim. Buildings leaned a few degrees out of plumb. There were few cars, many of those dented and scraped; traffic was mostly taxis, buses, motor tricycles, and dozens of a creation that Dalzell called a jeepney: like a stretch Jeep with a pair of facing bench seats in the back, most of the bodies bright unpainted steel, each decorated with combinations of pennants and reflectors, chrome ponies and gamecocks, and klaxon horns. They had names—

CHICKS BUSTER

VIRGIN BIRTH

BLUE THUNDER

TOTO BOGART FIVE SISTERS TWO BROTHERS

—on signboards above the front seat.

I didn't see one that wasn't completely crowded. Seven, eight heads, sometimes more, rose above any single seat. On the sidewalk, shoulders butted shoulders, arms brushed arms. That was the biggest difference, the physical closeness of the people. In the States we'll veer aside on the street, shrink in an elevator, anything for a buffer. But here individual space was reduced to the body's displacement, or less, and nobody seemed to mind.

We stuttered through the congestion for a few minutes and then swung out onto a wide boulevard, jumping to freeway speed. On our left, across a concrete divider, I could see wide water. Manila Bay, Dalzell said; I thought of my sixth-grade history book, a tintype of Admiral Dewey. Ahead of us a taxi bounced as a wheel slammed into a crater in the asphalt. Dalzell whipped over to the next lane, but there was a minor canyon in that one, too. We hit hard, and the Dodge slewed for a moment before it straightened itself out.

Ahead a light turned yellow. An unmuffled bellowing gathered up behind us and a Chevy Impala, a '62 or '63 with crumpled fenders, came rapping past on the right. The driver leaned forward, peering over the front panel, clenching the wheel and sawing it back and forth in wide arcs that didn't seem to affect the car. It boomed ahead us, wallowing, pitched across lanes and flew through the changing yellow, and was gone.

"If a traffic cop costs twenty pesos," I said to Dalzell when we were stopped, "how expensive is a captain of the customs police?"

I thought Sanchez must know somebody like that if he was smuggling rifles off a ship.

"Manny? Manny and I have an ongoing relationship. That gets a little more complicated, when you have favors going both ways."

"But everybody's got a price."

"With no exceptions." He sounded enthusiastic. "Filipinos are great at establishing the exact value of goods and services. They do it every day of their lives."

"What would it cost to bring in some guns?"

"Guns are touchy," he said. "Like what? What are we talking about, a couple of pistols? Some freelancers do that—Filipinos, I mean. You can just about cover your air fare to the States with a nice pistol. The customs inspector finds that, though, it's worth a hundred to him."

"A hundred pesos."

"*Dollars.* I told you, guns are touchy."

"Say about sixty assault rifles."

"No way," he said. He gave me a sidelong glance. "You trying to bring in some guns?"

"It was hypothetical."

He watched the light.

"That's some hypothesis." I didn't say anything, and he said, "So why do you ask?"

"Collins was over here trying to locate an individual. I don't know how much you were told."

"I knew that."

"I had an idea the individual might have brought in some guns."

The light changed, and we lurched out into the intersection.

"Assault rifles," he said. "And this guy is what, your average Filipino cheat-and-chisel artist?"

"Looks like it."

"You realize, you're talking *crates* of guns. *Cases* of ammunition. Have to bring that, too, 'cause ammo's just as hard to get. Crates and cases of stuff so hot, the money involved—forget money, it would transcend money—no way. And what would he do with it anyhow? Enough to equip two platoons of infantry. No way."

He looked over at me.

"No way," he said.

The Silahis was in a strip of high-rise hotels strung bayside, facing the water, just below downtown. They are slick, bright places, set in the belly of Manila like faceted quartz in dirty fieldstone. An attendant was at the curb. His white glove was on my door before the Dodge had stopped.

When we were out of the car, Dalzell pulled a wad of peso bills from his pocket, notes of red and blue, green and brown. He passed the attendant a blue one—blue, I would learn, is the color of twos—and flicked a finger at a Jeep in dark drab, parked in front of the Dodge.

"Whose is that?" he asked.

"Sir, that belongs to a colonel of the Philippines Constabulary, and a captain, I believe."

"That has to be them," Dalzell said to me. We climbed the steps. "The P.C. is the national police, but they're military—lots of juice. Hot to trot, what'd I tell you, they wheel out a P.C. colonel and a captain. You must be Queen for a Day. Now, I know you're feeling wiped. But you should talk to them before you check in. You cannot let these honchos sit around waiting for you. It isn't done."

The lobby was brass and marble and polished wood. To one side was a coffee shop, slightly elevated on a low balcony. The two officers were at a table by the rail, wearing khaki, sprawled in their chairs, holding cigarettes and tipping squat brown bottles of San Miguel beer; they were watching women walk by in the lobby, smirking, and we were at the table before they noticed us. Then they rose, not too quickly or too steadily.

Dela Cruz was the colonel's name. The captain was Agoncillo. Dela Cruz was spare and dark, and nearly six feet tall. Agoncillo was round-bellied, light-skinned, and short. But to me they were of a piece, the heedless way they sat and stood and spoke.

"A terrible tragedy," said Dela Cruz, and while he took my hand, he reached to pat me on the shoulder. It felt like a practiced move. We all sat. The captain raised a hand and snapped his fingers to bring a waitress.

How was your flight? Dela Cruz asked, and Agoncillo wanted to know if I had been to the Philippines before, and what were my impressions?

Everyone seems friendly, I said, and Dela Cruz said, Filipinos are world-famous for their hospitality.

"You visit these small towns in the provinces, you don't have to worry about your next meal," Dalzell said. "You'll have people come up asking you to dinner. They'll kill their last chicken so you have something decent to eat."

"That's true," the colonel said.

"Beautiful people, the people of the provinces," said Agoncillo.

A waitress took away the bottles and emptied the ashtray, brought a new round and clean glasses, a bowl of roasted peanuts and another of what looked like hot pork rinds.

"Delicious," Agoncillo said when he grabbed a handful of the rinds. "You should try it."

I felt tired, suddenly, ready to fade out any time. I watched Dela Cruz pick a speck of food from his front teeth, and in a corner of my mind tried to calculate the hours since I had slept.

"Maybe you could tell me what you know about the murder," I said.

"By the way," Agoncillo said. "My condolences."

"We weren't close. I just want to know what happened to him."

"His body was discovered yesterday morning," Dela Cruz said. "He had been dead several hours. We can't be exact." He flicked the speck off his finger. "One shot with a .45 automatic. The shell casing was recovered."

"Can I see the report?"

"Our information is secondhand from Bacolod," Agoncillo said. "This is only preliminary."

Two days and they had no report. I looked at Dalzell to see how he took this. He was watching the women in the lobby. There was almost a stream of them, young Filipinas going to the elevators with men, Americans and Japanese mostly; going up with men and coming down alone, walking quickly across the marble and out into the night.

"The report is due in Manila tomorrow morning," said Dela Cruz.

"Where was he found?"

"I understand it was a squatters' area on the fringe of the city," said Dela Cruz.

"Is that a bad neighborhood?"

"All squatter areas are bad," said Agoncillo.

"What about witnesses?"

"There are none, we understand," said Dela Cruz. "Since he was not found until several hours after he was killed, we can assume there are no witnesses to the actual crime."

"You mean nobody has rushed out and said they saw it."

"That is correct." Stiffly.

"It doesn't mean witnesses don't exist. They just haven't been found."

"True."

"What's a squatters' area—some kind of slum?"

"It is a place where people have erected unauthorized dwellings," Agoncillo said. "They pay no rent and their homes are ramshackle."

"Crowded, then," I said. They didn't disagree. "A .45 goes off near a crowded area, plenty of people must have heard it. You should be able to fix time of death, at least. But you'd have to canvass the area. People living in a squatters' camp—that kind of individual—they probably wouldn't jump to help the police, would they?"

The two officers didn't answer, and Dalzell, who now was paying attention, said quickly, "We'll have a lot more to go on when the report gets here."

"We are making every effort," Dela Cruz said. "Political cases have our highest priority."

"You think this is political?"

"Almost certainly."

This wasn't what I had expected to hear. All through the long flight I had been nursing the idea that the killer was Lito Sanchez: Lito who for years had lived outside the law, who lied and defrauded and trafficked in weapons, who would lose fifty thousand and see his sister jailed if Collins got too close.

"Political," I said, "I don't see how."

"Look at the circumstances," Agoncillo said.

"He's walking in a bad neighborhood late at night, somebody blows him away, that's political?"

"Over here it is," Dalzell said.

"Communists," the two officers said.

"Communists," said Dela Cruz again. "The NPA. New People's Army. They have guerrillas in the countryside, but they also have armed cadres in the cities. Assassination units, Sparrows. You know, because they're like birds." His right hand made darting movements in the air. "They fly, whoop, they hit, whoop, they are gone. Many of their hits they do from a motor sidecar. Their weapon is frequently a .45 auto."

"Unfortunately this exact crime is very common in our country," Agoncillo said. "Wherever the communists are established."

"Are they established in Negros?"

"Unfortunately yes."

"And they'd kill an insurance investigator?"

"An American," said Dela Cruz.

"The NPA hate Americans, of course," said Agoncillo.

He made this sound like fundamental truth, so complete that it left nothing else to say. Dalzell and the two officers began to play who-do-you-know in the military, ours and theirs.

After a while Dela Cruz and Agoncillo got up to leave. When do you expect the report, I wanted to know, and they said tomorrow morning. What time tomorrow morning? Perhaps nine, perhaps ten—but not to worry, they would send a copy to the hotel and another to the embassy.

"Rest, relax, enjoy our city," Dela Cruz said. He patted me on the shoulder again when he said good-bye.

"A word of advice," Dalzell said to me when they were on their way out. "A fella will get a lot farther in this country if he doesn't get pushy. Especially with P.C. officers. Directness is definitely not a virtue here."

"He's been dead two days, nobody knows anything."

"You're in a tropical climate now."

"Do you believe the communists killed him?"

"The Sparrows are homicidal little fuckers. Whacked-out kids, glue-sniffers—it isn't hard to imagine."

"He was an insurance investigator."

"They wouldn't care what he was."

"I still don't see a motive."

"Listen, the communists'd love to drag us into a dirty little war here," he said with sudden force. "Turn us into the bad guys, get every peasant in the boondocks whittling punji sticks—oh, believe me, they'd love it. That's the day we lose this country." He was loud enough, people were beginning to notice. He reined himself in. "See, when we put troops in somebody's backyard, even when we're trying to do him a favor, we can kiss his heart and mind good-bye. It only took us about fifteen years to learn that one, but we've finally got it down."

He sat back and hitched his pants.

"We're in the neighborhood, y'know," he said. He jerked his thumb toward the front door. "The Nam is only about six hundred miles on the other side of the South China Sea. Philippine Airlines flies once a week to Ho Chi Minh City."

"But why kill an insurance investigator?"

"An *American*. Provocation. It makes sense."

"I guess that was Collins's bad luck. To be the one they start with."

"You sure it hasn't happened before?" He sounded confidential. "People get shot here all the time. Even Americans. No passport can stop a bullet. But how it's perceived—it's all in the spin, my friend."

I felt tired, and a long way from where I had last slept. Cigarette smoke was more bitter here. Assassins rode motor tricycles. Money came in crayon colors, the Spanish fleet lay rotting across the road, and the place they used to call Saigon was an hour's jet ride distant.

I reached for the check, but Dalzell got it first.

"We'll let everybody's favorite uncle handle this one," he said. "I'll call you tomorrow."

"Not too early. The way I feel, I may sleep past lunch."

"You think so. Most of the time, though, first night in from the States, a fella will wake up around three in the morning like he's been zinged with a cattle prod. And that's it—rest of the night, his eyes are wired open."

"I'll take a hot bath. It usually helps."

"Personally, I recommend some deep muscle therapy with one or two of the local practitioners."

He was watching the women again.

"Till you know your way around, your best bet is the clubs up in Ermita, Del Pilar Street. You walk in, have a look, tell the mama-san which one you want, pay her bar fine, that's it. Half an hour, you're back here with Suzie

Wong and she's all yours till breakfast. Beats the hell out of trying to find a Nembutal at this hour."

He offered me a ride up Del Pilar, but I told him I needed a shower and a shave.

"Okay. Ermita. Any taxi driver knows it. Hell, it's like a shuttle service, back and forth. Ten pesos—don't let 'em charge you more. And watch out for the Aussie joints. They can get rowdy."

Up in my room I pulled the drapes open on the boulevard and the black void of the bay. I unpacked, holding off sleep, drew a bath, stretched out in the hot water and dozed at once. I might have laid there for hours if I hadn't heard the rap at the door. I cinched a towel around my waist, opened the door with the chain on and looked down on a straw fedora.

"Bembo Rojas," he said.

I opened the door.

"Oh!" he said when he saw the towel, the wet footprints on the carpet. "I have disturbed you."

"It's all right. Come in. But I can't talk for long. I'm very tired."

He stepped inside just far enough for me to close the door.

"Of course you are fatigued," he said. "The great trip from the States. How often I have dreamed of making that same journey myself. In the other direction, of course."

"You should. You'd have a good time over there."

"Perhaps some day," he said.

"The telephone," I said. I got my wallet. "What, five hundred something. Five twenty-two. Am I right? That'd be about twenty-six dollars, why don't we make it thirty and call it even?"

He was slow to go for the money. Finally he reached, took it and put it away.

"I don't have pesos yet. I'm sorry. Dollars, is that all right?"

"Dollars are excellent," he said. "Thank you. My cousin is not a wealthy man."

"I really do have to get some sleep."

"I believe I can be of some value to you here," he said. "I have a background in investigation."

"I don't expect to be in Manila long. I may be going to Bacolod."

His face got grave.

"You know Negros is an unsettled place," he said. "I can be of much assistance. I am a native son of Negros Occidental. Ilonggo is my native tongue. That is the local dialect of the province. English may be sufficient in Bacolod, but in the hinterlands few people are fluent in anything but the dialect."

"Were you in Bacolod with Collins?"

"He wished to use me in Manila only."

"Doing what?"

His face set hard for a moment and he said, "I helped him with some personal arrangements. But I can do much more."

"I'll think about it," I said.

"If you are going to be in Bacolod for any length of time, you should have help."

"I'll think about it."

I reached around him and opened the door.

"Please do. Let me give you a number." He took out a business card, and with a ballpoint pen crossed through a telephone number on the front and wrote another on the back. He gave it to me.

"One of my enterprises," he said. "No longer extant. This number is my cousin's. I can usually be reached there. Are you planning to leave soon?"

"I don't know. A couple of days, if I go."

"You must call me before you do." He was backing slowly out the door.

"That's a promise."

"As I told Mr. Collins, the situation in Negros can be precarious for a stranger."

Thank you, I said, and when I saw that he was past the jamb, I closed the door in his face. It was rude but I was tired, and much taken with the idea of being tired. I slipped the chain on, flipped the card toward the bed, and went to the tub, opened the drain.

And then I heard what he had said. Precarious for a stranger. As I told Mr. Collins.

The elevator doors were sucking closed when I stepped out into the hall. I went back to the room, searched on the bed, found the card on the floor.

ROJAS TOURS
PERSONAL GUIDE SERVICE
TO THE PHILIPPINE ISLANDS

"YOUR SATISFACTION IS OUR GOAL"
"YOUR SMILE IS OUR SATISFACTION"

VIRGILIO "BEMBO" ROJAS, PROP.

I stuck a corner of it under the telephone and turned out the lights. I tried to sleep, and maybe I did in brief fragile passages, but mostly I looked at the darkness above the bed and listened to the voices of men and women passing in the hall.

Sometime in the night I got up and went to the window. The boulevard still had traffic. Directly below was a street corner and a traffic light. I watched it go green on the boulevard, red on the intersecting street. A taxi bucked to a stop at the light and at that moment several figures came out from along the sidewalk.

They went up to the taxi, moving with great effort. One was hunchbacked, two walked as if they were very old; another had an arm and a stump on one side, a leg and no stump at all on the other, and stood with a crutch. They were begging. I saw the taxi driver make small brushing movements out the window, as if shooing flies.

A second taxi pulled up, and the one on the crutch lurched over to it. I saw that his crutch was the carved fork of a sapling. He propped himself against it at the open rear window, leaned nearly inside. Then drew back, extended his hand off the crutch and accepted a couple of coins.

He touched his hand to his forehead. The light changed. The taxis bellowed blue smoke. The beggars scurried, ragged wraiths moving in streetlamp penumbra, fleeing back into the shadows. They went out of sight, under the cover of some shrubs that grew high and weedy behind the sidewalk. The bushes hid them, but I knew they were there, dark within the darkness, and it filled me with a dread I could not name.

· 4 ·

I have never had a lot of friends. I have never been close to many people.

Not that I'm unfriendly, or especially difficult. My problem is putting forth. I am reluctant to infringe—I would not presume to breach boundaries.

My father, who was the only adult I knew well until I had nearly become one, was not nearly so punctilious. His name was Earl. He traded oil field hardware in Kern County, California, and played steel guitar in a country-and-western band that sometimes shared a bill with Buck Owens in Bakersfield. He bought a new Cadillac convertible every September, he wore old pawn turquoise, and he smoked Camels down to the shortest butts I ever saw.

And he had friends, friends close and distant, constant and occasional. He reaped affection. I knew his secret;

could have done it myself; but it seemed so simple, I disdained it.

Weekends and summer days I would ride with him on business jaunts, father and son together, widower and only child of a woman who had died when I was two. He was supposed to be buying and selling, but it seemed to me that mostly he talked, aimlessly and too much, not only with equipment wholesalers and rig foremen, but with truck stop waitresses, highway patrolmen, newsboys, roustabouts—he knew hundreds of people. He talked hard, listened hard, too; swapping jokes and ironies and pieces of lives while I shredded toothpicks or scuffed my toe in the dirt.

I could see that he was trying to be liked, *pushing* to be liked, putting out the way he did. That bothered me. I doubted the value of any affection so transparently ac-quired, ignoring the fact that he tried just as hard with me and that I loved him wholly. When he rubbed my head I could have kissed those brown-stained fingers.

For his funeral they filled three-quarters of the pews of the biggest Catholic church in Bakersfield, and there was plenty of crying, not just women. It was an eternal lesson in the value of effort in friendship. By then, though, I was confirmed in my reserve. I would not presume.

And yet I am not at all put off by those who do; without them I'd be barren. I am happy to be violated. I am charmed, I am touched, by those who try and absorb rebuff and keep trying.

This may explain the flush that I felt, my first morning in Manila, when I saw Bembo Rojas sitting in the lobby. He was reading a newspaper, calm as an old dog curled up on the front porch. His suit was the sharkskin again. The cuffs of his trousers were hiked up a few inches, and I could see his stringy legs above black socks. If not for his fresh shirt, he might have been there all night.

I had been up with dawn, wondering what was a decent hour to telephone a Filipino home. I had tried his number;

a woman told me he was gone. I could hear children playing, a baby's cry, traffic noise, the crowing of a rooster.

I left my name and waited, ate breakfast in my room, watched a morning news broadcast. Two teenage assassins had ambushed an army major and his driver in Manila. A spokesman for the president's office downplayed rumors of a military coup, but acknowledged that loyal military units had taken up positions guarding the palace. Flooding from a recent typhoon had uncovered a mass grave believed to contain bodies of missing left-wing activists. The army reported skirmishes—the news anchor called them "encounters"—with communist rebels in the provinces of Cagayan de Oro, Nueva Ecija, Samar, Leyte; and Negros Occidental.

Outside, jeepneys wriggled along the boulevard like spawning salmon packed in a stream.

Around mid-morning a clerk at the front desk rang to tell me that an envelope had been delivered. I dressed and went downstairs. That's when I saw him, sitting in a corner.

He looked up as I approached.

"Mr. Rojas," I said.

"Ah no, Bembo," as he stood.

"I've been trying to get in touch with you."

"I am here," he said. His face showed sly delight. "You wish to speak with me?"

"I think I need you."

"I am at your service, of course."

My right hand kept wanting to do something, so I put it out. It seemed a feeble gesture when I did it. But he grasped it anyway, and pumped it.

We went up together after I got the report. It was in a brown envelope, and it came with a cover note on letterhead that said P.C. Headquarters, Camp Crame, Manila. The colonel exclaimed his pleasure at meeting me, hoped to see me again before I returned home, and invited me to call him if I had any questions.

Clipped to it were two pages of onionskin paper, carbon-copy flimsies. One was the police report, the other from the medical examiner. I gave that one to Bembo and took the other. It had been single-spaced on a manual typewriter, and I had to look close to make out some of it.

Anonymous telephone call at approximately six A.M., 12 Mar. . . . elements of Bacolod Police, Precinct Six . . . edge of a gully beside the Granada Road, near the five-kilometer marker . . . body of white male, identified from passport . . . shot in face at close range . . .

"This man is not the coroner of Bacolod," Bembo said. He seemed indignant. "This is a military document."

"The P.C. is handling it."

"They are responsible for crimes of national significance."

"That's what this is—that's what they said last night."

The little moustache wrinkled, but he said nothing.

I went back to my page. Single shell casing, caliber .45 ACP, recently fired, discovered within three meters of body . . . notification made to Philippines Constabulary, as evidence suggested involvement of communist armed city partisans . . . extensive interviews of nearby habitations disclosed several local residents awakened by gunshot. Residents Arnulfo Militante, Modesto Echevarria, and Pert Eval placed time of gunshot at approximately two-thirty A.M.

"This is pretty good," I said. "Last night I gave them a hard time because they didn't have anybody who heard the shot. This morning they've got three. Looks like they talked to half the neighborhood overnight."

"Nothing happens that fast."

"What are you telling me, they made it up?"

"Why not? Who's going to correct them?"

When we were both finished, we exchanged sheets.

Caucasian male, said the medical report, approximately forty-five years of age. Height 1.92 meters, weight 93 kilograms.

A big guy, about six feet three, 200 pounds.

Entry at lower right maxilla, wound approximately one centimeter diameter . . . exit upper right parietal, approximately six centimeters . . . angle approximately fifty degrees . . .

The slug went in his cheek and came out the top of his head. A little guy pointing a pistol in a big guy's face.

Bembo put the paper down.

"The communists are supposed to have killed him?" he said. Now definitely indignant.

"Sparrows."

"Yes. In Bacolod there are many. But why would they do such a thing?"

"Because he's an American."

"Trash," he said. "Americans are killed occasionally, those connected with the embassy or the military bases. A casual visitor, never. Besides, the Sparrows' targets have to be approved by a committee. Adding a name to the list can take weeks. Collins was in Bacolod four days."

"Don't ask me," I said.

"Trash."

"You know a lot about this."

"Everyone knows these things, anyone who cares to know. It is our life."

Find out what happened, Gilsa had told me. He had been offended, Collins leaving on company business and coming back in a coffin. If it's Sanchez, he'd said, find Sanchez. If it's a thief, all right, it's a thief. But find out what happened. So at least I can tell his wife.

"I have to go to Negros," I said.

"Are you certain?"

"I need answers. I've got to know who killed him. I don't even know what he was doing there, two-thirty in the morning, or whenever it was. Do you know that place?"

"Five kilometers east from the center of town, the Granada Road, there are several squatters' areas in that vicinity."

"That's what the colonel said, a squatters' area. Can a man go there to get laid?"

His look was level.

"Yes of course," he said. "Squatters are very poor."

"Would an American go there to get laid in the middle of the night?"

"Never."

"So why was he there? I mean, it's a hell of a good question, but I'll never find out in Manila." I think I was trying to convince myself. "I have to go there, I have to ask some questions. Will you help me?"

He nodded without a word.

"You know Bacolod well?"

"Negros is my place. My family has been in Bacolod for four generations."

"How do we get there?"

"Philippine Airlines has several flights a day. They are often heavily booked. When do you want to go?"

"As soon as we can get seats."

He gave a dry little snicker.

"With sufficient capital one can get a seat at any time."

"Let's say tomorrow afternoon."

"Very well." He went to the telephone beside the bed. "I know a travel agent. A nephew, to be frank. He can purchase our tickets and add our names to the reservation list. Then, tomorrow, we should arrive early. A small consideration for the individual at the check-in counter . . ."

"The company can handle it."

"Excellent."

He dialed the number with deliberate, precise movements. That was how he moved, how he talked, careful and quiet economy. He said a few words to the other end that I didn't understand—Filipino, I guessed—then tipped his head to me and said, "A few moments."

"That's all right."

"We will make your reservations at the Green Fields hotel."

"Whatever you think."

"Nothing else is suitable."

Back to the phone. Some more words, slightly less calm. Back to me.

"Unavoidable delays."

He pursed his mouth and held the receiver to his ear. Some moments passed. He took out a cigarette but didn't light it, only tapped one end and then another on the bedside table.

"I've been meaning to ask you," I said—trying to ease him with conversation—"how hard is it to bring guns through customs?"

"Very difficult," he said. "Guns are the raw material of revolution, and the communists have many more volunteers than they have arms. Therefore guns are highly restricted. But it can be done."

"Even rifles?"

"Rifles are the most difficult. But it still can be done. You see, guns and money and influence are all the same. If one has guns, he has influence. If he has influence, he can always get money. Or money and influence, you see, can be converted to guns. They are all forms of power, yes?"

Back to the phone. A couple of sharp bursts, then to me with an expression of chagrin.

"My apologies," he said.

"You worry too much."

"Family."

"Then if somebody had connections and money, he could bring in rifles."

"Large amounts of money and very very good connections."

"I was told it couldn't be done."

"That is trash. No offense."

"A week before he left the States, Lito Sanchez bought sixty assault rifles and had them shipped to a warehouse near the docks. Ammunition, too."

He had been about to speak into the receiver. But he looked at me and put his hand over the mouthpiece and said, "He transferred them here?"

"I don't know where else."

"After a while, huh?" he said into the phone, and then covered the mouthpiece again.

"Do you know the vessel?" he said.

"I'm not a hundred percent sure. There was nothing direct from California to Manila around that time. But if he was sending it out as soon as he could—I assume he would—there was a ship to Yokohama a couple of days later. Then it would have gone here on a feeder line."

"When does that arrive?"

"About three weeks ago."

His mouth formed a small thoughtful O.

"I don't believe we should travel by air," he said.

"Whatever you say."

"There is an inter-island ferry twice a week, Manila to Bacolod. It leaves again on Wednesday. The passage is twenty-four hours. It will not be so unpleasant if we book a first-class cabin. As for lodging, my sister and her husband have a spare room. Their home is unpretentious, but clean."

"It's up to you," I said. "Why?"

"If you arrive by air, if you stay at the Green Fields, they will know immediately that you are in Bacolod."

"Who do you mean?"

"The friends of Lito Sanchez." The question seemed to surprise him. That I would have to ask.

"Who are they?"

"Of course I do not know," he said. "But they must be very powerful, and the longer we can keep them from knowing we are there, even for a day or two, the safer we will be."

· 5 ·

An undertaker in Bacolod prepared the body. It arrived in Manila that afternoon and went out a few hours later. I never would have known if I hadn't called Dalzell, to tell him I wanted to look through Collins's effects.

He asked, why would you want to do that?

I said, because I sure would like to figure out what he was doing there in the middle of the night.

That's when he told me that the body was coming in and his stuff ought to be with it. He said he'd go through and pull out anything that looked as if it could be business-related. It would be late, though. Why didn't I meet him tomorrow for breakfast?

He gave me the name of a restaurant on Padre Faura Street. Or I took it for a restaurant; it turned out to be a go-go palace off Del Pilar, with a facade of gold-tinted plastic. Next door was a medical clinic: Dr. Lorenzo Suarez, Specialist in Diagnosis and Treatment of Sexually Transmitted Diseases.

I walked out of the steamy morning, opening the door and pushing aside a black curtain. Inside it was dark and cool and still, no music, no dancers. At the back, beyond many tables where the chairs pointed their legs to the ceiling, was a horseshoe bar with a lit TV on the wall. That's where I found Dalzell and ten or twelve other Americans, perched on stools, watching basketball.

First round of the NBA playoffs, he said. From Oakland, on the Armed Forces Network. We ordered food from the bartender, and Dalzell reached under the stool for a portfolio tied with a string.

"This is it," he said. "Not much. If it tells you anything, you're a better man than I am."

It felt empty. I stuck it under the stool and watched the game. A shot from outside the arena showed the Bay Bridge, an orange sun low behind it. I thought of places that I knew well, thousands of miles distant, where the sun was now setting on yesterday.

"Are you going down there?" he said.

"Negros."

"Negros. You planning to go down there?" He kept watching the game.

"I don't want to."

"But you are. What, chasing some con artist."

"He was worth looking for in the first place."

"I'm not telling you you can't do it. It's a free country." He gave a grin that made him look like a perverse little boy. "Well, maybe not free. But extremely cheap." The grin gradually faded. "No, really, it is a free country, and even if it wasn't I couldn't tell you what to do. It's not our country. But, see, that's the point all the way. It is not our country. We are guests here. You can't forget it."

"I realize that."

"My interest is in keeping Americans out of harm's way and making sure that friends stay friends."

"There must be other Americans in Negros," I said.

"Damn few. And most of them know how to take care of themselves."

"I don't want to go."

"You will, though, I can tell. I don't know what to say, except don't do anything dumb, stay off the streets at night, and watch your back."

"Collins got shot from the front," I said.

"Yes, shit, see what I mean?"

We watched the game for a while, and ate. Night came on in California. The bridge lit up. I left with Dalzell. It was jarring, out into sunlight and damp heat and stink, jeepneys rattling past on Faura, turbid water standing in the gutters.

We shared a cab as far as the embassy. That was just four blocks. It sat bayside at the head of the boulevard's curve, behind concrete barriers and a fence of high black shafts. Filipinos stood in a line that wobbled out of the front entrance and far down the sidewalk.

"Visa applicants," Dalzell said when I asked. "That's just tourist. We reject four out of five—we know they'll try to stay if we let 'em in. Next door, that's the immigrant section. Most of those get the visa, but they've got to be petitioned from the States first, and then the waiting list is in years, unless it's for a spouse."

The taxi pulled to the sidewalk.

"They're trying like hell to get away from where you're going, so they can get to the place you just left," he said. "I want you to think about that."

He took a piece of paper out of his pocket and gave it to me.

"A Filipino," he said, "owns some land down there. You get in trouble, he's the guy to help you out. So happens he likes Americans. Oh, and you want to stay at the Green Fields. It's the only place fit for human habitation, and I mean just barely."

He got out but leaned back into the cab. His hand went to my elbow.

"You spend time over here, you hear English spoken, you see Colgate in the drugstore and Stallone in the theaters, you can start to think this is just like home. But it isn't, this place is not like home, no way shape or form, and thinking otherwise can be the worst mistake a fella ever made."

The portfolio contained Sanchez's old passport, a printout from the case file in San Francisco, and expense receipts from Manila and Bacolod. One was handwritten, three thousand pesos for a car and driver, three days. I couldn't read the straggly signature, but Bembo said the receipt was probably from one of the drivers-for-hire who congregate around the Green Fields. Bembo promised to find him. If he had driven Collins for three days, he knew things we needed to find out.

We were several hours out of Manila, in our first-class cabin on *Princess of Negros*. The cabin was a steel cubicle with two iron cots and a small metal table, all bolted to the deck plate and coated with thick gray enamel. It looked like a cell in a county jail.

Bembo's forefinger moved the pieces of paper around on the table, the way old men's fingers push checkers or dominoes. He turned one of them over, a bar tab from the Green Fields. "Geraldo Martinez" was written there, nothing else. I had missed it.

He picked up the passport, fixed on the photo for a few moments, then put it down. He went to the printout, ran his eyes up and down it, said "Ah, very nice," and began to copy it into a small notebook.

"Do you know the barrio?" I said. Sanchez's birthplace.

"Barrio Lanao, Hermosa town," he said. "I don't know that barrio, but Hermosa is in the interior. That is a critical area." Before I could ask, he said, "A critical area is a region where the military and the NPA are contesting for control. A nervous place."

"A war zone," I said.

"Yes, but it is an odd kind of war. Most of the encounters are not very large. More on the order of ambushes and skirmishes. Sometimes a skirmish develops into a running battle. But that does not happen every day."

He looked to see how I took this.

"Sanchez must have family there," he said.

That reminded me. I got the photograph from my bag. Lito and Vangie, the school.

"Do you recognize this place?" I said. "It's supposed to be in Bacolod."

"I am not sure. My sister will know. Is it important?"

"That's his cousin. She teaches there."

"A beautiful girl."

"We want to talk to relations, there's a place to start."

"That's a real *probinciana*." He held the photo almost at arm's length. "They aren't like modern girls, you know, their attitudes. That's a real Filipina treasure. Do you want me to interview her?"

"I can handle it," I said. "Soon as we figure out where the school is."

"Ah."

"She ought to speak English, a schoolteacher."

"Yes, her English should be good."

"I have to do something," I said. "You're going to find the driver, right, I'm not just sitting in the house all day."

She could almost have been his daughter, the fond little smile on him.

"The province-reared girl is very hard to get," he said. "She is *malambing*, that's tender-hearted, she is *mabait*, that's patient and kind, but she is also *mataray*, that's strict, and *pakipot*, that's hard to get."

"I don't want to jump her bones, I just want to talk to her."

"A genuine *probinciana*, she may not even let you do that." He didn't seem to be joking.

"I'll figure something out."

"This kind of girl is not like other women. To pursue a girl like this requires much patience and hard work."

"For crying out loud," I said. I felt myself get hot, and didn't know why. His certainty, I guess, so sure of her and me and of what would happen between us. "I'm just going to talk to her. I don't want to spend the rest of my life with her."

He held the photo out to me between two fingers, and his voice was mild but serious.

"Of course you do," he said. "Every man wants a woman like this, whether he knows it or not."

At sundown a ship's officer said a rosary over the P.A. system. I stood beside Bembo at the rail outside our cabin, watching the sky purple overhead and the water go black.

The engines thrummed under our feet. Bembo had called it a ferry, but it was a ship, and not a small one. In the morning we had watched the passengers push up the two gangways and disappear below. I had guessed two thousand, Bembo said closer to three, and I believed him after I went down there in the afternoon, to get sandwiches at the canteen. Through an open hatchway I glimpsed a huge cavern full of triple-high bunks, each occupied, lit by pale green fluorescent.

The prayers were tinny on the loudspeaker. I held the rail as a long strip of an island slid along to the east. The island seemed a very lonely place, no other land in sight, and I wondered if it had a population, a name. I was suddenly conscious of places and their names. Until two weeks before I had never known of Bacolod or Negros.

That morning Bembo had brought me a color brochure from the Ministry of Tourism. It showed green panorama, wide cane fields that lapped into the horizon. A red steam locomotive hauled a shaggy load of cane stalks. Two lovely women beamed on a city street.

Negros Occidental, it said, Bounteous Sugarland of the Philippines.

Bacolod, it said, City of Smiles.

I turned to say something to Bembo and found his lips moving with a Hail Mary.

From page three of the next day's *Bacolod Daily Star*:

Passersby discovered a headless corpse at the edge of a cane field early yesterday morning in Sitio Cagbungalon, Bago. The unclothed naked body was that of a man believed to be about thirty-five years old. He had been dead for several days already. The victim's hands were tied behind his back, and bore multiple stab wounds, characteristic of so-called "salvage" murders by anticommunist factions. The remains are available for inspection and identification at Guzman Funeraria in Bacolod.

· 6 ·

Vangie stood framed in the light of a tropical afternoon. It flared through her hair and wept a glow along her bare arms.

Nobody can tell you about sunlight in the tropics. You can read about it, hear people rave about it, but no words are true enough to the hotness of that light, the heavy way it sits on your shoulders, the dazzling liquid whiteness. At that moment it flowed over Vangie and fired the edges of her dress: a red dress, vague as the one in the photo.

She was alone in a classroom, by a long window that dropped almost from the ceiling to a knee-high bookcase. She held up a hooked pole and deftly snagged the eye of the window's topmost section, tilted inward for ventilation. It snapped shut when she gave the pole an effortless push.

"Miss Flores?" I said. In the principal's office I had learned her full name. "Evangeline Flores?"

She turned a perfect quarter turn to look at me. I couldn't see much detail, back-lit as she was in the brilliance.

"Vangie," she said.

I walked across the room. My path took me gradually out of the glare until I was standing beside her.

"My name is Jack Hart."

"You are an American."

"Through and through."

I tried to grasp all that the snapshot had missed. The clear depth of her skin. The slight, elusive folds of eyes that could have been Chinese or Malay or Polynesian, depending on the way she moved. Her absolute composure.

"Can I help you?" she said. She seemed to gently rock the words. That lilt, and an almost imperceptible heightening of some vowels, was all she had of an accent.

I gave her a business card.

"I'm investigating your cousin's case."

"Sir, I have many cousins," she said, but not at all in a snotty way. She read the card as if she had never heard of the company and had no idea why it would want to talk to her. She didn't seem threatened.

"I mean Lito Sanchez. Your cousin Preciosa filed a claim for benefits under a fairly substantial life policy that he just recently purchased. We think there's reason to question the claim."

"I don't understand."

"Lito's alive," I said, and waited.

She peered at me as if my head had sprouted clover. I would remember it days later, after I had discovered her gift for parrying and deflection, her bedrock reserve. After maddening hours of trying to meet her eyes for more than a flicker, I would recall that moment in the classroom when she had stared at me so openly, and the memory would amaze me.

That's how it is with the madonnas of the Philippines.

Like Filipino guerrillas, they show themselves when and how they choose.

She peered, she peered, and I felt myself squirm.

But her mouth was forming a smile. The smile broadened and she put up her free hand to hide a giggle, laughing not just at the folly but at the fool who had proposed it. Even so, I didn't mind. It was a lovely laugh, and I knew I'd do almost anything to hear it again, to see her hand go up once more in that uncontrived way.

The laugh wasn't all gone when she lowered the hand and said, "I'm sorry. I wish it were true. I loved my cousin very much."

"You think he's dead?"

"I know he is dead."

"How can you be so sure?"

She frowned as if the question deserved some thought, abruptly seemed to remember the window pole in her hand, turned and carried it to the nearest corner of the room. She walked with a slow sway that tossed the skirt of her dress. It would have been provocative if it had been conscious: but I could believe that she had never once considered how she walked.

She leaned the pole into the corner and turned back to me.

"What can I tell you? Lito is dead. Everyone knows it. I cried all night when I heard of it. I went to his funeral. I light a candle for him in the cathedral every Tuesday and Friday. He is dead."

The way she said it, I could see the funeral. A sleepless night of tears—I could hear that in her voice. I wondered if it was possible.

I walked up to her again.

"You saw him in the coffin?"

"Yes—no! No, of course I didn't. He was burned. The coffin was closed."

She was tentative now, maybe a little hurt, thinking that I had tried to trap her. I had.

"The reason I ask, he's done this before. At least twice that we know of, taken out policies and collected on false evidence of death."

"Oh Lito." Fond chiding.

"He walked off on thousands of dollars in debts. He lied and cheated."

"He did that to you?" she said.

"I never met the man."

"That's too bad. You would have liked him. Lito was warm and affectionate, and he made people laugh."

"His creditors aren't amused."

The room was hot, growing hotter with the windows shut. A bead of sweat had formed below her left ear, and now slid along her jawline to her chin. She brushed it perfectly with the back of her fingers.

"I think Precy is here now," I said. I looked at the spot where the sweat had been.

"Yes. She is with her parents in Hermosa."

"In the barrio."

"No, the town proper. They bought a small house with money from Lito and Precy. Mostly Lito. He was a good son. He was generous to all, especially his family." Her tone told me that I should pay attention. "Lito took care of the people who depended on him. He provided. I don't know about America. But here, that is the highest compliment for a man. He provided. Nobody who knew Lito well would betray him. He had earned that kind of loyalty. If he were alive, you would never find him."

"Then he might be alive."

"Oh no. Lito is dead. But if he were alive, you would never find him."

Even if none of it was true, I didn't care. She could tell me what she wanted. I was tired of badgering someone I wanted to kiss.

"I might like to look in on Precy," I said.

"You knew her in the States?"

"We met a couple of times. I'd need her address."

She gave a why-not shrug and went over to her desk.

"Hermosa is about fifty kilometers from here," she said as she began to write. "An hour by jeepney, a little less by car. Do you know Negros?"

"This is my first day."

"Welcome." The ballpoint traced a careful diagram. "You came here just because of Lito?"

I said yes. She shook her head at the notion.

"Do you have a car? Or will you hire a driver?"

"I don't know yet," I said. Truth was, I had no plans to see Precy. She wasn't likely to tell me anything else. But I wanted to filch some more seconds here.

I stepped closer when she was finished. She held the paper to show me.

"Six kilometers south of the city proper, along the coastal road," she said, "you will pass the entrance for Pahanocoy beach. Another four kilometers, a bridge across the river, into the town of Bago. The road to Hermosa is the first left intersection in Bago. There is no sign."

It was all there in neat strokes and compact handwriting. She reached briskly to point with the tip of the pen. I could feel the heat of her arm. I caught a lavender scent, too faint for perfume. Maybe soap—I imagined her that morning, lathering her skin, languid and unguarded.

"Pass through the sitio of Cagbungalon and the town of Palo. Continue into Hermosa, around the square. One block more, you will see a statue of Our Lady. As it happens, her right hand points to the corner of Bonifacio Street. The house of my auntie and uncle is the fourth on the right."

She caught me studying her instead of the paper. In a businesslike tone she said, "Travel during the day. It is safer. The road is narrow, and the situation . . . travel during the day."

I said, "Lanao. Where Lito was supposed to have died. Where is that?"

She looked back to the paper. The pen made a faint, diffident extension of the road that she had drawn.

"In the mountains," she said. "A few kilometers beyond Hermosa."

She handed the paper to me. I took it without looking. I was watching her.

She said, "Is something wrong?"

"Nothing. I was just wondering if I'd see you again."

"I don't know what else I can do for you."

"We could talk," I said. "Get to know each other a little better."

It came out glib, the way I said it. I didn't mean it that way. My mouth was dry and I might as easily have stammered. But somehow I sounded glib.

"For what reason?" she said. She folded her arms and seemed to withdraw behind them, created a few more inches of space between us.

"I think you're an impressive young woman. I'd like to spend some time with you."

"Thank you. That is not possible." Her look was stolid, and then she denied me even that, dropping her eyes. Watching her, I became a voyeur.

"I'm not such a bad guy," I said. "I won't bite."

Her head moved side to side.

"Dinner. That's all. I can be a gentleman."

"No," she said. She sounded firm, not at all regretful.

"You don't wear a wedding ring. But maybe it's a fiancé. A boyfriend. If you're committed just say so."

"I am not committed," she said, "but I am not available for casual engagements."

I wanted to tell her it felt anything but casual.

"I'm not married, if that's what's bothering you."

"Please go."

"Sorry if I upset you."

"I'm not upset. But you should go."

She wouldn't look at me, but she sounded firm.

I said, "Thanks for your help."

My card was on her desk, where she had put it. The dress had no pockets. I went over and wrote the address and telephone of Bembo's sister.

"This is where I'm staying," I said. "If you need to reach me for any reason."

I'd have done the same at the end of any interview. I suppose I was already trying to convince myself that's what it had been, just another contact.

Her head bobbed without coming up.

"I'm glad I had a chance to meet you," I said, "brief as it was."

"Good luck in Negros," she said. Her eyes rose, gave me a quick knock, and dropped again.

I left the room, hurried down the corridor, stung and flustered. Several children sat on the front steps, eight or nine years old, the girls wearing plaid jumpers, boys in white shirts and pants of navy blue. They watched me go by.

Hot sun was in my face as I started down the walkway. Unreal, I told myself, the past few minutes. Unreal, the way she had affected me: she was attractive enough, all right, but I thought that I must have needed to find her beautiful—that I had wanted to be stunned, therefore she had been stunning. Unreal, too, the way she'd rebuffed me. Women turned me down often enough, but never so hard, with so little to cushion the fall.

Naive and unexposed, I thought, literally a provincial. She had been unready for me, I too-ready for her. That sounded right. It was neat, it fit, and I had it all boxed in by the time I approached the end of the walk, where it met a gap in the stone wall of the photo. A few more steps and I'd be gone, when a boy's voice behind me yelled, "Hey Joe." The phrase called up a newsreel memory of G.I.'s marching through a bombed-out town, kids running up to touch the soldiers.

Hey Joe, he yelled again, and this time I knew he meant me. I turned, the boy waved, I waved back.

That's when I glanced to the window, her classroom. The sun broke bright off the glass, but I saw her through the glare. She was standing there, watching me go, lovely beyond my imagination.

I expected her to move away, but she didn't, not at first. We took each other in. She seemed wistful. I couldn't believe that my leaving had touched her, but she seemed wistful all the same, and forlorn and very much alone.

Only later did I understand that she must have seen the same in me.

We watched each other for a long moment that ended too soon. She backed away and was gone, and I was left with the empty window, its splashy reflection of the sun.

From the *Daily Star*:

VILLAGERS ESCAPE

Reports have reached Bacolod of the mass exodus by residents of a remote settlement in central Negros. Carmen Villanueva, of Sitio Dagad in rural Himamaylan, claims that she and ninety other refugees fled their mountain homes after the village was attacked one night last week, purportedly by an anti-communist vigilante company, the Sacramentong Dugo, led by a certain Baldomero Capas.

She said the villagers reached Himamaylan Town after an exodus of four days, during which they traveled only in darkness, out of fear for their lives. Six residents of Dagad are said to have been killed in the midnight raid. Mrs. Villanueva says that she and her neighbors despair for the future, as their homes were burned in the raid and they have lost most of their possessions and livestock.

"We have a garrison army," said Bembo's brother-in-law, whose name was Rogelio Herrera. He was a thin man with a hawkish look, hair slicked back close to his skull. He owned a hardware store.

"It sits behind walls and waits. Behind walls it is always ready to fight. But the Nice People do not pay house calls at garrisons."

He saw that I didn't understand.

"That's what a lot of folk call them, the NPA. Nice People Around. With No Permanent Address."

It was evening. He had taken me around the corner to meet his friend Nanding. At a table on the sidewalk we drank beer and ate skewered chicken livers from a charcoal grill. Young boys dribbled a tennis ball under a clothes-hanger hoop. The only traffic was three-wheel pedicabs that teenage drivers whirred around cracks and potholes.

"Our soldiers are bodyguards for the generals," said Nanding. "Every brigade commander has five hundred bodyguards."

"There are some fighting officers," Rogelio said. "They patrol, they're ready to pursue. But when they're in the countryside, it's the guerrillas who more or less choose when the fight will be. If they don't like the odds, they don't fight. If the situation is favorable—"

"Bap!" said Nanding, pounding the table so hard that the bottles wobbled and the chicken livers jumped.

"You can't blame them for being reluctant to expose themselves," Rogelio said.

"The communists are based up there," said Nanding. He pointed his chin at the mountains east of the city.

"At the beginning of this year," Nanding said, "the

army tried a big offensive in the mountains down south. They got pinned down the first day, and it took them three days to get unstuck. They hauled bodies out on carts because helicopters were being shot down. The NPA own the mountains."

The mountains were the spine of the island, a long unbroken series of steep humps. You could see them from almost anywhere in Bacolod, looming in the east. I could see them now, vaulting above the roofs and the power lines. Their thick foliage gave them the color and texture of a ripe avocado's skin.

"Really," said Rogelio, "nobody cares about the mountains. If it was just the mountains, the NPA could have them. But from there they influence the rest of the countryside. Many settlements are under communist control. I'm not saying they fly the hammer-and-sickle. But day to day the NPA are the authority. The army might come through on a patrol, and any guerrillas that happen to be around will disappear for a time. But the army cannot stay, you see, because if they do, the NPA will gather to attack."

"To kick their ass," Nanding said into the bottle raised at his lips.

"So the army moves on and the NPA is free to return. Most of them are local boys. Who is in control? The army that shows up once in a while and then rushes back to the garrisons? Or local boys with guns who come and go as they please?"

Nanding said, "That's where the vigilantes figure in. They are local boys, too. They live in the hills just the same as the NPA. There are many groups with many names. Alsa Masa—Masses Arise. El Tigre. The Tadtad, it means chop-chop, they hack their victims with bolo knives. The S.D., Sacramentong Dugo, holy blood. They're choppers too."

"The vigilantes kill communists?" I said.

"They think they do," said Rogelio.

"Oh yes, they have methods," said Nanding. "They hardly ever make a mistake."

"The NPA isn't just guerrillas," Rogelio said. "In their consolidated areas, the barrios and towns they control, they have a structure of leaders and supporters. That's who the vigilantes go after. Some are known but many others aren't."

"Yes," said Nanding. "But that doesn't bother the vigilantes. As I say, they have their methods for detecting communists. They are guided by God."

"Most vigilante bands start as cults," Rogelio said. He stopped. He looked unhappy.

"Tell him," said Nanding.

"These are religious cults," Rogelio said. "Very superstitious. They use amulets and incantations to make themselves invisible during battle."

"And for finding communists," said Nanding.

"They carry vials of holy oil," said Rogelio. "Some of them believe in knee bones—in Mindanao there's a big problem with desecration of graves, vigilantes stealing knee bones to wear on necklaces. They make bracelets from the shells of one-eyed coconuts. They believe, when they get near a communist, the bracelets get tight. The bones jump, the vials boil."

"What did I tell you?" said Nanding. "Infallible!"

A Jeep with some soldiers turned the corner a block away and began trundling in our direction, picking a course around potholes. The boys stopped playing. As the Jeep got closer, Nanding picked studiously at his chicken livers while Rogelio made patterns in the wet circles that the beer bottles had left on the tabletop.

I was the only one who watched the Jeep. There were five soldiers and the driver. They had M-16 rifles across their laps or propped up on butt stocks. The Jeep went down the street, and when it was gone, the boys began dribbling their ball again.

"Country folk are not sophisticated," Rogelio said. "If

someone tells them that God wants them to kill communists, they believe it. If the NPA get to them first, they turn into communists. They don't know anything about communism, but now they're communists. Country people kill country people, local boys kill local boys, poor folk kill poor folk. Their lives are cheap. We don't know a tenth of what goes on up there."

He took a long self-conscious pull at his beer, as if he didn't often give speeches. We all drank, and I watched the mountaintops become coppery in the falling light. Lanao and the hacienda were up there somewhere, at the end of the thin line of road that Vangie had drawn. I imagined ragged bands moving cautiously under the canopy of the high trees, nasty bloodlettings, the sounds of battle and of dying that the distance smothered.

Rogelio and his wife, Bertina, lived on the south side of Bacolod, in the home that had belonged to Bembo's parents. It was a two-story house with bars across the windows and a six-foot fence that heavy vines overwhelmed.

They lived alone, six kids married, and rented out the top floor. It needed paint outside. The furniture was simple and sparse: in our room the mattresses were foam pads, and the decoration was a paint company's photo calendar—scenes of Yellowstone—and an old wedding portrait. You flushed the toilet with a pail, filled the pail from a tap in the shower stall.

But the place was clean, Bertie cooked a good meal, and it wasn't the fault of the mattress that I was still awake in the darkness when Bembo came in.

I knew it was late. He made indefinite shuffling noises, bumped my bed once, rustled his clothes. The room was small enough, I could smell the stale bloom of rum.

A match flamed. He was sitting at the edge of his bed, in boxer shorts and sleeveless T-shirt, a stick figure under loose skin.

"You are awake," he said. "You should be sleeping. Don't tell me you waited for me."

"I was thinking."

"You think too much." He put a cigarette in his mouth and slowly, intently, brought the flame to the tip of the cigarette. When it was lit he blew out the match.

"What about the driver?"

"I did not speak with the driver," he said.

"Let's keep at it. We need him."

"I know what we need." The end of the cigarette glowed hot as he inhaled. He held the smoke. So long, I thought he had swallowed it. "This is my place, you know. Bacolod is the city of my birth."

"You told me."

"I have many many friends here in Bacolod. Tonight I was given a homecoming celebration. My evening was superlative."

"I can tell."

"Oh, are you jealous?"

"Just tired."

"No wonder. I noticed you didn't sleep worth a damn last night."

I didn't say anything.

"How did it go with the teacher?" he said.

"She told me Lito is dead. She said she went to his funeral. Is that possible?"

"Anything is possible. That's not what I meant. How did it go with the teacher?"

"It went all right," I said.

"It went all right. What passion. I don't know how your girlfriends can get enough of it. It went all right."

He stretched out on the bed; I could tell by the red glow when he brought the cigarette to his mouth again.

"Is she beautiful? Or just all right?"

"She's beautiful. I felt like I was thirteen years old. She's beautiful and smart. She has a world of class. She was born with class—I can tell."

"That's better."

"She also told me to go to hell."

"Whatever for?"

"I asked her for a date."

"You asked her for a date? You think you can just meet this girl and ask her for a date? Oh my God. This is a province-bred girl, a true Filipina, you think she is going on a date with some stranger, some *American*, whom she does not even know? I suppose you expected that after you bought her dinner and a couple of cocktails, she would just lay down for you."

"No. Not her. It does happen, though, you know."

He laughed a fierce low laugh.

"If that girl was still living in the barrio, and you wanted to talk to her—just talk—you know what you would do? You would go to the home of her parents. Every day you would fill their water jar and cut cooking wood for her mother. If her brothers liked cigarettes, you would buy them cigarettes. If you were very diligent, after about a month, she *might* sit with you for a few minutes. In the presence of a chaperone, naturally."

"It doesn't matter. She wasn't interested."

"How can you know that?"

"She wouldn't even discuss it."

"Of *course* she wouldn't discuss it. Of *course* you are expected to pursue her. Of *course* you are expected to go to extraordinary lengths." He dragged on the cigarette with a rattling noise. "The proper approach is for you to call on her at her residence. I will obtain her address tomorrow. That is what friends are for."

"We're supposed to be finding Lito Sanchez."

"Lito Sanchez," he said. "Yes. I did not speak with the driver, but I did interview his wife. His name is Nemesio Puyat. He got some Japanese tourists who wanted to go to Negros Oriental. He is with them there and isn't expected back for two days. As to Collins. One of my companions tonight was a police lieutenant attached to Precinct Six, the station that was said to have investigated when his body was found. Do you know what he told me? He said that the police were never called. The P.C. came directly to the scene. Don't you find that curious? Oh, and I learned that Lanao is part of a large sugar plantation, Hacienda Paz. We will need permission to go there. I assume you want to inspect the site of the fire. You see, I was not an idle drunkard tonight."

He took a last puff and mashed the butt out in an ashtray on the night table.

"A drunkard," he said, "but not an idle drunkard."

"The barrio's on the hacienda," I said, "the owner of the hacienda owns the barrio? The whole place?"

Vangie hadn't mentioned that.

"A large hacienda will have several barrios and sitios, maybe twenty to two hundred families each. They provide the farm labor. The hacendero allows them to build their huts on his property, without deeds or leases, of course. They have no means to exist except by working on the farm. If they leave the job, they must relinquish their home also."

"That's a pretty good system, you own the town, you just about own the labor, too."

"The Correon family is very powerful," he said. "Luis Correon owns Hacienda Paz, that alone is thousands of hectares, and they have others besides. Luis gave his son a large hacienda on his twenty-first birthday. If you include cousins and relations by marriage, the clan owns much of what is worth having in this province."

"I know that name," I said.

I got my wallet and fumbled through it in the darkness. Bembo sat up and fired another match. It showed me the slip of paper stuck between credit cards, the paper that Dalzell had given me in the taxi.

It said "Luis Correon," followed by a five-digit phone number.

Bembo took the paper and held the match in front of it.
I told him how I'd gotten it.

I said, "So Lito must have worked for Correon."

"One of thousands. I wouldn't make much of it."

But he kept looking at the slip. Trying to see something
more than ink on paper, I thought. He looked until the
match burned down to his fingertips, and he blew it out
with a breathy curse.

SARGE SLAIN

Two unknown assailants, thought to be
members of an NPA assassination team,
shot P.C. S/Sgt. Ramon Padilla to death
before dozens of onlookers yesterday afternoon at Bacolod City Plaza. According to
witnesses, the sergeant was approached
from the rear by two young men, who bran-
dished automatic pistols and shot him
point-blank in the head. The assassins
removed his sidearm and briefly shouted
revolutionary slogans before running away,
north up Lacson Street. Police recovered
.45 and 9mm cartridge hulls at the scene.

· 7 ·

The scion of the Correon clan hated surprises. I saw it
when I met him. I approached him from behind. He didn't
notice me until I was almost close enough to touch him,
and then he twisted suddenly in the chair. For an instant
his face showed a feral displeasure, like a big cat startled,

and I thought he might do anything—might even shoot me with the pistol in his hand.

The morning started with Bembo up before I was. He showered and came to breakfast looking fresh. Between tidy bites of fried egg and rice he said he was going to visit the squatters out on the Granada Road. He also wanted to follow up on what the lieutenant had told him.

That left Correon. Bembo didn't want to visit Correon, though he never said so. Once I knew Luis, I understood Bembo's reluctance: the lambs of this world have little to gain from venturing into a lion's den.

We had to see Lanao. I got up from breakfast, went to the telephone and dialed the number Dalzell had given me. The line crackled. I got first one woman and then another who didn't know English—maids, I guessed. I asked Bertie to help. She took the phone and spoke for a few seconds, and then gave her number and hung up. They will call back, she said. A few minutes later they did. She answered the ring, gave the receiver to me, and on the other end a man said perfectly, "This is Nonoy Paloma. Mr. Correon wishes you to be his guest for lunch, if you're available."

"It just so happens."

He asked the address and told me to expect a car at eleven-thirty. I told Bembo about it when I was back at the table.

"I never saw an hacienda before," I said.

"That wasn't the hacienda," he said. "That was a local number. The hacienda is in the countryside, an hour away. All the hacenderos have come to Bacolod, to keep from being killed by communists. Correon has a villa here in the city—I'm told it's beautiful."

"Well, a villa. I never saw one of those, either."

A black Mercedes 500 with blacked-tinted windows pulled up exactly at eleven-thirty. Out in the street kids gaped at the car but didn't glance twice at the Uzi carbine that the bodyguard carried when he got out and opened a back door.

I slid in and found myself beside a Filipino about thirty, his face round and open. He wore a cotton version of the blousy Filipino dress shirt called a *barong*, worn outside the pants. His slacks were pressed and his loafers were polished. Nonoy Paloma, he told me; assistant to Mr. Correon. The way he said it left no doubt that the car and its glory belonged to someone else.

Another bodyguard, this one with a Streetsweeper shotgun, sat on the other side of him. A two-way radio in the front console made the sound of gravel shaken in a pan. Someone was talking about platoons and companies. A military frequency.

Rogelio and Bertie lived south of downtown; the Mercedes headed north. Nonoy wanted to talk about San Francisco. He said he'd been there with Correon a few years before, San Francisco, Carmel, L.A., Las Vegas, a three-week swing.

"The greatest three weeks of my life," he said. "Bar none."

"Your English is terrific," I said. And it was.

"English is taught in the schools from first grade on." A self-dismissing shrug. "Anyone who finishes college will have had sixteen years of it."

"You got a degree?"

"Yes. Mr. Correon paid for my education. It would have been out of the question otherwise—my parents were workers on his hacienda." A wry wrinkle of the lips. "Farmworkers' kids do not aspire to higher education. If it weren't for him, I'd be cutting cane at this moment."

He moved his hands when he talked, earnest little gestures, as if he wanted to leave me none of the effort of communication. He was trying hard. He struck me as a careful man who probably tried hard all the time.

"What does an assistant to a sugar planter do?" I said.

"My job is to help things come out right."

The car was solid and silent, air-conditioning cold, windows very dark. It made the city remote as we pushed through downtown. That didn't take long. Bacolod was maybe three miles across, and downtown was just a few blocks anchored by the town plaza, a cathedral, and the countless stalls of the central market. It was decaying and crowded, with that look of being overdrawn on every account, a town where too many people have brought too little money.

After a couple of minutes we turned off a main road and down a rutted back street where the pavement was reduced to islands of broken concrete. To the left was a long row of what I had begun to recognize as standard Bacolod shacks: graying wood, rusting corrugated roofs, small weedy patches between the front door and the street where barefoot children scrabbled in the dirt. To the right, shards of glass topped a high blank concrete wall. Then we were at a steel gate in the wall. Two men with shotguns stood there. They opened the gate, we drove in—and suddenly, barefoot kids and broken pavement seemed as distant as stars.

The lawn hit me first. Lush, neat as a country club fairway but much more expansive, punctuated by thriving trees and disciplined stands of shrubs in bloom. The wall enclosed it as far as I could see, enough acreage to make a respectable cornfield in Iowa. The road was unblemished tarmac. It crested a swell in the ground, and down on the other side we began to pass buildings. A chapel, two cottages, a six-bay garage, all low and stocky, ochre tile roofs over white stucco with black wrought-iron trim.

The road ended in front of a big house that might have spawned the outbuildings. I followed Nonoy through mahogany doors. He took me down a long hall with a floor of polished hardwood, past a row of old straight-backed chairs the color of slaughterhouse walls. At the end of the hall an archway opened up on a patio shaded by an overhead arbor and hemmed in by bougainvillea. We slid open a glass door; and the moment we stepped out into the mottled light, a gunshot barked close off to our left.

It was the throaty blast of a big pistol, the first shot I'd heard since the one that almost took me out. My heart tumbled, but Nonoy only picked up his head at the sound and said, "Oh. This way."

Shots rolled in about a second apart as we went along a brick walkway, around to one side of the house. A firing range stretched back there, hidden from the drive by a tall hedge. One shooter was on the line. He was a big man, pear-shaped and flabby. The seat of his pants bulged as he crouched with an automatic pistol at the end of two beefy arms.

A second man sat at a table with boxes of ammunition and several pistols spread in front of him. I could see just his shoulders and the back of his head. The firing masked our footsteps, and we were almost to the table before it ended and he heard us.

That's when Luis Correon twisted around in his chair and I saw the scowl of surprise and the pistol he'd been loading.

But the scowl vanished in a blink. He put the gun down and he was up to shake my hand, a man about in his mid-fifties, with thinning hair and a discreet pouch of fat at his waistline. His movements were easy and direct, like someone whose path is never cluttered. He said, "Welcome to Bacolod, welcome to my home."

He was a white man.

Nothing would have pleased him more, I'm sure, than to have me note it so baldly. But it was startling, after nearly a week of Filipinos whose skin ran butternut to bronze. His was pink as a newborn mouse, and not just by accident. Later that day I would see five pale generations of Correons in a wall of photos. They had come here with their Castilian blood unsullied, and I could imagine that they had gone to a lot of trouble to keep it that way.

"Do you shoot?" he said.

"Not if I can avoid it."

The one at the line had pulled off his ear protectors, and as he walked to the table he said too loudly, "You're wrong, shooting isn't a chore. It's one of life's pleasures."

He was young, though at least ten years past the age when adolescent fat might yet turn to muscle. His face, too, was pink and soft. He had a hog's jowls.

"My son Baby," Correon said. "If Baby had to rank guns and screwing, he'd have a hard time figuring which is second to whiskey."

"No," Baby said. "Whiskey is third. A drink is a drink. I put shooting ahead of pussy, because a good gun is harder to find than a good piece of ass."

"You want a beer?" Correon said. "Some finger food? We won't eat for a while."

"Iced tea, if you've got it."

"Yes, you're an American, iced tea. Plenty of ice."

He looked past me. A maid had followed us out of the house. He said a few words to her in what I supposed was Ilonggo, smooth and rhythmic.

"You want to go up to Paz," Correon said to me, "it's no problem."

"I appreciate it."

"You worked with the American who was killed. He wanted to go up to the hacienda, too. He had it arranged. The night he was killed, he was supposed to go the next day. But I don't want to hex you."

"You met him."

"He sat there in that same chair. He shot with us. He couldn't shoot worth a damn."

"What did he tell you?"

"He was looking for the same Carlito Sanchez. That's all. I tried to tell him he was wasting his time. Lito Sanchez is dead."

"You knew Lito?"

"I know the family. It so happens, I knew Lito in particular. He was a bright kid. I took him out of the fields, and he did some work for us in the office. But I know the entire family."

"I understood," I said, "that there are hundreds of families on your property. You keep up with them all?"

"That's right. What do you think, a family lives on my land, works my land for fifty years, I don't know who they are?" He was not a large man, but there was a largeness about him. His voice wasn't loud, but it did command. "These are my people. Shit, they're my children. I feed them when they're hungry. I bring the doctor when they're sick. When they get married I give them money to make a house, and when they die I buy their coffin."

"You bought Lito's coffin?"

"Lito was home from the States. He had money. I sent flowers, though. Nonoy represented me at the funeral."

Nonoy nodded on cue.

"Did you see him when he came back?"

"No," he said. "The ungrateful little bastard. I didn't know he was here until he was killed."

"I'd still like to see where he died."

"It's up to you, you want to waste your time."

"I'm getting paid for it."

"Okay, no problem. We'll arrange it after a while, huh? But first we shoot. Come on, take one."

He waved an arm at the little arsenal on the table: three revolvers, an Ingram machine pistol, a Smith & Wesson .45.

Baby said, "Have a look at this one."

Two black leather clutch bags, like big shaving kits, sat on the table. Baby unzipped one of them and pulled a semiautomatic pistol from it.

"This looks like quality," I said.

"You have an eye. That's the nicest one of the lot. That's a Detonics Combat Master. Not many of those in the country."

"Beveled magazine well," I said, "polished feed ramp."

"It'll feed anything," Baby said. "Hardball, hollow

point, you name it. Most people go for Colts when they want a .45, but even a modified Colt isn't as nice as this one."

"Adjustable sights. It must be the Mark Four."

"You know your guns." He turned to his father. "The American knows his guns."

"You find a little sweetheart like this in the local gun shops?"

"Local gun shops, there is no such thing," Baby said.

"Go ahead, shoot," Luis said.

"Is that right? How do you come by all this?"

"Anything can be had," Baby said confidentially.

"*Shoot*," Luis said.

I picked up ear protectors and took the pistol to the line. Baby followed me up and stood at my elbow as I bumped in a magazine. He was closer than I liked.

"You were a friend of the murdered American," he said quietly. As if it was between us two.

"Just a colleague. I'll bet it's almost a year since I capped off a round."

"Nobody forgets how to shoot—it's like forgetting how to piss. It wasn't in the newspaper, you know, or the radio. But we heard. We have contacts. The P.C. thinks it was Sparrows."

"That's what they say."

"You have reason to doubt them?" His bulk made me feel crowded.

"I'm a stranger in this place," I said. I put the plastic muffs over my ears and lifted the pistol and sighted it down the alley. "I'm the last person to know."

They were using silhouette targets—human silhouettes. We sometimes used to shoot silhouettes on the police range. I always thought it was silly. Punching holes in two-legged paper images as if that will help you one day when you must draw down on human flesh.

I thumbed off the safety.

Baby wasn't exactly right; a few months will erode a

shooting touch, if you have one. But the basics do stay with you. I knew the basics. Grip the pistol firmly but don't choke it. Pull in a breath, look through the notch of the rear sight, lay the bead of the front sight where you want to hit, steady, meld bead and target, steady, hold, squeeze.

It was a light gun, short-barreled. It roared and jumped. I brought it down and stayed focused on the target—a circle over the silhouette's left breast, about four inches across, tiny at twenty-five yards—and though it didn't feel quite right, I squeezed again.

Baby was even closer now, leaning in toward my shoulder. I wanted to tell him to back off, but I stayed on the circle. His breath puffed on my cheek. I squeezed and fired. The shot was far wide, I could tell.

"Oof," Baby said.

Good shooting is a glissade. This felt like falling down a long flight of stairs. I fired, exhaling at the wrong time, I fired, yanking the trigger too hard, I fired, as the muzzle wavered.

I lowered the gun to get a better view of the six holes of daylight that showed through the paper. Two were in the circle, barely, three more were scattered outside, a sixth was completely off the black figure.

"One more," Baby said. "Seven-round magazine."

His pudgy arm pressed at my elbow. I could have moved, I considered slapping it away, but instead I brought the gun up and found my spot fast and fired the last round. It made a hole in the upper center of the head, about where the bridge of the nose would be, and I turned to Baby and said, "That's how it's done here, I remember now," swallowing a fury I couldn't fully account.

Correon had lied to me—that was part of it.

We sat for lunch in a dining room where big roof timbers angled upward from clerestory walls. Luis's wife,

Ofelia, was there. Her talc-colored skin was taut over high cheekbones. It seemed to have been stretched by the knot of black hair behind her head, so tight it must have hurt.

Maids carted in trays of baked chicken and tiger prawns, and egg rolls they called lumpia, and steamed rice, and a sour fish broth. Correon passed on gossip about an ambush in the south which overnight had turned into a full-blown battle; heavy casualties. Ofelia announced plans for a shopping trip to Manila. Baby bragged about molasses earnings from his farm's latest mill report.

Nonoy sipped his soup without a word. When we were finished, Correon got up and said come with me, and Nonoy followed us both to a room down one wing of the house.

It was Correon's office. He sat behind a desk and told me I could visit the hacienda whenever I wished. He wrote a note on his personal letterhead. Please render all possible assistance to the bearer, my dear friend Mr. John Hart of the United States of America. He would arrange a checkpoint pass with some contacts in the military. A bungalow on the farm was available for my use. I was welcome to borrow a pistol. I could have Nonoy as an escort whenever I wanted. Or not, as I wished.

"I don't want you to think I'm interfering. So if you want to go up on your own, you have the paper."

Open as a poker player who has just turned over his hand.

But I knew: he had lied.

The pistol could only have come from Lito. Yet Correon had told me he hadn't seen Lito. He had no reason to suspect that I knew about the pistol, so it must have seemed a lie without risk, the cheapest kind.

" 'Noy," he said, "make sure our guest gets whatever he needs."

"Yes boss," Nonoy said.

Worth telling, though, all the same.

"The hacienda should be quiet," Nonoy said. We were in the Mercedes, near downtown. "Luis accommodates the NPA."

I told him it sounded like bed-and-breakfast. But the joke didn't reach, or Nonoy had reason not to laugh.

"He pays them. They demand what they call revolutionary taxes from the landholders. Some pay, others don't. Luis pays."

He glanced over the driver's shoulder, toward the road ahead. He did it often, a brood hen's watchfulness, the tic of someone who worried for a living.

"If you don't pay?"

"You must be ready to fight. They burn trucks and equipment, they try to destroy the crop. Some planters bribe the military to defend their farms, but the military has its limitations. To do it right you must have your own troops. I know planters with a platoon of their own infantry. It may not sound like much. But if a hacendero has just thirty or forty well-trained men with military weapons . . . that's power."

"Warlords." I remembered Collins using the word, how exotic it had seemed.

"We have them. It's not a profitable undertaking, though. The overhead is high. Even more than the money, a warlord is automatically a target for assassination by the communists. Mr. Correon would rather pay for his peace of mind."

"Why the guards," I said, "the guns, if he's not worried?"

"A show of force. It's expected of him, a man in his position, to flex his muscles. People would be disappointed if he didn't. Noblesse oblige."

"Somebody told me, the communists have chased all the hacenderos down into Bacolod."

"That's true in many cases. Not of Mr. Correon. He

lives in Bacolod here because he wants to live here." A whiff of testiness wafted into his voice. "It *is* a shame that landlords don't live on their farms anymore. There's a great distance—the farm is another world—but you'll see that when you go up there."

He picked invisible pieces of lint off his dark trousers.

"Every Saturday, when he isn't traveling, Mr. Correon spends the night at his bungalow on the farm. Every Saturday night without fail. He tries to stay close. Sometimes I think that's what he sees in me. I'm a link to the farm, the people." His fingers ground the lint and released it into the air. He looked straight at me.

"He is not afraid. You must believe that. Mr. Correon fears nothing from no one."

Beyond downtown we waited to cross the coastal road from the south. Busy as it was, the intersection had no signal light. We waited for motorcycles, for swaying cane trucks piled top-heavy with sheaves of brown stalks, for jeepneys that had brave boys standing on the bumper, pigs and rice sacks lashed to the roof.

Down the inbound lane I saw black smoke and a blocky green shape. It got bigger fast, swung out to pass a motor tricycle, and loomed up on the intersection: a truck, a diesel six-by-six, devouring pavement with a turbocharger whine. As it passed I caught the army's white-stencilled markings.

The truck flew through and was gone so fast I had only a couple of seconds to see the cargo under a canvas canopy. It was men in camouflage fatigues. Some were sitting or standing with rifles, with weary postures and distant stares. Others were down and splayed out in the impossible repose of those who will never get up again. How many, I couldn't tell. They were in a heap.

"From the south," Nonoy said.

The driver got a break in the traffic. He hustled the Mercedes through, but not so fast that I didn't see the droplets that must have dripped through the bed of the

truck, making splashes that were deep red deepening to
black.

· 8 ·

In the afternoon two soldiers in olive drab came up the
front walk to deliver my papers. One said SAFE CONDUCT
PASS and OFFICE OF THE COMMANDER, TASK FORCE SUGAR-
LAND. The other was authorization to carry a firearm.
Both were signed by someone with "Brig. Gen." at the end
of his name.

Evening came and went. Bembo didn't appear. We ate
dinner, and I was thinking about sleep when a man came
to the door. Bertie gave him a hug. Her cousin Franklin,
she said. He was moon-faced, with the flattest nose I could
remember, and he wore a T-shirt with a fading portrait of
Ferdinand Marcos.

"Sir," he said to me, "with your permission, sir, my
cousin Virgilio has retained me as your driver. Yours and
his, as circumstances warrant."

"Bir-*hil*-i-o" was how he said it, and I didn't catch on at
first.

"For the daily fee of five hundred pesos, sir, plus expenses. My automobile is a Ford Cortina, most reliable."

"Do you know where he is?"

"He is conducting an investigation, sir, he asks you to
come along with me."

He dipped his head in what might have been an absurd
little bow, and sent a whiff of booze my way.

"Should you be driving?" I said.

"I am an experience driver. I am driving thirty years
already."

"But you're drunk."

"Hardly a little. That arrangement is satisfactory, sir? Five hundred a day, plus expenses?"

"Maybe. I don't know. Where is Bembo?"

"Four fifty."

"Take me to Bembo. We'll talk about it later."

The Cortina had rumpled sheet metal at two corners, an old chintz bedspread on the backseat, and a small plastic fan on the dash that blew directly into Franklin's face. On the front dash, constructed of foil and blue cellophane and twinkling Christmas lights, was a small grotto where a statuette of the Virgin stood.

We drove first to the central market, and he asked me for two hundred pesos. Instructions from Virgilio, he said. He got out and went inside and came back with three liter-size bottles of Añejo rum and a plastic bag that contained about a dozen fish the size of brook trout. He put it all on the seat between us.

He turned east, down a street I hadn't traveled yet. The streetlamps came farther apart, then not at all. We were on the outskirts of Bacolod. In the fringes of our headlights scruffy shrubs and walls of tall cane stood up to the side of the road.

He drove. The headlights pointed up a white kiosk beside the road, two men inside. I recognized P.C. khaki. Checkpoint, Franklin said, and I took the general's envelope from my shirt pocket. I had brought it, with my passport.

Franklin slowed. The two soldiers waved us through without leaving the shed or glancing at the papers.

"The last outpost before the countryside," he said. "Past here is no-man's land. They are very nervous. They are not armed."

"That would make me nervous, too."

"But it is safer. If they were armed, the NPA would kill them for their guns."

Franklin drove another two or three more minutes

before he parked in a bare patch beside the road. He got the fish and the rum.

"He is here," he said. I could see almost nothing. I never knew night like those tropical nights, the air viscous and murky, nights dark as day was brilliant.

A path poked into a grove of low trees. As I followed him through it I heard a man singing against the ring of a guitar. It was an old rhythm-and-blues ballad—the Platters, I think.

His voice was high and steady. It slid and bounced and caught in all the right places, and it got louder as we came out of the trees to the edge of a ravine. It was at least fifty feet deep and at least twice as wide. The music came from a clump of twenty or thirty shacks on the other side. Men were gathered around a table in an open space between huts, lamplit. One of them was strumming and singing.

I stopped. Franklin didn't. He climbed onto a swinging footbridge and began to walk across. It was a ridiculous contrivance, a B-movie bridge of narrow planks suspended by fraying hemp. Franklin strode over and waved me on.

The light looked good on the other side. I stepped on. I had to bend some at the knees, to grab the low ropes that served as handholds. It creaked under my weight. A stream ran below, throwing back moonlight, and I could see more shacks stubbed into the sheer side of the ravine. Then I didn't look down again until I reached the other side.

The guitarist rang off a last chord as we got to the little table. About ten men sat there, filling up all the space around it. Bembo was one of them. I expected at least a hello, but I got a cocked-head wolfish leer I'd never seen from him before. It contorted his features. Except for the fedora, I might not have known him.

"The 'Cano favors us with his company," he said.

One of them stood to give me his seat. He pointed to the empty spot with the exaggerated gestures of someone who doesn't have the words. With my own gestures I told him, No it's yours, I'll stand.

Bembo said, "He's trying to be your host. Granted he's not a Correon, but you can at least sit on his bench, surely you can give him that much."

I wedged myself in and said hello.

"Hey Joe," said two or three of them around the table.

Most of the men were young, twenties and thirties. One, beside Bembo, had to be at least seventy. All wore T-shirts, gym shorts or baggy trousers, and rubber sandals. Their faces and shirts were wet with sweat. Mine were, too; but their discomfort seemed perpetual.

The huts were scrap wood and bamboo and woven grass panels. Through almost every window I could see women or children. A sewage smell crawled through the torpid air. The night pressed down hard on the lamplight.

"Unless you are unwilling to sit with your little brown brothers," Bembo said.

I said, "I can't stand peevish drunks. They remind me of my mother-in-law."

Bembo ratcheted his face. A couple of them laughed, one put it into Ilonggo, then the others laughed. A woman came out and took the fish from Franklin. He put the bottles on the table.

"You are married?" said the man with the guitar.

"Divorced."

"Ah. In de P'ilippines we have no divorce."

There was a single drinking glass on the table. Somebody splashed a couple of fingers of rum into it and put it in front of me. Bembo watched me and seemed ready to snarl again; he relaxed a little when I took the glass and drained it, put some more rum in and handed it to the man beside me.

"The American is in love with an Ilongga," Bembo said. "Raised in the hinterlands, now a schoolteacher in Bacolod."

That got loud exclamations of delight, in the original and a few seconds later in whispered translation.

"Deh Ilongga is loving, but very hard to get," one of them said.

"I just met her," I said. "It's not like I'm going to marry her."

"She is a probince girl, what else you goin' to do wit' her?"

"He wanted to take her out," Bembo said. "The first time he met her, he asked her to go out to dinner."

"Oh."

"Oh no."

"Oh my God no."

The little man, I wanted to throttle him.

"You cannot do det. Deh girl from deh countryside is *very* hard to get."

"I'm just a visitor, see, I thought she was nice, attractive, I wanted to know her better."

"She is beautiful?"

"Yes," I said.

"Beautiful," Bembo said. He looked at me sidelong from under the straw fedora. "Intelligent also. She speaks English like a native."

I hadn't told him that.

"I saw her," he said when he saw it dawn. "I have been very busy in your behalf."

He said this as the glass arrived in front of him. He lifted it carefully and drained it in a long and steady sip.

"You get any busier," I said, "I'll have to carry you home."

He set the glass down as if he hadn't heard, filled it and passed it on.

"You have no fucking respect," he said. He seemed to be addressing the bottle. "Not that I expect much from an American. But even so. How can you have gotten this far in life without knowing whom to treat well?"

The others must have noticed, but they made a show of

not noticing. The one with the guitar fingered a chord and slid into a slow croon. It took me a few bars to recognize it. "Smoke Gets in Your Eyes." I hadn't heard it in years.

"Do you know where you are?" Bembo said. He opened his hands slightly to show that he meant right now, this place. His voice was husky, as if there were still some emotion behind it. The acid was gone, though.

It came to me.

"A squatter's camp," I said. "Where Collins was killed."

"Among the invisible," he said. "Squatters have no voice or substance. But they have eyes."

"You found out something?"

"If you hear it now you will have no reason to stay. And if you leave quickly you will insult these good people."

"I'll wait."

"Good. Tell me about Correon."

I went over the pistol and the lie. I told him what Correon had said about Lito: the flowers, the funeral. I described the scene in the office.

The singer reached for a sweet high note behind me as I handed Bembo the letterhead note and the military papers. He went through them quickly, a sardonic rumple on his face.

"With this you could get away with murder," he said. "You could carry the gun, you could escape through the checkpoints, and that note from Don Luis would get you out of custody if you happened to get caught."

The glass came around to me again. Somebody else began to sing an old rock ballad called "Donna." I could remember slow-dancing to it when I was a teenager. Now a kid with a livid wen on his neck was stroking the song, pure and perfect, as if nothing mattered more at this moment than getting it right.

He knew all the words, all the notes. Everybody seemed to know all the words and the melodies, must have sung them dozens of times on nights like this. I drank and put the glass down and thought about poor men sitting under the sky, giving life to soulful old songs that the rest of us had forgotten.

The glass went 'round and 'round. They sang more songs. A woman brought some fish, charcoaled whole. In the shacks the kids ate, too, tearing through crispy black skin for white flesh underneath.

They sang, we drank. My bladder started to ache; I went to the edge of the ravine and launched into darkness. I felt free and unknown.

When I came back to the table, Bembo had an arm around the old man beside him. His drawn face and sunken cheeks showed his age, but his back was still straight and his calves were knotty muscle. He smiled a lot but had said almost nothing.

"This is my friend Galicano," Bembo said to me.

His hand was tough as stone when I took it.

"Galicano used to work on a plantation up in rural Talisay, but because of the troubles, the owner doesn't plant it anymore, and now Galic is down here living with his grandson. I met him when I came here this afternoon trying to find someone who had heard the shot.

"Almost everyone had, it seems. But when I asked for Pert Eval, Modesto Echevarria, and Arnulfo Militante— from the report, remember?—nobody knew them.

"I must have been making a pest of myself, because one kind lady finally told me that I should speak to her husband's grandfather. That was how I found Galic."

The two of them beamed together.

"Galic keeps a little garden over on the other side. Sometimes, if he has trouble sleeping, he goes there to tend it when the moon is out. He was there the night—tell him, Galic."

"Very poor, my English," Galicano said.

"It's fine," I said.

"Four men," he said. "One automobile. White, nice."

Bembo said a couple of words in Ilonggo, Galicano

answered him, and Bembo said, "They had clean clothes. They wore leather shoes. He admired their shoes."

"Four men," I said, "one of them was an American."

"Yes. Very big man. His hands behind his back." He kept his voice low. "They make him go down, like to pray. One man have a gun. He shoot the big man in the behind of the head."

"The face," I said, but Galicano tapped the upper back of his skull. Entrance at parietal, exit at maxilla, the report should have said.

"They argue," Galic said. "Not suppose to shoot him back there. Suppose to be the face. They remove the rope from his arms. They return to the car. They go."

"Did you tell that to the police?"

"Police do not come. P.C., next morning, they stay a short time only."

"Nobody here called the police?"

"Nobody see, me only." He showed a few yellow teeth, set in his gums like stumps. "Nobody here will help police."

"What time did it happen?" I said.

The two men traded scraps of Ilonggo, and then Bembo said, "About three hours before first light. Maybe two-thirty."

"At least they got that right," I said. I was thinking about the report.

"Yes, very disturbing," Bembo said. "I was not aroused when they created three witnesses. I thought, maybe they were just too lazy to find out exactly when the crime occurred. But now we see, they had the time right. They knew it without asking."

He waited for me to catch up. The rum, the sultry darkness, the image of Collins being shot as he knelt: I was trying to wade through it all.

"The P.C. killed Collins?" I said.

"P.C. or army or police, their allies, their friends, their sponsors, friends and allies of their sponsors—"

He might have gone on if I hadn't stopped him.

"Sponsors," I said. "The military and the police have sponsors?"

"In a manner of speaking. The salary of a P.C. captain is perhaps fifteen hundred pesos a month. You pay him fifteen hundred a month, he owes you as much as he owes Madame President."

"This is some place you have here," I said, before I could censor it.

His face got hard again.

"In America," he said, "nobody pays police officers? Or is it the price that bothers you, that we come so cheap?"

The wolfish look came and went. He was more hurt, I guessed, than angry.

I didn't say any more, but looked across the ravine and thought of Collins, now at the elevator making lewd gestures, now kneeling with a cop's gun at the back of his head, his flip confidence dying in the dust with all the rest of him.

The bottles and the women's indulgence gave out around the same time. Wives with crying babies in arms scolded husbands from doorways and windows. Goodbyes were lengthy and effusive. I crossed the bridge with laborious caution, Bembo behind me murmuring no problem no problem no problem.

I got in the front seat beside Franklin. Bembo sat upright in the back. The road was empty. So was the white kiosk.

"Lito Sanchez may be dead," Bembo said. "I want you to consider the possibility."

"I've thought about it. But it looked like a scam for sure." The crystalline view from the thirtieth floor.

"They had a funeral. They buried a coffin. The death certificate is registered—I checked. Granted, they could have buried an empty coffin. He could have paid someone in the registrar's office. But Vangie is certain that he is dead. She isn't acting, she believes it. She would never believe it if the rest of the family did not."

"He's pulled it before," I said.

"Not this way. If he is alive, he has cut himself off from his friends and loved ones. That I cannot accept. It would mean trading his family's love for money. No. A Filipino would never do it."

His head shook with a quick shiver.

"Not for money," he said.

"For what?"

"I cannot imagine. My God, think of what he'd be giving up. Vangie, I saw how she loved him. The light in her when she talked about him, that's priceless. If I ever found that he had traded on that, I swear to God, I myself would put a bullet in the son of a bitch."

"You saw the girl," I said.

"You can say her name out loud. You're among friends."

"Vangie. Quite a lady."

"Hunh! She is a treasure!"

The car dropped hard and thumped. Franklin was working hard to keep it straight, and sometimes he'd drive it straight into a pothole.

"Her home is in the barrio, Lanao," Bembo said, "but during the school term she lives in Bacolod, at a boarding-house on Gonzaga Street, two doors down from the southwest corner of Cadagat Road."

"How do you know that?"

"I asked her, naturally."

"Did she know you work with me?"

"I made a point of it. 'Miss, it is my great pleasure to be associated with the American whom you met yesterday. He is an upstanding young man of unimpeachable charac-ter.' Tomorrow is a Saturday, she will be there. Most weekends she returns to Lanao to stay with her mother, but tomorrow she will be there, I believe. She will expect you."

"You told her I was coming."

"Don't be foolish. She never would have given me her address if I had told her that it was for you."

"Then she's not expecting me."

He blew a derisive snort.

"Americans know *nothing* about courtship," he said.

We were back in the realm of streetlamps again, passing shuttered shops and apartments. Still there was almost no traffic. Franklin clipped through three red lights without slowing.

"If Lito is dead I'll probably be going home soon," I said.

"It might be for the best."

"I'd still have to go to Lanao, look around."

"If you want." The car jolted us again, and he said, "What about Collins?"

"Collins, I've been thinking about the people who sent me out here, let me tell you. They'd like to find out what happened to Collins, but they're not burning to find out. If Lito's dead, we're out of easy answers, and that's the only kind they really want to hear."

"That bothers you."

"It pisses me off, that somebody did it and is going to get away with it."

"He was your friend?" Franklin said.

"I barely knew him," I said. "That's not the point."

"Jack is afflicted with the need to know," Bembo said. "He lusts after the truth. Am I right, Jack?"

I said, "Not bad for a stab in the dark."

"Furthermore, he has an acute sense of right and wrong." His voice had a tinge of amusement. "He is offended that he might have to leave here without seeing the killers of Collins brought to justice."

Franklin looked across the seat at me, incredulous.

"This is true?" he said.

"True enough."

"Oh my God. There is no justice."

"There is no justice," Bembo said.

We rattled through the south side of Bacolod, past the Green Fields, a four-story island of light and life in the dead night. The entrance was wide plate-glass, the lobby big and bright behind it. I saw a clerk behind the desk, three bellmen in front of it, several gents lounging on banquettes, laughing with man-about-town insouciance. Two young women wore dresses like candy ices, peach and raspberry, and when they opened a set of doors near the back, I got a strobe-lit flash of a crowded dance floor. Several expensive sedans were parked in the drive out front, and men in short sleeves held rifles and shotguns as they struck poses against the fenders.

"You will still see Vangie?" Bembo said.

"I might as well. Drop in, say hello. Is that it—you stop by the house, you sit down and have a little chat?"

"Exactly."

"You don't call ahead or anything?"

"If you told her you were coming, she would be obliged to leave."

"I see," I said, though I didn't.

"A favor for me," he said. He looked and sounded grave. "Do not take advantage of her."

"Don't worry. She isn't buying anything I have to sell."

"Say it."

"Okay. I won't take advantage of her."

"Do you mean it?"

"I told you. Anyway, it doesn't matter. If I had ten years I might not be able to wear that one down. A few days, I guarantee I'm not getting anywhere."

"Don't be surprised," he said.

The Philippines might have more loud, ugly dogs than any other place on earth. I think several dozen of them roamed the block where Bertie and Rogelio lived, and they all woke up when I slammed the door of Franklin's Cortina.

Their yapping crescendoed as Bembo and I came up the front walk. I went straight to the bedroom. Bembo came in a few minutes later.

He gave me an envelope, sealed. My name was written on the front in plain block letters.

I opened it and saw a single sheet inside, folded once. I didn't take it out. Bembo hadn't moved. He had something to say.

"Is something wrong?" I said.

"My sister is worried. Guns, soldiers at her home."

"I don't blame her."

"They are ordinary people. They do not make trouble and they do not want to be recognized as troublemakers. They would rather not be recognized at all."

"Of course not," I said.

"That is one of the tragedies of this conflict, the way motives and allegiances are called into question."

At last I understood.

"You think it would be better if I didn't stay here."

"I am ashamed to ask—"

"I don't mind," I said. "I hate imposing anyway. I can go to the Green Fields, right? They must have space."

"I am exceedingly regretful."

"You shouldn't be. We were just trying to buy a couple of days anyway. It's not like the company can't pop for a hotel room."

"Thank you."

"First thing in the morning."

"No hurry. But thank you."

I took the paper out. It was a page torn from a spiral notebook. The lettering was the same as on the envelope, a hand that could have been masculine or feminine, young or old.

I said, "I wonder who knows I'm here?"

He said, "By now, anyone who cares to know."
I showed it to him. It said:

Persist

· 9 ·

Rooms at the Green Fields ran from four hundred to six hundred a night. They took plastic, so I registered for the best. A bellman named Eddie bustled my bags to the room and pointed out hot water from an electrified shower head, a telephone that looked roughly forty years old, a black-and-white TV nearly as decrepit, a fourth-floor view of corrugated roofs that threw off ripples of mid-morning heat.

He left the door open behind him.

"I drove past the hotel around midnight last night," I said. "Everything else was dead, but this place was still wide awake."

The planters' social center, Bembo had called the hotel. Where they drink and scheme and screw. One of the few places in Bacolod where they feel safe at any hour.

A chiffon rustle outside snagged my attention, and I looked past Eddie to the door. In the hall I glimpsed tottering peach and raspberry.

Eddie saw them too, their slurred makeup, tangled hair, gave them a glance, came back to me with a flat look and said: "Yes, this is a very lively place, sir."

I walked up the steps of the boardinghouse on Gonzaga Street, two doors down from the corner of Cadagat Road. Where I was expected because she hadn't been told I'd be coming. I held one box of a dozen roses and another with a big chocolate cake.

Bring her flowers, Bembo had told me, and for the others in the house something good to eat. He approved the cake but howled when I left the florist's with a bunch of chrysanthemums. It has to be roses, he said. To a Filipina nothing else is a flower.

I balanced the boxes and knocked. It had a hand-lettered sign, LADY BEDSPACERS WANTED. Bembo and Franklin hadn't driven away yet. I was aware of them behind me, watching.

I felt silly but I knew there was no other way.

The door opened. A woman in her thirties, wearing a housedress, pushed her hair back to see me better.

"Hi, I'm Jack Hart," I said, "I'm looking for Vangie Flores."

"I know," she said.

Her name was Mrs. Guanzon. She sat me in the sagging middle of a sofa in the front room, what Filipinos call the *sala*. She took the cake and left me the flowers, and shouted upstairs for Vangie. Young women began to appear, and Mrs. Guanzon introduced them. Rose and Tessie, Len-Len and Fe and Wilma and Christine and Guia.

They lived three or four to a room, Vangie told me later. Meals and a cot for four hundred pesos a month.

Vangie was shouted for again. Marivic and Chona and Divina came in. The cake was lavishly admired. Len-Len was dispatched for Vangie.

"And how do you find the Philippines?" Rose asked.

At that moment Vangie came down.

"Everyone has been friendly," I said. She wore a cotton duster, a floral print. You can buy them anywhere in the Philippines for fifty or sixty pesos, but Vangie made it seem rare. Her hair was long and straight, and it shone.

I stood. She stopped at the bottom of the stairs. I expected her to act surprised, maybe a little miffed, and I was ready to give her that. But she didn't even try, just showed a smile so slight it betrayed nothing, and said, "You found me."

She owned the moment the way she owned herself.

I held the box out for her. She came and took it, opened it and made a sweet little cluck when she saw the flowers. She cradled them for a moment, the way a mother holds an infant, then gave them up to Mrs. Guanzon.

She took a chair across the room. I shared the sofa with Guia and Tessie. It wasn't a large room, and we filled it up, the women and I and Mrs. Guanzon's two-year-old, Wilfred. I enjoyed it. Any man who likes women would have enjoyed it. They asked me polite questions about life in the States, paid attention when I answered, even laughed at my jokes: everyone but Vangie, who wasn't going to let me have anything so dear as a laugh so easily.

Wilfred sat on the floor, wrapped his arms around Rose's legs, and glared at me with the spite of a displaced lap dog.

Mrs. Guanzon brought out the cake, and it was much admired again, and we ate. When they were finished they carried out their plates, one after another, and they didn't come back. We were alone before I knew what had happened.

It felt golden, being with her again. She held her hands in her lap. Her back was straight, head poised.

"Well, you're here," she said.

"I hope you don't mind."

"It's up to you—"

"I wanted to see you again—"

"—although I don't know why."

I said, "Come on, I thought we covered this last time."

"You seem to be a nice man," she said. "I don't want you to waste your time."

"Everybody is worried about that. It's my time."

"And mine."

"Tell you what. I'll do my best to see it's not a waste for either one of us."

She tightened the hands she was holding in her lap. I reminded myself, she must detest glibness.

"You're a visitor," she said. "How long will you be in Negros? A few days? Maybe a week or two?"

"It could be more."

"You would still be a visitor. You must see it from my point of view."

"You're thinking, what, I'm going to give you the big rush and dump you? You're afraid as soon as you start to like me I'm going to get on a plane, is that it?"

She didn't speak. I knew she'd never admit that she might be vulnerable to me. Or maybe it was implicit.

I went to her, stood over her for a moment, sat in a chair beside her.

"I don't know about days and weeks," I said. I hadn't thought about this—it was just coming out. "I want to be with you while I can. I have no expectations. I only want to watch you and listen to your voice, really pay attention, so when I can't be around you anymore at least I'll have that to keep, I'll be able to remember you for a long time."

"Oh," she said, a surprised little yip, the involuntary sound you might make when someone touches you unexpectedly in an unexpected place.

"The way it feels," I said, "I'm the one taking the risk. I need you, not the other way around. But if I ever think it's not just me, it's in you, too, and something was happening between us, God, I'd never let us be apart. I promise you that."

She turned a few degrees away from me, breaking contact. It was how she composed herself. When she came back to me she would be all straight lines and solidness again.

"Nothing is going to happen between us," she said. "You have to know that. It's a good thing you have no expectations, because nothing is going to happen. I'm telling you now, so that if you're hurt, I'm not responsible."

She will turn you down a hundred times, Bembo had

said. Maybe a thousand. She will do her best to sound discouraging, but you must never be discouraged, because the next time can always be yes.

But he hadn't said how convincing she would be.

"I'm a big boy," I said. "I'll take my chances."

I won't try to catalogue her evasions, the demurrals and denials and conversational dodges by which she made me understand that she was granting me nothing but her presence, and only on loan.

We could be friends, she told me, and she was genial, even warm, as long as we stuck to the script. But that day and for days afterward she stepped aside when I pushed, backed away when I reached, wriggled free when I tried to grasp.

Understand, this had nothing at all to do with putting a hand on her.

I might have resented her rigidity if I'd thought she was playing at it. But she was no coquette. She seemed to need the distance for good reasons of her own. I understood that she did whatever had to be done, that she asked and took what she required—exactly and no more—and that through it all she stayed truer to herself than anyone I ever knew.

"I'm going to Lanao," I said. Tomorrow or the next day, I started to say. But then I knew where I would be tomorrow.

"Monday morning," I said.

She seemed to cringe at the idea.

We had been alone for more than an hour. Now the others had begun to drift in and out of the room, and I knew I was supposed to go soon.

"We are quite poor in the barrio," she said.

"It's nothing to be ashamed of."

She nodded but didn't look convinced.

"Most of your family is still there," I said.

"My mother. Most of my aunts and uncles and cousins, too, except on Lito's side." Her father had been dead for almost ten years; Vangie was his only child.

"This'll be my first time on a hacienda."

"Believe me, it isn't nearly as grand as it might sound." Her mouth turned down and her eyes got that hidden look I knew from the snapshot. She said, "You ought to get permission before you go up. It's private, you know."

"The Correons," I said. If her face showed anything, I didn't catch it. She seemed subdued. But on her it seemed natural. "I met them yesterday."

"You met Luis."

"The whole bunch."

"Nonoy must have been there."

"Nonoy Paloma—he was there the whole time."

"I grew up with Nonoy," she said. The memory seemed to lift her. "He was a few years older. He was best friends with Lito. There were four of them, really. Lito and Nonoy and Remy Ortiz and Geri Martinez."

It went right past me. "Geri" was what she said, but "Harry" was what I heard.

She said, "Four bright boys. They were in trouble all the time. Full of mischief. I suppose Lito never gave it up."

"Nonoy sure grew out of it," I said.

"And Remy—you think Lito was bad, do you know what Remy is up to now?"

I didn't. She was about to say it, I think, but changed her mind.

She said, "Tell me what Lito did. I want to know."

I told her some. I tried to keep it short because it sounded tawdry, out loud that way. She kept asking questions, though.

"Filipinos do this often?" she said when I told her about the Death Kit.

"Not just Filipinos, believe me."

"Lito too?"

"Twice that we know of."

"He stole thousands. Thousands and thousands."

"It isn't like he mugged some widow for her pension check. Corporations in the States make that kind of thing so easy, it's like picking cherries."

Her expression was solemn.

"It was wrong," she said. "He was a good man. Poverty, the things people do—but it's no excuse. You must think we're irredeemable." Not at all, I started to say, but before I could get it out, she said, "You may be right. You may be right."

REBEL RAID IN LA CARLOTA

An NPA party numbering about thirty overran an outpost of private security forces at Hacienda Clara, in rural La Carlota, in the early hours of yesterday morning. Two hacienda guards were killed and two others wounded. The guerrillas seized five Armalite rifles and some six hundred rounds of ammunition.

They proceeded to burn three trucks and two storage sheds belonging to the hacienda, wreaking about P1.5 million in damage. Elements of the 119th Infantry Brigade arrived around dawn, but their pursuit of the brigands was fruitless.

Purportedly the raiders were led by Remigio Ortiz, a.k.a. Kumander Rocky, whose guerrilla contingent is one of the most active in central Negros.

· 10 ·

That afternoon, we sat and watched people walk in and out of the hotel. Or I watched; Bembo burrowed into the *Daily Star*. At one end of the lobby the Negros Sugar Producers Association met behind closed doors in the Azucar Room; at the other end, in the Planters' Ballroom, the reception for the Lopez-Lizares nuptials was hitting full throttle with ice carvings, roast pigs, a ten-piece orchestra, and an Everest of gift packages.

We were waiting for Nemesio Puyat, who was supposed to be bringing his customers back to the Green Fields. When he arrived, he was easy to spot: he was the unhappy man who stalked two Japanese couples past the front desk, complaining that he didn't know what to do with travelers' checks in yen.

The men were brush-cut and dour, and built like Greco-Roman wrestlers, seventy-kilo class. One had tattoos swirling up his arms. Their ladies were miniskirted lollipops with glazed lips and huge sunglasses and pink Eurotrash plastic sandals over lacy white anklets.

They all just walked away from Nemesio Puyat, left him standing in the lobby, looking mad at the world.

My first patrol partner used to say: Never expect much cooperation from a man whose dog has just pissed on his morning newspaper.

Puyat looked even more upset than that. But Bembo went up to him, spoke to him in commiserating Ilonggo, had an arm around his shoulders as they spoke to a clerk at the front desk. Yes, the clerk said, he could cash the yen; Puyat bleated at the rate only for form's sake. He got his money, Bembo took him aside, and after a short conference they both came up to me.

"We have time to visit Palo, I think," Bembo said.

Franklin had left; the Cortina had carburetor trouble. We went with Puyat in his Isuzu sedan, a smoking diesel. We took the two-lane highway south. The asphalt was littered with crushed cane stalks. Past the entrance to Pahanocoy beach, another four kilometers to the bridge. We turned eastward, toward the mountains.

"I pick him up at deh airport," Puyat said, "he ask me if I know where to find girls, I say yes, he hire me six hun'red a day."

"I thought it was a thousand," I said.

"No, he tell me to write t'ree t'ousand for t'ree days, but he give me one eight only. I say okay, no problem, he pay in advance."

We were beyond city air now, and the mountains looked sharper, punching up into blue skyline. Cane fields grew up on both sides of the road, making a thick, high wall. Small settlements interrupted them, brown burps in the green where gleanings of rice and coffee lay spread to dry on the edges of the pavement.

"I take him to the Green Fiel's. It's deh afternoon, he don' need me no more. Nex' day, we drive to Hermosa, he go into deh town hall, he come out talking to some man, I don't know who. Dey say good-bye. He want to drive to a house in Hermosa, he got direction. We drive by deh house two time."

"Bonifacio Street," I said.

"I t'ink you're right."

"The parents' place," I told Bembo.

"Now he want to go back to Palo. Okay, we go back. He got more direction, somet'ing, we drive around, try to find deh place."

"What place?"

"He don't say."

"Did Collins have a contact in Hermosa?" Bembo said.

"No way. He must have gone to check the death register."

"When he was there," Bembo said, "he met someone who knew about Lito. Someone who told him how to find the parents' home and . . . something else."

To Puyat I said, "Did he tell you what he was doing?"

"No. He jus' want to talk about what great pussy he been having las' night."

"Wait a minute, you didn't take him out, how did he get a girl?"

Puyat shot me a look of disbelief, and Bembo said, "It is not necessary to leave the Green Fields for that."

"No problem," Puyat said.

"All right. He had directions."

"Yes. Come to fine out, it's by deh church. Deh back of deh church in Palo."

"What is?"

"I don' know. Across deh street from deh back of deh church is some stores, some buildings, he make me drive pas' t'ree or four time, he looking at somet'ing on dat side of deh road."

"But you don't know what it was."

"I don' know *exac'ly*."

"He didn't stop at any of those shops or buildings?"

"He stop at deh church." Puyat accelerated to pass a motor tricycle that carried seven people and a goat. "He go into deh church, he come out, he go to deh little house beside deh church, you know, where deh pries' live. He knock on deh door, deh pries' let him in, dey talk for a while, he come out and we leave. He tell me, Tomorrow in deh afternoon, you gonna bring me back here. Den we go back to deh Green Fiel's. Dat's all for dat day."

"What day is that?" Bembo said.

Puyat paused just long enough to tap out a cigarette from a pack. He offered them around, and Bembo took one.

"T'ursday," he said, "one week back. Dat's my novena night, T'ursday."

"Thursday the tenth," said Bembo. "He was killed early on the twelfth."

"He saw Correon at some point."

"Deh nex' day," Puyat said.

"Friday the eleventh," Bembo said.

"I am suppose to pick up him after breakfas'. But I go to deh desk, he lef' a message, be back at four. Deh lady at deh desk say he go to Correon."

"You met him at four?"

"Oh yes, right on time. We go to Palo, deh church. He tell me to leave him dere, meet him around six or seven, nex' morning."

"He went into the church again?"

"Deh little house beside."

"You never saw him again."

"I go back deh nex' morning, I wait. I don' see him. I go into deh church. I go to deh little house."

"But no one was there," Bembo said.

"Dat's right," Puyat said.

"Morning of the twelfth," Bembo said. "Nobody at all was there."

"Dat's right."

The mountains were much larger when we got to Palo. It was a somnolent town that seemed to molder in the deep afternoon sun, flaking outward from a plaza rimmed by coco palms, with a dry fountain at one end and a chipped figure of the revolutionary, José Rizal, at the other.

The church was out of the old center of town, five or six blocks from the plaza, about as far as it could get without drifting into the clumps of grass-and-scrap huts that puddled around the outskirts. Cinder block showed in the cracks of its pebbled facade. The rectory sat close by, whitewashed concrete block, no more than two rooms.

"Dis deh place," Puyat said, and he steered around a corner, down an alleyway. On our right side was the church lot, on the other a cramped row of homes and small businesses. A furniture maker with bamboo tables and rattan chairs stacked outside. A bakery with a front window that was more duct tape than glass. Then—as the back of the rectory crept by on the opposite side—a tire repair shop.

Geraldo Martinez Vulcanizing.

I said, "Shit, that's the guy from Collins's file, Geraldo."

I still might not have made all the connections if Bembo, with a Filipino's bent for the amiable demolition of formality, hadn't said, "Our friend Geri."

I heard "Harry" again, but this time I knew what it meant, and I said, "Shit, that's Lito's friend from way back."

Puyat slowed even more. Bembo said, "Drive, drive." Through an oversize door we could see a man about thirty years old, swabbing the inside of a tire carcass. Channels of sweat ran through the black dust that coated his face and arms. He looked up, and when he saw we weren't bringing business, he went back to work.

Puyat drove around and stopped at the front of the church. Bembo got out with me and we went down the open space between church and rectory. We stopped near the back of the lot. We could see directly across the alley to the Martinez place. It was in a two-story building with the shop downstairs and rooms up.

We walked a few steps to the back of the rectory. Through a window, I could see a wooden desk, a single chair, a cot, a crucifix on the wall.

I looked back to where Martinez was rolling the tire to the back of the shop. The floor above, a woman stood at a stove. A smell of frying fish vaulted across the alley.

"Lito knew Martinez well?" Bembo said.

"Best friends when they were teenagers, according to Vangie."

"Collins went to the town hall in Hermosa to check the death certificate," he said. "By chance he met someone who knew Lito. Probably someone in the office who heard him say the name. A few questions, he found out the parents' address and also about his friendship with this Martinez. He drove past both places but he did not disturb anyone because that would have alerted Lito."

I picked it up: "He doesn't want to spook Lito. He assumes the guy is out and about, just waiting to collect on the policy, having a good time. He figures, sit in the right spot for a little while, Lito will come around, that's the ball game. He'd want to stake out the parents' place, but maybe it didn't look right. He drives by here, though, he sees this, this is perfect."

Bembo said, "Most priests would cooperate once the situation was explained."

I said, "He goes to the padre, tells him what's up, the father lets him hole up in his room and watch Geri's place. And then sometime in the middle of the night, what? Lito spots him and sends three assholes to come and get him, kill him? What the fuck is this? Or the priest is a friend of Lito's, the priest turns in Collins? To who? I tell you what, the goddamn priest ought to be able to answer some questions."

The bedroom looked empty, but the front door of the church had been open. I started to go there. Bembo took my arm.

"You did not see today's newspaper," he said.

"Not yet."

"The priest cannot help us," he said.

PRIEST CONFIRMED DEAD

A decapitated corpse discovered earlier this week near Cagbungalon, Bago, has been identified as that of Father Diosdado Cortez, pastor of Holy Name Church in Palo. Family members, who arrived lately from Dumaguete City, made the identification from birthmarks upon the back of the victim.

Father Cortez was last seen alive the evening of the eleventh this month, when he left rural Palo after administering last rites to a dying lady. However, his automobile was found parked as usual near the church. He was reported gone the next afternoon.

Since his disappearance, unsigned leaflets have been posted around Bacolod, claiming that the cleric was a secret member of the NPA and the Communist Party of the Philippines. They describe him as a "traitor to his Savior, his religion, and his nation, fully deserving of a traitor's end."

In the past two years, three other priests in the diocese have been abducted and murdered by radical anticommunist elements. The mutilations of the body of Father Cortez were characteristic of anticommunist salvage squads.

A statement from the diocesan office condemned the killing and denied that any priest under its jurisdiction is associated with the insurgents.

"We most vehemently condemn the continued violence against servants of the Lord," the statement said. "Indeed we decry all instances of political violence."

The body of Father Cortez will be removed to Dumaguete.

The rectory was locked. The church was dark and almost empty. Two wizened gray women knelt along a side aisle, buzzing prayers at one of the Stations of the Cross.

I was ready to leave. Then a black curtain moved at the confessional, and another woman, also gray and shriveled, came out and walked to the altar rail.

Bembo went in where she had been. The two worshipers in the aisle stopped buzzing and scuttled on their knees to the next station. The black curtain moved again. So did the wooden door beside it. It was a priest, a tall one with red hair and a florid nose. Bembo followed him to me, and he introduced us.

Father Brendan, Bembo called him.

"You want help. I don't believe I can give you much in the way of that," he said. He was Irish, and he had the Irish way of making every word seem specially weighed and custom-rolled.

It was a good voice, but strained. And not just the voice but the way he stood, too, a tightness.

"This is not my parish," he said. "I'm here as a temporary replacement. I did know Father Dado. We worked together in Bacolod until just last February. I cared about him. I'm sure I have two questions for every one of your own."

"I'm hoping to find out who might have come into the rectory on the night of the eleventh."

"That's at the top of my list, too. Already chasing our tails now, aren't we?"

He didn't like me.

"Somebody else was in there when it went down," I said. "An American. He was killed too."

"He told me." With a nod to Bembo. "If so, you know more than I do. Maybe you should be the subject of this interrogation."

"I'm just trying to understand," I said. "The way it looks, some people were after the father, they came in, my associate happened to be there, he and the father both ended up getting killed."

"I've seen the posters," the priest said. "Diosdado Cortez was no communist. More to the point, nobody would believe that he was. He hated politics. Activism made him nervous. To the oligarchs and their goons, anyone who gives a bowl of rice to a starving man must belong to the NPA. But not even they would have mistaken Dado for a communist."

"Did you tell that to the police?"

"Nobody cares! Why should they? People are murdered here all the time. Dado will be forgotten soon. I'll have other friends to grieve, and problems of my own to worry about."

He brightened.

"Have you considered," he said, "that Dado might have been a casual victim? Maybe it was your compatriot they wanted, and Dado only happened to be there."

I realized then, it wasn't me that he disliked, so much as Big Blue in my shirt pocket, with the gold eagle on the front cover.

"And if they wanted him, they may want you, too," he said. "Wouldn't that be poignant?"

"I've had people hate my guts," I said, "and some of them had pretty good reason, but just because I'm an American, that's a new one."

"You must not have traveled much," he said.

"I don't see that it has anything to do with me."

"Americans have been leaving their dirty fingerprints on the Philippines for ninety years."

His anger baffled me. I thought, *I just got here.*

He said, "You made this place. The way a pusher makes an addict, you made this place. You convinced them that they wanted what you had. How they crave it now. They'll do anything for it. They'll do anything to please you. Don't you know? People are dying here so America can have dead communists."

"I don't know anything about it," I said.

"Not only is ignorance no excuse, it compounds the crime."

I turned to go.

"Wouldn't that be poignant, though?" he said. "Wouldn't it be just poetic?"

· 11 ·

Some times you feel the emptiness more than others. I got stabs of it that evening, after I said good-bye to Bembo at the front door of the Green Fields. Sundown, strange city, empty hotel room: bad combination.

Of course, the impulse is to fight it with doses of noise and people. But that cure, I've learned, can be worse than the malaise. Better to batten down, ride it out. It ends. It always ends. Whereas acts of desperate escape tend to have gnawing long life in memory.

Although I speak only for myself.

I took a shower, my fourth or fifth of the day. I ate dinner in the room, watched an old episode of *Dallas*. I kept thinking of Collins and the dead priest, how methodical and purposeful their executioners had been. Serious men, Bembo had said, doing serious work for important people. Collins kneeling in the night so far from home. A beheaded priest rotting in the cane. I remembered the squatters' sweatiness, the stink of shit where their children played. The sunset as we drove back from Palo, soft and buttery; sinister, too, when I imagined bands of killers waiting for darkness.

Wouldn't it be just poetic?

I was in bed with the lights off, but miles from sleep, when a thumping beat began to bump up from below. Only the bass made it up through the floor. Disco beat. I had always hated disco. Tonight it seemed suicidally right. I got up, dressed, and followed the beat down.

It came from behind the two wide doors at the back of the lobby, throbbing through the door handle when I held it. Strobe lights pounded on a packed dance floor inside. Packed, I saw, mostly with young women. The room had forty or fifty tables. Young women filled many of those, too, and still more stood lined up along the walls. They wore dresses, or skirts or slacks. They might have been nurses and secretaries out for the evening, trying to look smart.

I didn't catch on right away. Because they really were young, a lot of them just teenagers. Because they really did look winsome and not at all wanton. In this case the local usage was apt; by their age and freshness they were not so much women as girls.

A hand took my elbow and a female voice said with false delight, "You're a newcomer."

She was in her forties. Her hair was dyed the color of dark copper, and she had a beauty mark painted on her chin. By the time she gave me a second aggressive glance, I knew that I had been typed and appraised.

Chan is my name, she said. Floor manager. The girls call me Mommy Chan.

"You want a girl?" she said. "I'll get you a table, I'll find a nice girl to sit with you, good English. There's no charge for sitting and talking."

Then I understood why Collins hadn't left the hotel that first night.

"If you want to go with the girl," she said, "the fee is three hundred for a short time, six hundred until morning."

I thought, perfect. The best hotel in Bacolod is a brothel. Perfect.

It shouldn't have surprised me. It definitely shouldn't have shocked me: me, eighteen years a cop. But somehow it snuck through and scratched me deep. That, on top of all the rest. Dozens of them, their youth and expectation available for the price of a steak dinner—perfect.

Nonoy Paloma called my name before I could say anything to Chan. He was wending around the tables, waving to me.

"Luis is over there. He asked me to get you," he said when he got closer. Almost apologizing. "If you don't mind."

"Ah, you are a friend of Mr. *Correon*," Chan said.

Correon sat against the back wall, at a table with his son and two other men: a Filipino and an American, both about my age.

Penney was the American's name. He was slight and trim and natty. The Filipino introduced himself as Julio Ferrar. English Leather, Pancho Villa moustache. There were three black clutch bags on the table, and one of them sat in front of him.

"Julio is down from Sagay for the planters' meeting," Correon said. "And to give his bird a workout."

I said to Penney, "What about you?"

"His bird doesn't get out much," Correon said.

"I do business around the country," Penney said.

All of them but Penney were drinking Black Label in tumblers topped with crushed ice. Penney had a beer in front of him that he didn't touch. Correon filled a tumbler and gave it to me.

He told them why I was there.

Ferrar said, "How do you find our country?"

I said, "Everybody has been friendly."

"You don't look like you're having a very good time," Correon said.

"Oh, I guess it's the water," I said, "the food is different, maybe it's a little bit of culture shock."

"I felt the same way last year when I went to the States," Ferrar said.

"Culture shock," Correon said. "Sounds like you've been to visit my farm already."

"Not yet. Monday, I think."

"You know," Ferrar said, "you Americans live in a

commando society. You give a command, you have to do it yourself."

"Most foreigners aren't comfortable on the haciendas," Correon said. "They see just the surface. It bothers them. They don't understand. You must have *context.*"

"Things are expensive over there," Ferrar said. "In Las Vegas I met a prosty who wanted three hundred dollars to spend the night."

I thought that Correon had been trying to make a point with me, but he seemed to give up.

"No bitch is worth that much," he said.

"She was blond. Her tits were huge. I never saw tits like that except in the magazines."

"She probably knew that," Baby said.

"You're right. She probably knew there wasn't a girl like her within three thousand miles of where I live."

"Did you enjoy yourself?" Correon said.

"I tried to. But I kept thinking of all I could buy here for that money. Three hundred dollars, six thousand pesos. I pay my brigadier general six thousand a month. All the time I was pumping away I kept thinking, a blond bitch for one night, or a brigadier for a month. That spoiled it for me. It didn't seem right."

"Your brigadier general," Correon said, "that's another waste of money."

"You pay him too."

"Not like that. It's nice to have friends in the military. But not for six thousand a month."

"What am I going to do? I need what he's got."

"That's your mistake," Correon said. "You put yourself in a position where you need something from the bastard."

Baby said to me, "Julio keeps a platoon of private infantry on his hacienda."

Tossing it off like a cartoon caption in *The New Yorker.*

"Almost two now," Ferrar said. "Fifty more or less."

Penney broke in: "In my opinion this kind of sensationalism is one of the reasons overseas capital gets nervous over here."

Nobody seemed to notice him.

"That must be expensive," I said.

"It's not so bad," said Ferrar. "Some of them are patriotic volunteers who just want to fight communists. They're happy to have rice three times a day."

"They still need guns and bullets."

"That's the problem," Ferrar said.

"How does that work?" I said. "Outfitting your own infantry?"

Nobody seemed to think it was an unusual question.

"I pick up what I can," Ferrar said. "You get shotguns without too much trouble. There are some old M-1 Garands left over from World War Two."

"You can't fight the NPA with just shotguns and old M-1's," Correon said.

"That's why I need my brigadier," Ferrar said. "He arranges, ummm, a long-term loan of some Armalites, M-16's, from the brigade armory. Fifteen thousand pesos a rifle, when I can get them. The drawback is that the army doesn't even have enough for its own soldiers."

"And what they do have is shit."

"Most of the Armalites the army uses are made under license in Bataan," Nonoy said.

"Piece of shit local products," Correon said.

"Awful," Ferrar said. "They break, they jam all the time."

"Everybody uses M-16's?"

"People use what they can get," Ferrar said. "But mostly Armalites they pry away from the military."

"And what about the guerrillas?"

"The NPA uses what they take from our side."

"Any AK-47's around?"

"Very few," Ferrar said. "Naturally everybody wants to get his hands on an AK. You see them every once in a while."

"A very great while," Correon said. "In fact I don't remember the last time I saw an AK."

Correon let the bottle drip dry into his glass. He said a few words, and Nonoy got up and went away.

Correon motioned to the girls on the dance floor, and said to me, "Do you see one you like?"

"Naturally he does," said Ferrar.

"It's been a long hard day," I said.

"Christ. Another straight-backed pain in the ass. What is it with you Americans? Don't you know how to have fun? You visit my farm, I don't want you to give me any shit afterward."

"That's not what I'm here for," I said.

"I'm looking at you," he said. "I see the way you're sitting, you've got your back up straight, like you want to keep your nose out of the garbage. You don't approve."

"Let yourself go," Ferrar said. "You're not at home now. Nobody cares."

Chan came to the table. She leaned over the table while Correon and Baby and Ferrar made their choices. It took several minutes and much back-and-forth in Ilonggo. Then she left. She stopped at three tables, and twice more on the dance floor. Each time she said a few words, each time a girl went straight across the room and out a side door. Five of them.

"Don't you like to dick around?" Ferrar said.

"That's between me and the staff at the V.D. clinic," I said.

Correon's laugh began as a belch and ended in a startling roar.

"Fair enough," he said. "Just remember, when you're on my farm, bear in mind that dominion is a natural state. That's all I ask. You're an American. You should know that."

He pushed away from the table, and they got up and left me with Penney.

He said, "Well done."

"How is that?"

"You have to maintain your distance with these people. They'll try to drag you down with them every time. Especially when it comes to appetites. They'll chew you alive if they think you're no better than they are."

I said, "You give me too much credit. It really has been a long hard day, that's all there is to it. Catch me next week, you might not be so proud of me."

I got up and said good-night. I didn't want any more Scotch, and I wasn't going to wait for him to finish that beer.

I went to my room, unlocked the door and opened it, and stepped on the envelope that someone had shoved underneath.

A plain envelope, blank. Inside, a single sheet of paper with a few words in block letters.

Sgt. Benito Padilla/3rd Precinct
Hurry
"You Are My Hope"

REBS, S.D. CLASH

Information has reached Bacolod about a major encounter between an NPA force and the vigilante group, Sacramentong Dugo. Reports say that several nights ago the NPA attempted to overwhelm a suspected vigilante holdout in a mountainous region of rural Hermosa. Apparently several combatants died on both sides. The raiders withdrew after a firefight of nearly an hour's duration.

· 12 ·

For once the telephone connection was clear. I could hear someone call Padilla's name in the Third Precinct house, a set of footsteps approaching across the floor, a low exchange in which I caught the word "Americano."

It was Sunday morning. Bembo sat beside me in the room and knit his forehead. His friend the police lieutenant had known of Padilla. A hard man, was the report. A career cop whose brother, Ramon, equally hard, was in the P.C.; or had been; both with a knack for pointed interrogation, specializing in subversives, that had landed them together on the Sparrows' hit list. Together no longer, though—it was Ramon who'd been shot down in the city plaza just a few days before.

"Padilla," said a voice on the telephone.

"My name is Hart."

He gave a noncommittal grunt.

"I want to meet you," I said. "We need to talk."

"What do you want to talk about?"

I guessed: "Lito Sanchez."

"What the hell do you mean?" he said, like someone who really didn't know.

In my head I scrambled and reached.

"Or the dead American," I said.

I heard long silence.

"You should talk to Orlando," he said finally. "It was Orlando's operation."

I reached some more: "You sure you want me talking to Orlando?"

A silence even longer.

He said, "Eight o'clock. Dee Tasty. Across the street from here. Dee Tasty."

"Dee Tasty," I repeated, and Bembo nodded as if he knew it.

"Damn it," Padilla said, "this was supposed to be fixed." And then he hung up on a connection so good, it seemed a shame to let it go.

I had planned to visit Vangie in the afternoon, but by mid-morning I couldn't wait. I got a taxi, stopped at a department store to buy a box of chocolates, then went straight to Gonzaga Street. I took the front steps of the boardinghouse two at a time.

We sat together again in the *sala*, far enough apart that I'd have had to lunge to touch her. We talked, but we didn't say anything worth repeating. The words were just a screen for our probing and gentle sparring; her evasions were masterful. Though she never seemed uncatchable. Simply uncaught.

At seven-forty that evening, Bembo and I were eating pork ribs in what had been a front seat to war just a few weeks earlier. Two platoons of NPA had ridden into town on captured cane trucks to assault Third Precinct head-quarters. That was at the north end of town, directly across Lacson Street from the open-air barbecue called D'Tasty Food Barn.

Bembo told me about it while we ate at a picnic table. I faced the precinct house. It was concrete, draped with grenade net. The windows were sandbagged, and it was encircled by a perimeter of razor wire atop more sand-bags. I could see pocked depressions in the walls. Rifle grenades, Bembo said.

A string of lights hung over our heads, suspended be-tween poles. Behind us was a gravel parking lot, beyond that huts and frowzy shrubs that quickly got lost in dark-ness.

I had never met Padilla, but when he came toward me I recognized a hard man. He was squarish, a short thick neck. He crossed the street with shoulders hunched, hands stuck in his pockets, eyes narrowed and lips clamped thin: like someone headed into a biting wind.

I stood up at the table. Bembo had told me I shouldn't be here; Bacolod, he'd said, is no place to trust your fate to anonymous notes that arrive in the night. But he had come because I did. I walked a few feet to the counter in front of the barbecue grills, enough to show Padilla that he was dealing with me alone.

The counter had five stools, all empty. I sat in the middle, facing Padilla as he came to me, with the street and the precinct house behind him.

He stopped beside me and stood watching a cook turn halves of chicken over the coals. He looked once at Bembo, but one look seemed to be enough. He wasn't interested anymore.

He picked up the way he had left it. "This was supposed to be fixed," he said. This time he sounded defensive. He wore a sport shirt, loose. Below the bottom of the shirt, at the hip closest to me, I could see the end of a pistol barrel in a holster.

"There are still a lot of questions," I said. "An American gets killed, there's going to be questions."

"Orlando didn't expect an American. He was surprised that anyone else was there. The priest was in a chair, sleeping. We got him tied up and everything was okay. Then the American came out of the other room."

His voice became urgent.

"Mon and I were in favor of getting out. Orlando said no, we had to have the priest. The American got pissed off, and Orlando hit him over the head and then, shit, what were we going to do? We didn't want to harm an American, you know that."

The chicken sizzled. Moths danced at the lights and drove berserk shadows.

"You had to kill him?" I said.

"He saw us. He would have known."

"Who pulled the trigger?"

"Mon," he said. "God bless his soul."

I thought: Mon. Ramon. The brother.

"But he fucked it up," I said. "He was supposed to do it in the front, instead he gives it to him in the back of the head."

His face went slack; the way it does when you learn that one of your big secrets has jumped the fence. Padilla was good—a pro, after all—and he put himself together quickly enough. But I knew what I had seen.

I said, "You think we don't know these things?"

He said, "Did Orlando tell you that? Shit. Orlando wouldn't tell you that. Somebody close to him. Somebody jealous. Shit. Somebody close to Orlando is talking about these things, Orlando blames Mon and me, but I know Mon didn't tell you that, and I haven't told anybody. Shit."

He turned to me. He began to sound plaintive.

"Socorro has to tell Orlando, I'm not the one talking. We heard—we have sources—our sources on the other side told us they didn't do Mon. Who does that leave? Somebody's talking, Orlando thinks it's Mon and me, but we wouldn't talk."

I'll do it, I could have said, and left. I knew plenty.

But I didn't know it all.

"Come on, compadre," he said. "My record is clean. It's the best. You have to help. If they did Mon they'll try to do me, too."

Flies cakewalked on the sticky countertop. My hands felt greasy from the ribs. I remember those flies, and the heat, and the crazy flitting shadows, and wishing I could get my hands clean.

I said, "Tell me how to get in touch with Orlando."

"You should know that," he said. His face curdled.

"For somebody who knows a lot, you don't know very much."

"I mean right now," I said. Trying to recover; I had stubbed my toe, or worse. "We've been trying to get to Orlando this afternoon, we haven't been able to reach him."

"You're not with Socorro," he said. He drew back, as if I might contaminate him. "I thought you were with Socorro, but Socorro knows how to find Orlando. Who are you?"

The thick fingers of his right hand made scratching motions below the holster. I was suddenly aware of movement behind him, and movement at my own back, too. Things were happening. But Padilla stood close and I couldn't take my eyes off the hand and the scratching motions it made near his gun.

"Who *are* you?" he said.

Behind him a compact young man, maybe twenty, was taking big strides toward the counter. His eyes were locked on the back of Padilla's head.

Bembo shouted, "Behind you."

He meant me.

I swiveled to see another young man, gaunt-faced, taller than the first, coming my way.

His right hand was under the bottom of his T-shirt.

He strode, he pulled out a semiauto pistol. I felt the sickening dread of a bad dream made real.

Two steps away he was slowing and straightening his arm and raising the gun. I watched. I watched.

Bembo was back in my vision now. He was moving toward us. His right hand made a quick tipping motion, as if he were throwing back the last mouthful of beer from a mug. Something bright flashed. He was holding a knife.

The gaunt-faced one noticed too late. He turned in a graceless pirouette as Bembo's blade made a brief, flat arc and slashed through his T-shirt, leaving torn flesh behind it, slashing across his chest and through his bicep. Gaunt-face grunted and lost his balance and crashed into me.

I caught him, and the stool tipped under us. I fell back holding him in my arms, the gun pressing against my ribs. He and the gun came down with me, and as we tumbled I got a look at Padilla. The compact gunman was on him, gun out, gun up.

My back hit the ground. The compact one pulled his trigger, and a roar blew apart Padilla's head and lifted him off his stool. His body thumped down.

Gaunt-face tried to roll off me. I grabbed the gun and let go of him, and he got to his knees. Bembo was standing at my head, sweeping the knife back and forth.

Around us people were shrieking.

The compact one held his gun and looked at Padilla, at me and the pistol I held, at Bembo with the knife. Gaunt-face looked down at his wound, put his left hand across it as if to hold it together, and he scrambled to his feet and started to run back where he had come from.

The compact killer saw him run, and ran, too.

Their footsteps slapped off toward darkness. Gunfire opened from across the street, the ripping of an M-16 on automatic, and the screaming swelled. Bembo dove to get low. Bullets gouged out sudden holes in the side of the counter above me and rained bits of plywood down into my face. I flopped my head to keep the shower out of my eyes, and found myself looking at the shattered back of Benito Padilla's skull, white bone and gray tissue and blood-matted hair.

The gunfire stopped, the running footfalls didn't; both pairs slip-slapped into the night, until I couldn't hear them any more over the gunfire and the shrieking.

· 13 ·

"Don't get the idea that I saved your life," Bembo said. "They only wanted the second Padilla."

We were in my room at the Green Fields, so soon after the shooting that my ears still rang. The police had relieved me of the pistol. They had taken statements for a couple of minutes and let us leave.

"I *thought* I was going to save your life," he said. "Then it occurred to me that he probably wasn't going for you at all, that they were both trying to kill Padilla. But by then I already had the knife out, so I cut the son of a bitch anyway. Once again my body moved faster than my mind. It's lamentable, especially at my age."

I stank of a sweat that seemed to have the odor of gunfire and adrenaline and blood. Grease from pig ribs still coated my fingers, and I still wanted to wash it off.

"At any rate, you shouldn't take this personally. You were only a bystander. Maybe their employers are not interested in you at all. Or maybe they are interested, but they did not expect you to be there."

Their employers. I had already told Bembo what Padilla had said. The cops had picked up a .45 shell from near the body. I had recognized the pistol that the gaunt-faced gunman thrust toward me. A Browning Hi-Power; a nine-millimeter. One of the cops had laughed out loud when I mentioned ballistics tests. But I could guess that Ramon's killers had killed Benito, too. And Benito had said that Ramon hadn't been killed by Sparrows. *Who does that leave?*

"Now Padilla," Bembo said, "Padilla could take it personally."

Bembo was serene and unruffled. No more than five

seconds after the shooting stopped he had stood and brushed the dirt off. He had taken out a pocket handkerchief, cleaned the blood and gore from his face, wiped the blade, and replaced it and the handkerchief in a back pocket.

The knife was a *balisong*, a butterfly knife: with a split handle that enclosed the blade and flipped backward in a blink. I'd seen them a few times in San Francisco, almost as fast and neat as a switchblade. I thought of him, moving with a speed that now amazed me when I saw it in memory.

"That was a brave thing you did," I said.

"That was a foolish thing I did."

"You carry a knife all the time?"

"One may have to slice a mango at any moment."

"You knew what you were doing. You haven't just sliced mangoes with that thing."

His fingers made a little backhanded flick, a dismissive gesture like sweeping crumbs.

"In the resistance," he said, "the first year and a half, we lacked guns and bullets. We manufactured our own gunpowder, and we cut cartridges from brass curtain rods. The blade was the only weapon most of us had."

The resistance. I shuffled back through decades.

"You fought the Japanese?"

"I was young and reckless. It was the thing to do."

"Here?"

"Sometimes in Bacolod, mostly in the countryside. Our bases were in the hills."

"The original guerrillas," I said.

"Not at all! Forty years before that, our guerrillas fought the Americans. Did you know that you and I were once at war? For three years. And then, before that, against the Spanish. Our revolution. That goes back nearly one hundred years."

The idea settled over me, a hundred years of fighting and dying, bridging generations. A hundred years of nights like this one. My appetite for answers seemed pathetic.

"Look what we've got so far," I said. "I came here to find out about Lito and Collins. Collins, we've just about figured out what happened to him. Renegade cops killed him. A hit got mixed up, people are hit over here every day for all kinds of reasons, Collins was just unlucky. Like me tonight. Wrong place at the wrong time."

Bembo said, "In Negros it is easy to find oneself in the wrong place at the wrong time."

I said, "We've got no reason to believe that Lito is alive, except that once upon a time he was a little prick. Nothing else fits. People that knew him, they all believe he's dead. I mean, they really do believe it. They can't all be great actors. If he's alive, he's not just fooling us, he's fooling everybody else, too."

"What else do you need?" Bembo said.

"Not a thing," I said. "We'll go up to Lanao tomorrow, take a few pictures of the fire site, not that I doubt there was a fire, but I do have a boss."

"Will he believe you?"

"He'll have to. 'Cause that's the way it happened."

"You'll be going, then."

"Not *right* away. I want to stick around a few more days." I knew I could finesse another week out of Gilsa.

"Ah. Vangie."

"I'd hate to bug out just when things are going pretty well. I'm not saying she's mad about me. Another week, though, then I go home, I write her some letters, call her—you never know."

"Our work is finished, however."

"After Lanao. Finished."

He didn't try to hide his relief.

"Bembo," I said, "you wanted to sign on for this."

"I had hoped to keep you out of trouble. Not help you make it."

"You could have quit any time."

"Oh no," he said. The suggestion seemed to shock him. "Sure you could."

"Never. You treated me with respect and kindness. You offered me your friendship. Loyalty is the least I can give you in return. It is a debt of honor."

I searched his face. The words were almost baroque—*loyalty, debt of honor*—and I wondered if he was being sly. But he looked grave. He seemed to mean it.

"You still could have quit any time," I said, "no hard feelings.

"Never." He was absolute.

"It's over now," I said. "Lanao. Then a week of R and R for me. Maybe you and Franklin can show me some sights."

"So long as we stop twitting powerful people."

I thought of him again, coming toward the assassin and me, the knife in his hand. The old man. I wanted to hug him.

"You have my promise."

He lifted his eyes to the ceiling.

"Thanks, God," he said, and he meant it.

· 14 ·

The road to Lanao lanced miles and miles through fields of cane that lay on the lowlands like big green lakes. The cane grew in rows, close and tight. From the car it looked like corn, though where it grew highest it was taller than any corn. The day was breezy, and when the leaves turned over and showed their undersides, the fields shivered the way water ripples in wind. Ahead of us were the mountains, looming closer and larger and clearer as we drove east.

Correon knew we were going to the hacienda today; Nonoy Paloma had phoned during breakfast to offer himself and a car. I said no to the car, yes to Nonoy. The hotel kitchen packed our lunches, and when Nonoy arrived we started up, he and I, Bembo and Franklin.

It had the feel of a lark, pressure off. Bembo had called Manila, and his nephew the travel agent had booked my return. I was leaving for home in ten days. With the date set, I was suddenly aware of my dwindling time in the place. Negros probably would never be on the itinerary of any package tour, but it was foreign and far away, and I felt obliged to soak up what I could of it while I had the chance.

I watched the scenery with a hit-and-run tourist's dutiful appetite for detail. Between Palo and Hermosa the lowlands gave way to rolling swells that lapped to the horizon. Coco palms rocketed into clear sky and flared exuberantly against the blue. Streams ran hard and cut deep; from an ancient steel bridge, I watched women squat at the edge of a gleaming stream, beating laundry against a stone. A water buffalo—Bembo called it a carabao—churned through mud like melted chocolate. Banana trees grew down in gullies, a deeper green than the cane, and the sun jumped off their shiny wide leaves.

We didn't see anything of war. There were settlements, but they seemed small and sparse against the breadth of the land. Mostly there was the brown earth and the green cane and the blue sky, undiluted color.

Beyond Hermosa the land buckled and rose, and we began to climb. The road got narrower. The pavement was broken. The world up here was darker, and more motley; trees grew thicker, papayas and mangoes and whole stands of bananas. The fields were still packed with high cane, draped over the hills, but it all seemed wilder than the flatlands below.

Ten or fifteen minutes, we passed a sign that said we were entering Hacienda Paz. A couple of minutes later an unpaved spur jutted off the road. Nonoy pointed us down the twin ruts.

Brush grew along the sides of the spur. A row of papaya trees threw shadows in our way. Beyond the trees were fields, and I could see a crew at work, twenty or thirty men. Some bent at the stalk and swung a broad blade, or stripped the leaves off the cut stalk with a hooked tip at the end of the blade. Others piled the stalks into sheaves, others carried the sheaves up a ramp to an old flatbed truck. All the men wore long shirts. They tied the cuffs of their shirts and trousers, and they wore cotton head-dresses that wrapped around their collars. I decided that cane leaves must be much sharper than corn.

The spur went on for about half a mile. It took a long deep curve that the papayas followed, and the curve ended at Lanao.

The barrio was a sorry heap.

I don't mean to be snide. I've seen pictures of tarpaper shacks in Mississippi that didn't look much worse. But those were pictures. This was reality, baking in the mid-day sun: maybe two hundred huts of bamboo and thatch, shed-sized, boxy and weathered, built on platforms about three feet high. They seemed poised to retreat before the first stray flame or strong gust.

They sat together on a bare spot of ground maybe a hundred yards across and almost as deep, surrounded by cane. Toward the site's front center, the huts sat close together, packed around a small clay courtyard where the spur ended. Farther out they were more sparse, with room between them for swatches of beaten grass, occasional palms and banana trees.

We pulled into the courtyard. Across the clay a boy dropped a plastic jerry can into a well. Several women stood nearby in the narrow rim of shade that one of the huts provided. Naked babies clawed the earth.

They all watched us as we parked and got out. Heads popped up in windows. An old woman waved from the doorway of one hut—there was no door, only a curtain—and when Nonoy started toward her, I remembered that he'd grown up here. He and Vangie, too; I tried to imagine them crawling in the dirt. The gulf across the courtyard suddenly seemed an ocean wide, but Nonoy crossed it with a few deep strides, as a dog nipped at the heels of his loafers.

He took the woman's right hand and bent and pressed the hand to his forehead. Then he hugged her. My auntie, he said when we followed him over; youngest sister of my mother. Children came out of nearby huts and took his hand the way he had taken his aunt's. Second cousins, he said, third cousins, cousins once and twice removed. For the first time since I'd met him, he looked happy and loose.

I asked him about his parents.

People don't usually stumble over that question, but it tripped Nonoy up, just enough that I noticed.

"Both gone," he said after a beat.

"Brothers and sisters?"

"One sister," he said. "Living in Manila."

He had brought a brown paper sack to the hotel, held it beside him in the car, carried it across the courtyard. Now he opened it. It held ten or twelve smaller plastic bags of baked rolls and cookies. He gave one bag to his aunt and passed out the others.

We drew a crowd. Most of them, when they weren't greeting Nonoy, were sneaking uncertain glances at me. Most were women and children and old people—the men were in the fields. They were all small, all thin. They wore rags, or what soon would be rags. Their shy smiles showed crooked and rotten teeth. I tried again to imagine Vangie here, and couldn't. So polished, so healthy.

Nonoy disengaged himself from a couple of kids. Time for business, he said, and we followed him as he walked down narrow pathways between dwellings. We came out toward the barrio's back side, where the huts were fifteen or twenty feet apart.

One space, between two coco trees, was wider than the

others. The ground there was smeared with soot and ash. Blackened stubs of bamboo poles stuck out of the earth.

This was the place, Nonoy said. I pointed my camera at pieces of charred bamboo that lay against one of the palms, at the carapaced trunk of the tree, singed from the ground to at least ten feet up. By now several dozen villagers were standing and watching.

Bembo said something to them, and a woman came forward. They spoke back and forth, and Bembo said, "This lady is a witness. She lives next door. Her husband was with Lito the night of the fire."

She seemed to be about forty-five. She had an infant in arms and a toddler clinging to her shift with one hand, gnawing a biscuit with another. I thought they must be her grandkids. Now, knowing what I know about the folk of the hacienda, I'd say she was no more than thirty; the children were surely her own.

"Her name is Imelda Sapa," Bembo said. "Meldy."

"You knew Lito?" I said to her.

She answered right away in Ilonggo.

"Her mother was a cousin of Lito's mother," Bembo said. "Lito was a friend of the family. Her husband was a friend of Lito."

"Tell me about the fire."

Bembo translated in bursts: "It happened in the middle of the night. Everyone was asleep. Meldy woke up and saw the light of flames inside her room. The hut next door was on fire. The flames were already high. They were flying out the doors and windows. The roof was aflame."

"Whose hut was that?"

"It belonged to a family that abandoned the barrio earlier this year. They left hoping to find work in Bacolod. As of the night of the fire, it had remained empty."

"I want to know what it looked like. A hut just like all the others?"

"More or less the same."

"What I'm trying to get at," I said to Bembo, "these

places have a door, three or four windows, you're not more than ten feet away from a quick escape. I can see how they'd catch fire, anything would do it, but I don't understand how somebody could get trapped inside."

Meldy must have followed it all, because she answered right away, emphatically.

"Lito was extremely drunk," Bembo said after her. "He came to visit Lanao around noon. It was Sunday. All the men were idle. Lito brought a number of bottles of rum, and he began to drink with quite a few of the men, his friends and acquaintances. They drank rum with coconut water all afternoon."

The ends of his mouth turned up. His brows rose.

"Quite a tasty concoction," he said, "rum with coconut water."

Meldy spoke some more, and I heard her disapproval. Bembo said, "After the rum was exhausted they obtained some tuba. That is a kind of coconut beer, fermented coco sap, the poor man's San Miguel. They drank until the tuba ran out, approximately at midnight. Everyone went to bed. Meldy's husband—Rafael—invited Lito to sleep at their hut, but Lito declined. He knew that Meldy was quite upset. Rafi fetched him a sleeping mat and a mosquito net, and Lito went into the vacant hut. According to Rafi, Lito was so intoxicated that he was barely able to climb the three steps up to the hut."

"Drunk," Meldy said firmly. Then she went back to Ilonggo.

"When she saw the fire, she tried to rouse her husband, but he was slow to awaken. She yelled out the window, and some other neighbors awakened. Nobody could get close, however. The fire was too large. She hoped Lito had managed to escape, but when they called for him, there was no answer. In the morning the ashes were cool. The men went through them and found the body."

"In net," a woman said from the crowd. Another said a few words of Ilonggo.

"The residue of the mosquito net enclosed the body," Bembo said. "They believe that Lito might have awakened, but was still inebriated, and became tangled in the net. He would have died quickly. You can see, the construction of the huts, one could hardly design a more efficient pyre."

I tried to think of another question. They all watched me.

"What happened to the body?" I said.

A quick exchange with Meldy, and Bembo said, "One of Lito's relations here went into town to notify his parents. The funeraria in Hermosa sent up a hearse, and took the body away."

"What about his car? He must've had transportation, getting up here."

"Jeepney," three or four voices said at once.

"A jeepney comes here?"

"Along the highway. It's their lifeline," Nonoy said.

Bembo waited, and I looked at all the faces looking at me. I thought of Gilsa and Collins and myself in the office, passing around the death certificate; I thought how far that moment was from the pile of ashes in front of me, a distance greater than just days and miles.

I said, "I guess that's it, then."

A woman brought fried bananas and coffee. Native coffee, Nonoy said. It was black, sugar-laden but still bitter. We sat on the steps of Meldy's hut, where a coco palm laid stripes of sunlight and shade. From there I could see across the low-lying cane fields to the east. Maybe half a mile away—maybe a little farther—a low, wide house sat on a knoll, spotless white, aloof. Deep eaves gave it a brooding, heavy-browed look.

"Luis's bungalow," Nonoy said. "He comes up here three or four times a month, Saturdays mostly. That's where he stays the night."

The crowd didn't get any smaller while we ate and drank. Most of the people watched me. You are a spectacle, Bembo whispered in my ear. They edged closer and began to ask me questions. How tall are you? Are those your real teeth? What is your salary? Americans eat bananas? Americans eat *rice?*

I was in the middle of an answer when a long wail rose from somewhere among the huts. The naked grief in the voice made me stop. The keening dropped and immediately rose again, even more wrenching. Nobody moved, nobody spoke, until it fell silent.

When it did I said, "What is that?"

Meldy spoke, and Bembo said: "A mother is mourning her son. He died last night."

Meldy said, "Vigilantes," laboring over each syllable.

"You have vigilantes here?"

Nonoy said, "Sometimes they come."

"S.D.," Meldy said. She spoke in Ilonggo, and I waited for Bembo to translate. But Bembo was mute.

"She says they came in the middle of the night." It was Nonoy speaking. He sounded almost bland. "The vigilantes were angry, and they shot up the family's hut. One of the bullets struck their only son. He was killed."

Meldy finished with a short phrase, and Nonoy said, "He was seven years old."

I said, "That's awful," and Nonoy, offhandedly, said, "Do you want to see?"

I didn't, but I heard myself say yes. The crowd shifted and began to move toward where the wailing had come, and we were up off the steps, following.

They took us around the periphery of the barrio, almost to the other side. I heard a hammering, and then the people in front of me stopped and parted and revealed a man nailing the top of a small plywood coffin; I could make out the stencil marks of a packing crate under a coat of whitewash.

The coffin was on a table between two huts. The man drove the nail with slight, careful taps. A woman stood beside him, wringing a handkerchief, absorbed in the man's work, her expression contorted. The keening must have been hers.

When she looked up she looked directly at me. I felt unnerved. Her gaze was steady. Not unfriendly; almost gracious. But in terrible pain. She made a small gesture, unmistakable. She was inviting me to come forward.

I did. I felt miserable and helpless, but I came up to the table. She held me with her eyes, until she looked down, and I did, too. A rectangle had been cut in the top of the coffin. A little boy's face showed in the opening, his eyelids closed, his face unblemished, exquisite.

"Fidel," she said, and the cloth twisted in her hands.

"I'm sorry," I said.

The hut was a shambles of torn thatch and splintered bamboo. It had been chewed by bullets. Dozens of bullets, I thought.

"I'm sorry," I said again. I backed away from the table. "I'm very sorry."

"They don't blame you," Nonoy said.

"Can we go?" I said.

"Whenever you want."

I said good-bye a few times to no one in particular, said thank you, and I'm sorry.

I was at Nonoy's elbow as we wended between the huts, through the middle of the barrio, toward the courtyard. Bembo and Franklin were right behind me.

"This is awful," I said to Nonoy. "This kind of thing goes on all the time?"

"Sometimes."

"Luis lets it happen?"

"They come and go at night," he said. Which, it struck me later, wasn't much of an answer.

"She said they were the vigilantes. S.D. Could that be right?"

"These people would know."

"They were looking for communists."

"That's what vigilantes do."

I tried to fathom his terseness. He seemed detached, but I didn't believe it could be. Something lay beneath it: anger, I guessed. At what, at whom, I couldn't say.

I heard a muffled jingling behind us, and a boy's voice said, "Hey Joe."

He was ten or twelve. His T-shirt was more holes than fabric, his bare feet were filthy. The jingling came from one of the plastic bags that had held Nonoy's baked goods. Now it was full of empty brass cartridge cases.

The boy held up two of the shells and said "One peso, Joe. Souvenir."

I got a good look at them. I gave him twenty and took the bag.

"From last night," I said. He lifted his eyebrows. Yes.

Some things you know on sight, when you've been around guns for a while. But I dug into the bag and pulled a casing out, just to be sure. I turned it upside down to look at the base.

Stamped into the brass were several Oriental characters that had to be Chinese, and the numbers 7.62–39.

"That is not from an Armalite," Bembo said.

"No, M-16 cases are longer than this, and the caliber's smaller, they're narrower in the neck." I pointed to show him. "This one, this is from an AK-47."

I kept the one shell and gave the others to the boy. He scampered.

The Cortina took us down the spur, toward the highway. None of us had anything to say. I felt myself detach from the barrio, the rawness and the misery receding. I was glad to be leaving, ashamed to be glad.

At the highway we turned east, and after a few seconds Nonoy said, "The bungalow is close by. Let me show you."

"I'd rather get back to Bacolod," I said.

"It's very close. Right up the road. At least let me introduce you to the caretakers. That way, you'll have a place to stay if you come up here again."

"I'm finished here. I don't think I'll be coming back."

"No? That's a shame. You have an opportunity. Not many outsiders get a chance to see life on the hacienda."

I thought that I had seen plenty. But Nonoy for some reason seemed to care. I can't say how I knew. A minute straightening of his posture, maybe, or a faint tincture of disapproval in his voice. By now I had begun to learn that among Filipinos you had to pay attention, for dialogue was conducted as much in silence as in words, through intuition and discernment.

Anyway, I knew it mattered to him.

"A few minutes won't make a difference," I said.

He pointed us down another spur off the highway. Wide, tall mango trees lined the road, regular as pickets in a fence. A breeze flung blossoms off the trees. At the end of the drive the bungalow sat atop a low roll of land. The road swung behind the knoll and climbed the gentler back slope, to a gravel parking lot.

Like the villa in town, it was whitewashed stucco, but plainer, less deliberate. The roof was thatch, raked low. Shrubs with dark glossy leaves and tiny ivory flowers crouched below the windows. At the front, two wide stone steps tiered up to double doors.

We followed Nonoy through. Inside, the place beamed. Burnished plank floors, wicker and rattan furniture. The *sala* occupied the front half of the house. A hallway bisected the back portion, to a rear door and a patio.

I went out there. A long set of rock steps, notched into the side of the knoll, ended at a tiny white cottage that was the bungalow in miniature. It was the caretakers' home, and the caretakers were coming up the steps. Vilma and Hector, Nonoy called them. They had tough, crumpled skin, as if suction had shrunk them from within.

We hadn't yet eaten the food from the hotel. Franklin got it and brought it to a white enamel table on the patio. Hector set up a big beach umbrella over the table. Vilma carried out cold beer and ice water, a miracle: I hadn't seen a power pole since we climbed out of Hermosa. There was a generator in the basement, Nonoy said; Luis likes his lights bright and his drinks cold. A few minutes later it cut in, thrumming somewhere under the house.

After we ate I went to the edge of the patio. Nonoy and Bembo joined me. From there you could see the carpet of cane that lay between the knoll and Lanao. You could see the barrio itself, absurd little figures fretting among toothpick huts, quaint as a museum diorama.

Some people seemed to be gathering. They were. They were gathering behind a white chip of a coffin set on four sets of shoulders, and the coffin was moving toward the spur road, in and out of view as it traveled between huts. The mother was right behind it, reaching up to touch it, her head thrown back.

Up here it was a silent procession. The wailing of the mother didn't carry this far. It seemed so soon. Dead twelve hours and buried. But I realized, no undertaker, no embalming. Luis Correon hadn't even had time to buy a coffin.

I fingered the brass hull in my pocket.

"The S.D.," I said, "the way I heard it, they were choppers. They were armed with machetes."

"That is correct," Bembo said.

"It used to be," said Nonoy.

That evening Vangie made me describe the man and the woman whose boy had been murdered. She wanted to know exactly where the hut was.

"It could be the Estero family," she said. "Or the Pacitas."

"I didn't hear any names. I could call Nonoy. He'd know."

"It doesn't matter. I'll be there tomorrow."

"What about school?"

"I cleaned out my desk today. The term ended on Friday—don't you know, our school year runs June to March? I can get out of the city for a while."

"You're going to stay in the barrio?"

"I'll be with my mother until June."

I saw the rags on the children, the dirt, the pitiful white-washed coffin. I blurted: "You don't belong there."

"That is my home," she said, stiffening.

"I don't mean anything by it. You seem so different, though."

"Better," she said.

"That's right, better, if you want to put it that way."

"I'm not. A little education, that's all the difference. I was born in Lanao. Until I came here to college, I never slept a night anywhere else. That's my place. You'd know it right away, if you saw me there."

I didn't say anything. I was thinking, that's what I'd have to do. See her there.

Quietly, gently, but with a firmness that scared me, she said, "I think you should forget about me."

It didn't sound like a gambit. I stammered before I said, "I couldn't do that if I tried."

"This can't turn out well for either of us."

"That isn't true. I happen to be sure about that."

"You don't know me. You don't know who I am. You have no idea what I am."

I know all I have to know, I began to say.

I stopped myself.

"I want to try," I said.

She sat back in the chair, and her face went through a series of subtle shifts that ended in the wary eyes and wan, troubled smile that I had first seen in the snapshot.

This time, I told myself, I could guess what went into it.

Her hands opened in surrender. I watched them spread like a flower. She seemed incapable of any action without poignant grace. Or without melancholy.

"It's up to you," she said. "Whatever you want, it's up to you."

"What I want," I said, "I won't get into that tonight. What I'll settle for, you let Bembo and me give you a ride home tomorrow."

I watched her catch a no on the lips. She held it and didn't say anything.

"How else will you get there?" I said.

"Jeepney."

"Jeepney," I said. "You're going to have clothes, am I right? Clothes, personal items, a few books—what are you going to do, put everything in boxes and suitcases, tie 'em on top of the roof?"

"One box, two suitcases."

"The jeepney stops out on the highway, you have to drag your stuff down the road to the village?"

"Once in a while a jeepney comes direct. Otherwise, yes, that's how we do it. We manage."

"But tomorrow you don't have to. Tomorrow, just once, you can have it easy." Before she could answer I said, "You don't have to show boundless enthusiasm. A simple yes will do."

I thought I saw some pleasure seep through around the edges of her eyes.

She said "Thank you," and "Yes."

The front desk clerk at the Green Fields caught me before I reached the stairs.

"Sir, for you," she said.

She held out an envelope, plain white with J. HART in block letters.

"When did this come?" I said.

"Ah, sir, that is delivered, perhaps, one hour after you left this evening."

"Who brought it, do you remember?"

"It was a boy from around here. He comes around trying to sell shoe shines, unauthorized. We're constantly throwing him out."

"Do me a favor. Next time you catch him, when I'm around, hang on to him and give me a call."

I didn't open it. I brought it to the room, threw it on the dresser. It sat there while I showered and watched the evening news from Manila. Two police captains and a lieutenant had been implicated in a car-theft ring, a leftist college dean had been ambushed in the Santa Mesa district, and the Sparrows had killed two army officers in Marikina.

I managed to turn out the lights and get into bed. I tried to ignore the envelope. I might even have slipped into sleep. But I heard a banging on the door, and if I had been asleep, I wasn't any longer.

I put on my pants, went to the door, and found Baby Correon outside.

He said, "Jesus Christ, you're not asleep already?"

"I was thinking about it."

"You can't! We're just getting started." He seemed extremely drunk. Even standing still he gave the impression of being all over the road. "You must let me show you some Filipino hospitality."

"I'll have to pass. It's been a long day. I wouldn't be much fun."

"Working hard?"

"I'm trying."

I could see him make the effort of centering himself, fixing me in his sights. He said, "Do you have something against me?"

"No." You make me want to kick you, I thought, bury my foot in that fat ass. But I don't know why and I wouldn't mention it even if I did.

"I thought you might have something against me, you don't want to drink with me."

"I'm just worn out. But I appreciate it. Thanks."

He said, "Hey, I want to talk to you for a little while."

"Tell you what, why don't we get together tomorrow

evening, we'll have a couple of cold ones, we can shoot the shit then if you want."

"Now," he said, more a plea than a demand.

I said, "Where, here?" and got out of the way as he lurched into the room.

He stopped and stood. For a few moments he looked around and paused at my clothes, shoes, luggage. I could almost see him adding me up.

"Busy, huh?" he said.

"They don't pay me to sit."

"Top-Siders," he said, pointing to the shoes beside the bed. He pointed to his own and said, "Bally. Swiss." Once again I got the sense of him racking himself into focus. "What have you been up to?" he said. The question didn't sound entirely casual, but I thought that might be the alcohol.

"I went to the hacienda today."

"Looking for Lito," he said dully. "Lito is dead."

"I think you're right."

"What does that mean? You're going home?"

"In a few days."

"Lito is dead, what else?"

"Is there supposed to be anything else?"

He spread his arms: "Just asking."

Neither of us spoke. I wondered what he wanted, but I didn't wonder too hard. It's easy to get lost in the turns of boozy logic.

"I'd kind of like to get back to sleep," I said. "You want to get together tomorrow evening or the day after, any evening you want, I'll make plans."

He didn't seem interested. He almost didn't hear me, I think.

"You don't have something against me, it isn't that?"

"Absolutely not. I'm beat, that's all."

"Don't work yourself to death." He said this as he wallowed toward the door. He got it open and went out and looked back in. "There's a lot of it going around."

He shut the door without saying good-bye. I was glad to be rid of him; too glad; I put him out of mind, turned out the lights, got into bed.

I tried to sleep, but couldn't. It wasn't Baby keeping me awake, but the envelope, throbbing in the darkness.

I got it and ripped it open under the light.

DANNY BOY'S DISCOPUB
SORBITO STREET CORNER OF LACSON

"WHO WILL BRING THE RICH TO ACCOUNT
FOR THEIR MONSTROUS EXCESSES?"

LITO LIVES

· 15 ·

I kept the note in my wallet. It had too much gravity just to discard, but I put it aside in my mind. That wasn't hard, next morning, when we drove up to Lanao with Vangie. She was a bright pleasing light, shy smiles and shining beauty, captivating.

Only once did I tell myself that I was looking at Lito's cousin. And reminded myself, Lito is dead.

Bembo and Franklin left us in the barrio courtyard; they claimed to have distant cousins in Hermosa, with whom they would spend the day. They drove off, and I carried Vangie's bags, following her through a maze of huts to her mother's.

Vangie skipped lightly up the two steps to the door, two

slab sides of a coco log. I carried the baggage in, stooping as I came through the door but banging my head just the same.

The hut was like all the other huts I had seen in Lanao, which is to say, small and mean. Two rooms with bamboo floors, together about the size of my living room. I kept thinking to myself, Vangie grew up here. Trying to make it seem real. Grass mats, two stools and a bench, a small corner table where a chipped plaster Santo Niño stood. A lithographed Virgin with a gilt halo, Christ with a flaming heart, potted vines in the unscreened windows, some glass jars, a few cups and pots and plates, an earthenware water crock. Not much else. This was what made me uneasy about the barrio, the way existence was stripped to its rude elementals, laid open like a cadaver on an autopsy table, its feebleness exposed.

"My mother," Vangie said. "Rosita Flores."

She was a tiny, withered woman. I took the parched skin of her hand, gently, as if a heavy touch might crumble it. She wouldn't look straight at me, but nibbled with the corner of an eye, diffident, abashed, then turned away and went into the other room to pour me a glass of water from the crock.

Vangie asked me to sit, and I hunkered on a stool. The thin bamboo slats of the floor bent under my weight. Through the gaps in the slats I could see hens pecking the earth below. Like the door, windows, and ceilings, the seat seemed about seven-eighths scale to me. Vangie looked at me spilling off the stool, and she smiled, and the smile rolled over into a grin that she couldn't contain. She put her hand up and laughed, the way she had the first time we met.

"*You*," she said with bemused wonderment. "*Here*."

When they knew I was there, friends and relations drifted through the hut most of the early afternoon. Vangie and I didn't get much chance to talk. For a while she sat across from me, while kids dashed between us, creaking the bamboo. They made a kind of screen, so that I could watch her without being obvious. I studied her, not only her face, but her movements and the innocent disclosures of her housedress, which covered almost everything and touched almost nothing. Still, when she shifted it gave away the swell of breast, curve of hip, flow of calf into ankle.

Later one of the nieces, a toddler, hunched in the farthest corner, chewing a stick of cane. She spit the pulp into her palm and made a heap of it beside her on the floor. I watched Vangie scoop up the pulp and toss it out the window in an offhand motion that seemed to belong to the place, and made her—dismayingly—seem to belong, too.

In the afternoon, pinpoints of sun strained through the warp of the woven-grass walls. The light outside was timeless and melancholy, and through the window, across the cane, Correon's bungalow scowled at the top of the knoll.

Bembo and Franklin came to get me. Vangie walked with us to the courtyard and stood near the well to wave good-bye. Leaving her there was hard. Even harder was the seamless way she seemed to fit among the thatch and bamboo, the barefoot children: the place so foreign to me, so much a part of her that she must be beyond my reach.

Bembo understood, and he knew how to draw me out. We didn't have much to say on the way down, but when we were a few miles from Bacolod he said, "They are very poor, the people of the barrio."

"It's pitiful."

"And it disturbs you, knowing that those are her roots?" Asking as though he knew the answer.

"They're good people, solid. It's not that. I could care less that she's poor. But it's easy to forget where she comes from, the way she speaks, as bright as she is. The education fools you. See her up there, you realize, that's her. It's really who she is. Then she seems that much farther away. The distance is what bothers me."

"The distance doesn't seem to have gotten in your way. In fact you've vaulted all obstacles so far."

"You think so?"

"If you only knew. She spent the day with you, didn't she? And rode in a car with you, too? Ah! To have come so far with a girl like that, in such a short time. Ah! A girl like that."

He closed his eyes and rested his head on the back of the seat, and took on a look of happy admiration. He held it for a few seconds. Then the ends of his mouth turned down slightly, and the skin gathered above his brow, and he said, "How did she afford it, I wonder? The education."

"I understand the local college isn't expensive."

"Not by your standards, maybe, four or five hundred dollars a year. But for a family in the barrio—that's immense."

"A scholarship, maybe."

"There are a few scholarships available. Very few. The competition . . ." He shrugged. "She must have been one of the lucky ones. What good fortune. And then she finds you—yes, yes, she's definitely one of the lucky ones."

We drove into the city. They dropped me at the front of the hotel and he said, "You are all alone again."

"I'm used to it."

"We will have dinner tonight. We will imbibe and carouse. We will be two carefree bachelors out on the town."

"I thought you had plans."

"Plans can be changed."

"Not on my account. I'm fine, don't you worry."

His face took on sour angles.

"Constant solitude is bad for body and soul," he said. "You must get that girl."

"I'm trying."

"Tomorrow night we will have dinner, yes? We will

discuss tactics and strategies in your blitzkrieg campaign to overcome the reluctant Vangie."

"I'd like that," I said.

I was bending to speak to him in the car. He reached through the window and scattered my hair. When he took his hand away I realized that the last person to do that had been my father, when I was no more than thirteen years old.

"Behave yourself," he said, and they drove away.

I showered off the day's sweat, put on a fresh pair of khakis and a clean shirt, went down, caught a cab out front. There was a steak house downtown that I wanted to try. It was evening, early for supper in Bacolod. The restaurant was empty, the food came fast, and I finished in a hurry. Ten years of meals alone, I had learned to eat at a sprint.

Darkness was fattening when I went outside, a few minutes from meaty fullness. The sidewalks were crowded, and in the street, jeepneys dashed from corner to corner in furious burps of speed. The air was smoky from the charcoal fires of the barbecue vendors.

I began to walk, grim with the utter freedom of having no expectations to meet, no promises to keep. I knew it well.

I headed north, past the cathedral, and kept going. When I put it behind me I lost the last landmark that I might have recognized, even in the day. This was blank territory, darker than downtown, away from all the jeepney routes. Shuttered shops gave way to tightly buttoned homes and boardinghouses. Block by block the crowds got thinner on the sidewalk, until my own footsteps were the loudest noise. Big black gaps of night lay between the puddles of yellow light that the streetlamps cast. I was alone, without reference. In the liberating darkness this could have been any place. I could have been anybody. There was only me and the hot darkness and the sound of my footsteps that echoed down long halls, the empty and featureless halls of my exile.

· 16 ·

"Tell me about San Francisco," Vangie said.

We were in the front room of the hut, the next morning. She was clean and scrubbed. In more than one way, she shone.

"San Francisco is a great city. I moved there in 'seventy. The old-timers told me, You should've been here ten or fifteen years ago, before the hippies ruined it. Now, when I meet newcomers, that's what I hear myself saying—you should've been here before the yuppies took over. But it's still the same place. Nobody's going to ruin San Francisco."

"Oh." A wistful breath of a word.

"You'd love it," I said. "I can see you over there. I can just see you."

I could, too. I saw her with me. I could imagine the sweet clangor she would make when she collided with the monuments of my history.

"It's a peaceful place, isn't it?" she said. "Not just San Francisco. The States."

I had never thought of America that way before; but there, at that moment, "peaceful" was exactly the word.

"Not a lot of shocks and surprises," I said. "Nothing much gets in the way of living. People can pretty much go their own way. Figuring out what you want can be the hardest part. Somebody as smart and sharp and good-looking as you are, you could have anything."

Her head dropped and she looked to the side, out the window. I thought I'd said something wrong. Her upper lip seemed to tremble.

With a yearning that pierced me clear through, she said, "Peace would be enough."

· 17 ·

Bembo and Franklin spent the day in Palo while a mechanic repaired the Cortina. Or at least tried repairs. On the way down, after they had picked me up, the engine overheated. It pounded us with hot waves that surged through the firewall, and we stopped at the garage. They had hard words with the mechanic. The argument lasted long enough for the engine to cool, and we drove back nursing it.

We were supposed to have dinner together. But we didn't get to Bacolod much before dark, and Bembo didn't fight me when I said maybe I'd just have an early meal alone and go to bed early.

I did have an early meal alone. I didn't go to bed. I caught a taxi in front of the hotel.

Lacson Street I already knew. It was the main drag downtown, where it clipped off one end of the city plaza and skirted the provincial capital grounds.

To the driver I said, "Do you know a street called Sorbito?"

"Yes I know Sorbito. The north end of Bacolod."

"It crosses Lacson."

"That is true. Near the boundary of the city proper."

I hadn't told Bembo about the last note. I didn't want him to feel obliged.

"What about a place called Danny Boy's?"

"Ho!" he said, and his hands jumped off the wheel for a moment. "Danny Boy's! Ho! Floor show! Bold dancers!"

In the Philippines they use "bold" for "nude."

"You want to go to Danny Boy's?" he said.

For a few seconds I peered at possibilities, reminding myself that I didn't have to do it, feeling poised at an edge.

The driver waited for an answer.

I said, "Look around a little, why not?"

It was in the same dark district where I had walked the night before. In the midst of shadows and shuttered windows it was a pond of seedy life, loud music leaking out into the night, out front a furtive bustle of cars and taxis and men. The building was concrete block, decorated with a mural of a Folies Bergere chorus line, dancers huge-busted and blond. The mural was soiled, defaced by graffiti, including the word "rebolusyon" stroked across the row of long legs in fishnet stockings.

The sign at the front door read: NO FIREARMS. Through a foyer, behind black curtains, was heavy cigarette smoke and the smell of stale beer, a couple of dozen tables, a small stage with a runway where a young woman in a red negligee was doing stretches and splits to "We Are the World." A hostess brought me to a table beside the runway. Everyone else in the room was a Filipino.

I asked for a beer, and while I waited I looked and found eight or ten young women sitting at the back of the room, prim as schoolgirls at a junior prom, and some just that young. Others were with men at the tables.

By American standards the place was a dive, the furnishings old and cheap, paint peeling on the walls. But in the Philippines you have to look past flyspecks and cruddy floors, and know what you're looking for. The beer ran twenty pesos, higher than at the Green Fields, and waitresses were carting it by the trayloads. The tables were mostly full with patrons who wore clean shirts and the same easy, smug expressions I'd seen on the two P.C. officers my first night in the country. At twenty pesos they were drinking a field hand's daily wages with every bottle: reason to feel smug, if you looked at it that way.

And black clutch bags on every table.

The song ended, the dancer unfastened her negligee. She was naked under a spotlight. With earnest determination she began to do the same stretches and splits.

I was watching her when a man's hand rested on my shoulder. It was a heavy hand, with a diamond solitaire in gold and a couple of bent fingers. At home I might have recoiled, a stranger gripping my shoulder, but here I was getting accustomed to touch. Filipinos like to touch— good friends, men, will hold hands in public.

"That's prime stuff," he said in my ear. "She's right off the farm, rural Cadiz. Six months ago she was planting cane points and pulling weeds in the fields. Her father would've cut your throat if you'd tried to kiss her. You don't have to worry about that now, I promise."

He dropped himself into the chair beside me, a thickset man about my age with a broad nose on a flat, squared-off face, narrow eyes that squinted between wide high cheeks and a low brow. A face like an Olmec head, I thought, and almost as baleful.

"You don't object," he said.

"Please." He was already sitting.

"You're an American, right? I like Americans. We don't get many in here."

"Not many Americans around," I said.

"Some. More than you might think. Where do you come from in the States?"

Without a reason to tell the truth, I said, "Portland. In Oregon."

"I know Portland. It's down the interstate from Fort Lewis, Washington. That's where I took Ranger training."

"You were in the U.S. Army?"

"Philippines. Some of our officers go through the program. I was there in the winter. It wasn't as cold as I thought it would be, but it rained every fucking day."

He was watching the dancer while he spoke to me; I was watching, too. He said, "What brings you to Bacolod?"

"My father was here during the war. I decided to see it for myself."

"A little sightseeing, play around a little, I know how it is. Americans like the Philippines because they can do things here they can't do at home. I say be my guest."

He had a jovial tone but his face didn't move. A smile would've been like cracking stone.

The dancer made quick, mincing steps to disappear behind a curtain at the rear of the stage. Another slinked out in a sequined gown. She wore her hair long, combed in a peekaboo style that was a parody of sultriness. She might have been a child plundering Mommy's closet.

"That one," he said, "that's another country girl. She's from down south, Binalbagan."

"You know them all?"

"I should. This is my place."

"You're Danny Boy?"

"That's me. I don't look like any fucking Danny Boy, do I? People hear the name, they think I ought to be singing in a choir." He made a sound of amusement that came out like hacking phlegm. "It's been a long time since I sang in a choir."

Within arm's reach of us on the runway, the girl blinked into the spotlight and reached behind her neck. The gown shimmered down to the floor. She wore nothing else. I thought of the shapeless dusters that the women wore in Lanao from about age eight until they died.

"She's young," I said.

"Fifteen. But I didn't tell you that. They're supposed to be eighteen to work. What can I do? She runs away from the farm, looking for a job, she comes in here—how can I say no? If I turn her down she'll end up blowing fishermen at the docks for ten pesos and a half a kilo of yesterday's catch."

"You like the country girls."

"They're fresh and clean. No bad habits or diseases. They aren't whores yet, if you know what I mean. I won't hire a girl who's been to Manila. Just off the farm they might be awkward, maybe they don't know all the tricks. But most men would rather plow new ground." His eyebrows came up in increments, as if they were being cranked. "That one is Maricel, if you're interested."

"I don't think so."

"Don't get me wrong. She's not *that* awkward."

He left me after a few minutes. I saw that when the dancers were finished they would dress and return to the seats, either at the back of the room or to a customer's table.

I stayed and watched for a while without knowing what I was supposed to be looking for. A couple of beers later, feeling a little heady, I paid and left. Danny Boy wasn't around when I went out.

The place was well out of downtown; no taxis in sight. I went to the intersection. I was looking up and down Lacson Street, pacing. The music stopped, maybe the pause between two dancers, and in its absence I heard a girl's voice: loud, insistent, a strong note of fright.

It seemed to come from behind the club. I walked down Lacson. An alley cut through and ran behind the row of buildings that included Danny Boy's.

A white sedan was parked at the back door of the club, pointed up the alley toward me. One of its rear doors was open. Danny Boy stood near it. A girl was there too, and when she shook her head I recognized the dancer named Maricel, her long hair pulled back in a ponytail, dressed now in baggy jeans and an oversized T-shirt, the way teenage girls dress in Bacolod when they have the money. She looked small. She was yelling at Danny Boy in the shrill way that a scared little terrier will bark from a corner.

Maricel yelled, and Danny Boy yelled back at her. I saw what was happening: Danny Boy wanted her in the car, and she didn't want to go.

Danny Boy spoke into the car, softly; somebody was

in the backseat. Maricel started away from the car, and
Danny Boy moved fast. He shot a hand out and
grabbed her by one wrist. He spun her toward him, off
balance, caught her and shoved her into the car before
she could shout. The way he did it, I knew it wasn't the
first time.

He gave an apologetic shrug into the backseat: meant, I
was sure, not for the girl but for whoever had received
her.

The sedan purred out toward me, picking up speed. I
gave it plenty of room. It swung by me and paused only
a moment before it turned out into Lacson Street. In that
moment, though, I saw that the man in the backseat was
Nonoy Paloma.

Danny Boy may have been watching it, too, following it
up the alley, because now he had noticed me. The impas-
sive face showed nothing—annoyance, amusement; nothing.

I was about to turn and go when someone stepped out
from the back door of the club. It was a white man. It was
Penney. He went up to Danny Boy and spoke, and looked
my way when Danny Boy pointed his nose up the alley. I
didn't raise my hand or say a word to Penney, and he
didn't acknowledge me. The three of us stood fixed there
for a few moments, united under the tropical night by
questions and surmise.

Though I assume they had more answers than I did, or
more to hide; or else it didn't matter to them. Anyway,
they broke off first. They showed their backs to me and
went inside together.

A cab came a couple of minutes later. I was glad to get
away. At the hotel I almost made it across the lobby
before the clerk spotted me and reeled me in.

Holding an envelope.

For you, sir. Yes, the shoe-shine boy, sir. Yes, if you're
around, I'll stop him the next time I see him, yes sir.

I took it up to the room, sat on the bed and opened it.

LORNA RODRIGUEZ
ALMA SOLANO
TETCHIE SALVADOR
VIVIAN MAAMO

VICTIMS

"IT IS INDEED A REVOLTING SPECTACLE
WHEN SICK APPETITES ARE BEYOND
REPROACH"

· 18 ·

By day, those few days in the barrio, I basked in Vangie's glow. The hours tripped over each other in a rambling lope, sun-drenched and lambent. By night, in Bacolod, I pursued wraiths into dark corners and cringed at what I found—until morning when I was back at the barrio again, once more before her, like reaching safe haven. She was sanity. There was day and there was night, and they were separate and whole unto themselves, the way night and day are in the tropics.

Back home I might call it schizophrenic, but in that place, that time, it made sense. I didn't imagine that night and day, Vangie and the wraiths, might overlap.

Mostly my memories of the days are soft-edged and plush, like the recollection of a childhood lullaby. One incident stands out sharp and crisp, though. It was the Thursday of that week, about midday. Bembo and Franklin were in Palo again. Vangie and I had walked out toward the courtyard at the front of the barrio, and we sat a discreet distance apart on a halved-log bench, in the shade of a clump of banana trees. Beyond the trees were the high cane and the arc of the spur road through the fields, motionless under the high sun.

Nine or ten women dawdled around the water well, chatting in gossipy tones while babies clung to their skirts. Half a dozen men perched on the steps of a hut at the edge of the courtyard, one of them—a hunchback in his twenties, with a crooked nose and jug-handle ears—singing soft a cappella. Elvis. "Love Me Tender." A small dog, bare in patches, slowly crossed the courtyard, tail slowly switching at flies.

Then a rustle of cane tops, movement near the front of the courtyard. A boy, a child, burst barefoot from the cane, dashed halfway across the hardpan clay, and stopped. I recognized him: the kid who had sold me the cartridge cases. I had seen him often since then. He hung around Vangie, jumping to do errands for her, entranced, as smitten as I. Alex was his name.

He froze for a moment in the courtyard. His head swiveled back and forth, eyes wide as a rabbit pursued. He turned and took off running again, across the clay, to the nearest row of huts, a few feet from where the hunchback was singing. Outside one was a woven grass basket, a couple of feet across and about that high. He ran to the basket, took off the lid, stepped into the mouth and folded himself out of sight. The men at the steps, women and children at the well, Vangie and I—we all watched as a thin brown arm snaked out for the lid and pulled it into place over the top.

The cane rustled again. The hunchback broke off his song; around the well the women stopped chatting and gathered up the babies. Vangie startled me with a firm push on my shoulder. In a schoolteacher's definite voice she said, "Jack, out of sight—behind the trees."

I did what she said. I stepped into the low cover of the banana trees, broad-leafed and cool. A heavier rustle off to the side, and half a dozen soldiers in green fatigue uniforms stumbled out of the cane, into the open. They were in a crouch, rifles ready, as if they expected to be fired on.

One of the soldiers wore a master sergeant's chevrons. He carried a pistol, a G.I. .45. He walked out into the middle of the courtyard and spoke loudly, forcefully; Ilonggo, Filipino, I couldn't tell, but I caught the sound of a question. One of the men at the steps shook his head, no. So did another, and so did three women at the well.

The sergeant crossed over to the huts. For a moment he seemed headed straight for the basket, but it was the men on the steps he wanted. He stood in front of them, bantering, cajoling, forced good cheer with a tint of menace. The men didn't smile. The sergeant's voice got more insistent as he asked a question. The men shook their heads. No. No.

He brought the pistol up and put the muzzle at the head of the one nearest him—the hunchback—and shouted a question. The hunchback showed rotten teeth as he grinned a nervous grin and shook his head. The sergeant shouted again, a short, hammering series of syllables. The hunchback closed his eyes and shook his head. I watched from the trees, conscious of the pistol and the stillness in the courtyard, of the hunchback's fear and the pregnant basket.

The sergeant thumbed back the hammer of his pistol; I could hear the click. The sergeant shouted his question. The hunchback cringed and shook his head, pistol's muzzle pressing into his temple, and the sergeant shouted again.

I stepped from the trees, and in what I hoped was a friendly tone said, "Hey, amigo, if I knew what you wanted I'd be glad to help."

Every head in the courtyard turned toward me. I kept walking toward him, toward the pistol and the hunchback and the basket.

I said, "I'm just a visitor, I don't know what I can tell you, but you never know."

"An American," he said. He lowered the pistol. I kept walking, and Vangie started to follow me.

"They're chasing communists," she said, loud enough for everyone to hear. "They think one of them ran into the barrio."

"No kidding."

"There was an encounter down in Curba—that's a sitio a few kilometers south. An ambush. One of their squad was killed."

We were close to the hut now. I stood between him and the basket.

"An American here?" he said. Astonished.

"I'm courting this girl."

"Courting this girl . . ."

"She's lovely, but she's giving me a hard time."

"Well, yes, the province girl is very hard to get. Not like Manila."

"I'm Jack Hart." I put out my hand. He had to holster the pistol to take it.

"Sergeant Emilio Segovia," he said. My breathing was tight. I tried hard to make it smooth.

"She says you're looking for communists."

"Yes!" This roused him again. "We are on patrol near Curba when the NPA ambush us. You did not hear the shooting? No? Well, the wind is wrong. Anyway, we chased them. One ran here."

"When?"

"Now! At the present time! You did not see him?"

I could feel all the eyes watching me.

"Nobody came this way," I said.

"You are sure?"

"I only know what I saw. I was sitting right over there."

"Maybe you aren't seeing very well. Maybe you're looking into the eyes of your girl."

"I wish. But she won't look at me."

"Yes, that's the way they work, isn't it? The more you

· 159 ·

love her, the more miserable she wants to make you. So you didn't see any NPA?"

"Not a one."

"Okay," he said, "no guerrillas here. My mistake." He spoke to the troopers, and they warily lowered their rifles. He turned away, and took my elbow as he did—I nearly jumped at the touch—so that we were walking together toward the middle of the courtyard. He tugged at my elbow again, pulling me closer, and very softly he said, "Did they t'reaten you?"

"Who?"

"The NPA—they're here, aren't they? Did they put a gun to your head, to say that? Go ahead, you can tell me now."

"There are no guns. I didn't see any NPA."

He looked bewildered.

"I was sure . . ." he said.

"You were chasing them through the fields?"

"Yes."

"The cane is tall. It would be easy to make a mistake."

"Yes."

"What happened in the field, I can't tell you. But I know what I saw—what I didn't see. I can tell you, definitely, no guerrillas came through here."

He tried to digest this.

"Truly?"

"No guerrillas. Truly."

A reluctant shake of the head.

"All right. No guerrillas. But you should be careful."

"Why is that?"

"This whole fucking place is full of them!" He threw up his arms. "Guerrillas, their sympathizers, it's a snake's nest. They hate Americans, you know. Nobody has harm you?"

"Everyone has been very warm. Everyone but the girl," I said.

"Yes, yes, the girl. My friend, some advice, let me tell

you. Much better you take her virgin'ty soon as you can. Then she'll have to marry you, and you don't spend any more time up here. It's the best way."

"I don't think she'd like that," I said.

"She'll thank you for it later. That's how they work." He looked back. To Vangie he said, "This is a nice guy, a nice American. Don't give him such a hard time." More loudly, he said, "The rest of you, watch yourselves. You help a communist, you are a communist. How can I tell the difference?"

They tramped off where they had come from. The cane swallowed them.

Vangie went back to the bench. I followed her. We discussed the weather. The women started chatting again, and one of the men started singing, but it was artificial, strained. The basket sat and didn't move. One by one the men got up and went away, and gradually the women took their children and left. Nobody came to take their places, and we were alone, except for the mangy dog. And the basket.

"It's hot," Vangie said. "Why don't we go back?"

We walked across the clay, past the basket, in among the huts.

"You took a big risk," she said when we had put the courtyard behind us.

"Don't scold me. I had to do it. He would've pulled that trigger."

"Perhaps."

"Or the boy—they'd have gotten him one way or the other—they'd have killed him on the spot. I wasn't going to stand around and watch that. The one guy who might be able to stop it."

A whisk of bare feet behind us. Alex passed us at a run, this time a kid's playful lope. He showed me a grin and a thumbs-up, and dodged out of sight between huts.

"I'm not being critical," she said. "Not really. You were brave. You made friends today."

We walked and I said, "After all, he isn't a guerrilla anyway. Is he? A boy that young?"

Her answer surprised me.

"No," she said, then, "I don't know, it's hard to tell, nobody is really sure. It doesn't matter anyway, does it?"

"I guess not."

"It doesn't matter to anyone here," she said. "He's one of us, he belongs to the barrio, that's all we need to know. Nobody would have given him up. Not even at the point of a gun, did you see? We take care of our own. We have to. Nobody else will."

I didn't tell Bembo about the boy and the soldiers; didn't want to worry him.

"The man should be shot," he said that afternoon as we drove back to Bacolod. He meant the mechanic in Palo.

Franklin's car was still overheating. The gauge was broken, but by sniffing the fumes coming up from the floorboard, he knew that the temperature was critical. Heading back to Bacolod, we crept up hills and drifted down in neutral.

On the flat stretch between Hermosa and Palo the smell got acrid, like baking rubber. We stopped at a bridge. Franklin went down to get water for the radiator. Near Palo the smell got strong again, and Bembo said we should storm the mechanic and demand satisfaction.

I said, "You can leave me out of it. Just drop me at the church if it's all right with you. Pick me up when you're finished."

"Why?" he said. Aroused.

"I want to talk to the priest."

"Why?"

I said, "Bembo, don't stand between a man and his confessor."

"What are you doing?" he said. And he said it again, *What are you doing?*, more emphatic with each word.

"There's just a couple of things I want to clear up with him."

"You told me, no more. You promised."

"It doesn't involve you."

"How can you say that? How can you insult our friend-ship?"

"It's not something I need you for, that's all I mean. I can wrap it up on my own."

"You know, we are in partnership. And you promised me, you *promised*, that it was finished."

His sternness was softening, though.

I said, "If you don't want me seeing the priest, I won't see the priest."

"Of course you must do what you must do," he said. "How can I help?"

"Nothing. If I needed you I'd say so. A few minutes with the priest, that's all."

They left me at the church. The windows of the little rectory were open, and Father Brendan, in gym shorts and a T-shirt, came to the door when I knocked.

"I want to talk," I said.

"I would have thought you'd had an earful last time."

"Not that. You want to get around to that again, okay, I'll stick around for it. But later. Right now I want to talk about Father Dado."

He didn't say a word, but opened the screen door and stepped aside. I entered a room that was combined kitchen, *sala*, and dining area. Books, papers, dishes, a typewriter, a small phonograph and some LP's. Dishev-eled. A place where a man lived without company. I thought of the countless hours that he and others had spent alone between these walls. The endless nights.

He was cooking dinner, rice and fish. He turned down the heat under the frying pan and took the rice pot off the burner, and he waited for me to speak.

I said, "Something's going on around me. I don't know

· 163 ·

what it is, but it's so close I can almost touch it. I can't let it alone. I tried, but I can't."

His face lost some of its hard set.

I said, "And not only that it's going on, but it's wrong. I don't care where we are, what language we're speaking. It's wrong."

I told him about Padilla, what he had said to me, and about Danny Boy's.

"You should see these," I said. The notes. I showed them to him; it was a relief to put them in someone else's hands. "This bastard, excuse me, this mystery man keeps sticking a needle in me to make sure I don't relax. It's like he's playing a game. He knows everything, but he won't tell me. That would be too easy. He's got to drag me by the nose the whole way."

He was reading the notes.

He said, "This is a tortured soul. The language. 'Monstrous excesses of the rich'—an anguished voice in the wilderness, if I ever heard one. 'When sick appetites are beyond reproach.' Whoever he is, he has seen too much."

Then he tapped a finger against one of the notes and said, "Her father was here last Sunday."

The finger rested beside the name Tetchie Salvador.

"His name was Jesus. Jesus Salvador—how could I forget it? He had come to see Dado, all the way from Hinobaan, in the south, six hours by bus. They met last year, when Jesus came to Bacolod to bring his daughter home. They had had a falling-out, and she had gone to Bacolod, looking for work.

"She was working as a prostitute. Conditions the way they are, how else can a girl from a poor family support herself when she leaves home? And with so many poor girls leaving home, looking for something besides a life in the fields.

"It's a national scandal. Filipinas grow up believing that they're destined for one man and a family. They're taught to love and care. There are no better wives or mothers.

One thing they aren't taught is hardness; the very quality a prostitute must have to survive. It's tragic for even one Filipina to end up whoring. But hundreds of thousands, great parts of whole generations—unspeakable.

"Dado felt this deeply. Until he got the parish, he ministered to the girls in the streets and the clubs. It earned him some notoriety. There were jokes. You see, part of the tragedy is that whores are pariahs. They're forgotten and neglected, even by those who should know better. Dado had an administrative job in the diocesan office, but during his spare hours he was in the streets and the clubs. There was gossip. But I knew him. I knew he was doing it out of Christian charity. He even persuaded me to help out.

"This is what Jesus Salvador told me. Last year he came to Bacolod to bring Tetchie home. At that time he met Dado. Tetchie wouldn't return with her father, but Dado persuaded her to write to her parents at least once a week. When the letters stopped coming, Jesus contacted Dado, and Dado tried to find Tetchie again. He couldn't. He told Jesus that he'd keep trying. When Jesus didn't hear from him any longer, he came here."

"Tetchie was working the streets?"

"She was better off than that. Apparently she was a beautiful girl. She was in a club."

"I don't suppose Jesus mentioned which one."

His lips were thin.

He said, "She was working at Danny Boy's, of course."

Bembo didn't ask me anything else. He didn't mention our dinner plans. For the rest of the ride into Bacolod, he gave me a verbatim account of the siege at the garage, which ended with the mechanic installing a new thermostat at cost.

"A triumph of righteousness!" he said.

But he hadn't forgotten. When I got out at the Green

Fields he said, "I assume you have intentions tonight. I gather that. Do you want me to come along?"

"No. It isn't much. I can do it myself."

"I would help if you needed me."

"I'd ask if I did."

"Do not be foolhardy. Please."

I took a cab out to Danny Boy's early, a couple of hours after dark. I told the driver to wait, went through the doors and stood inside the black curtain. The place was nearly empty. I didn't see Danny Boy.

When the hostess came to me, I said, "I want Maricel."

She said, "Fine, sir, have a seat, I'll bring her to your table."

"I want to take her out."

She was a short woman in her fifties, with a thick neck and heavy lids that drooped over her eyes. They made her look as if she were ready to catch a fly on the end of her tongue.

And she did poke out the fat tip of her tongue. She touched it to her upper lip while she formed what I took to be a suggestive smile.

"Americans are always in a hurry," she said.

"How much?" I had my wallet in my hands.

"We don't have carry-away service," she said. "This isn't McDonald's."

"Don't tell me those girls are just for decoration."

"We're a nightclub. Our profit is in the drinks, and the girls' table fee." The smile slunk out again. "What happens after closing is no concern of the management."

"But if nothing happens, the girl doesn't have a job for long."

Again the tongue peeked out.

"We have few complaints."

"The table fee is how much?"

"Sixty an hour."

"Say six hours. Two beers an hour, I make that six hundred pesos."

"But we lose a dancer in the rotation."

"A couple of hundred to the hostess should take care of it."

She reached for it and said, "In a few minutes. She will change her dress."

She stuffed the money down the front of her blouse.

"Americans hurry too much," she said.

I went out and waited. I didn't see anyone I recognized, until Maricel came out the front door, in jeans and T-shirt. She walked up to the taxi and got in beside me.

"You ask for me," she said.

"My name is Jack."

"Maricel."

She sat straight against the seat. Her hands were in her lap. Her eyes went everywhere but to my face.

"I wanted to see you."

She nodded stiffly.

"We go to where?" she said.

"I'm staying at the Green Fields."

"Yes." An almost imperceptible moue. "I know Green Fields."

The cab pulled away. I thought I ought to say something more, but she didn't seem to expect it. She looked straight ahead and sat silent and still, tiny, lovely, perfect as a bisque doll. At the hotel I expected everyone to stare. She was so young. Nobody stared. Nobody noticed, I think, except for the hall porter, who wished me a very good night in a voice that was heartier than usual.

In the room she stood by the bed. I told her to sit down and she did.

"You will bathe?" she said.

"I just want to talk," I said. She looked at me for the first time. "Nothing else. Is that okay?"

She didn't answer. I pulled up a chair in front of her.

"I noticed you last night," I said.

"I see you also."

"I'm wondering about Danny Boy's, do they treat you well?"

She shrugged slightly; silent, ambiguous.

"How long have you been working there?"

"Running on five months already."

"There's four girls, I wonder if you know them." I said their names without looking at the note.

"Alma and Tetchie I know," she said. "Tetchie lives with me in boardinghouse."

"Now? Tetchie lives with you in the boardinghouse?"

"No. In the past."

"Where is Tetchie now?" I said.

"Gone."

"What about Alma?"

"Gone."

"Gone where?"

"I do not know."

"They just left? They quit?"

"Yes. Very fast."

"They didn't tell you where they were going?"

"Very very fast."

"Fast, I don't understand. What do you mean fast? She was your friend, she must have told you where she was going."

"No. One night she works, next morning she is gone. She does not return."

"She went out with a customer, she didn't come back?"

"Maybe."

"You don't know?"

"I am also with customer."

"She never said anything? No good-bye?"

"No good-bye."

I was trying to speak softly, slowly. I was trying to be gentle. But her eyes were looking wet. They smeared when she rubbed them, and she unfolded a small lace handkerchief from the pocket of her jeans.

I waited while she dabbed at the dampness on her cheeks.

"She had clothes, right?" I said. "What did she do with her clothes?"

"The next day Sir Orlando comes for her clothes. He says she is gone and he will send them to her."

The name hit me late. She had finished, and I was trying to think of the next question, when I heard what she had said.

My voice sounded hollow when I said, "You know a man named Orlando?"

She looked at me as if trying to discern the joke.

"He is sitting with you last night," she said.

"That's Danny Boy."

"Yes. Sir Orlando. The owner of the club. Danilo Orlando is his name."

I had to get up. I walked around the room and tried to make connections. I saw Orlando and the two Padillas in the priest's room; killing the priest and Collins; and with Penney and Nonoy at the white sedan.

Touching my shoulder. It knotted me inside.

I sat in the chair again. She was holding the handkerchief to her face.

"Tell me about the American, Penney."

"Friend of Sir Orlando."

"What does he do there?"

"He visits there sometimes. They talk in the office of Sir Orlando."

"What about your customers? Do they treat you well?"

"Some are good to me. Some are not good."

"The one last night, he isn't one of the kind ones."

She didn't answer.

"Nonoy Paloma."

She kept her eyes down and said nothing.

"That wasn't the first time you met him."

"He is there before."

"You didn't want to go with him. You were with him before, you didn't want to go with him again."

She wouldn't look at me.

"Girls are disappearing from Danny Boy's. Something's happening, isn't it? Tell me. You can tell me. I'll keep your secrets."

"Please sir. No more."

She put the handkerchief down to say this, and when she did I saw the dark flower of a bruise high on one cheek. She had covered it with powder. The damp handkerchief had wiped the makeup.

She drew back when I reached to touch it.

"Who did that?" I said. "Your customer? Nonoy?"

She didn't speak, didn't move.

"Why won't you tell me? Are you afraid?"

No answer.

I said, "I think Tetchie's dead. Tetchie and those others. You do, too."

"Please sir, my head is pain," she said. "Very pain."

"I'm sorry."

"You have aspirin?" she said.

"You want some?"

She nodded. I went into the bathroom, got two tablets and a glass of water. When I came out the room was empty. The door was open.

I walked to the head of the stairs, where the hall porter stood at his station.

"Did the girl come here?"

"Yes sir. She is gone already. That girl, she didn't steal anything, did she, sir?"

"No."

"No problem with that girl?"

"No. It's all right."

Back in the room, I shut myself behind the door. Maricel had left the handkerchief on the bed; I picked it up, wet and mascara-spotted. It seemed pitiful. The feel of it in my hand suffused me with sadness for her, for Alma and Tetchie and all the others, for the people and the place.

I didn't know what was happening to me. I was never sentimental: never, never susceptible to the maudlin, for all my contact with other people's losses. How often had I fingered the tokens of tragedy—key charms, love letters, a child's stuffed toys—mundane relics that crime or accident had invested with poignancy—how often, without ever yielding to pathos? When it would have been so easy?

Now the handkerchief and its banal dampness bore me down with a weight of grief. I told myself that this was to be expected. Too much time alone and lonely in a bizarre hot place.

The handkerchief made a soft bump in the bottom of the wastebasket.

I wished she hadn't left so quickly. I wanted to tell her: I'm sorry about your problems, I really am sorry, I went looking for you and that was my mistake, but I can't do anything for you—I can't. I can't. I can't.

· 19 ·

"Tell me about your wife," Vangie said.

"You mean now or then? I don't even know her now."

"Before."

"It was a long time ago. It feels like somebody else's life."

"What you remember," she said. "Was she pretty?"

"She was pretty. I won't say she was a knockout, but she took care of herself. Men would look at her when she walked down the street."

We were alone in the hut. It was the hottest part of what might have been the hottest day so far. I sat on a stool, holding a glass of tepid water.

Vangie was by a window, swishing a paper fan in her face. I saw that tiny wet droplets had formed below her ears, running down the underside of her jaw. I wanted to brush my lips there. I wanted her to pull back her hair, the way she did sometimes, so that I could see the curve of her neck and the hollow at her nape.

"You loved her," Vangie said.

"In my way."

"Do you miss her?"

"I don't think about her. It's finished. There's so much behind each of us now, it almost doesn't matter. Life goes on."

"But isn't she still a part of you? She must be." I was already shaking my head. But she went on: "You were married for ten years. You raised a child. You must have feelings for her. How could it be any other way?"

"I don't miss her. I don't think about her very often."

"I'm disappointed to hear that. It would be natural."

The fan stopped. She watched me over the top of its curve. She gave away little enough any time, but with most of her face hidden, just the steady eyes on me, that look could have been scorn or puzzlement or disbelief.

"How did it happen, the divorce?"

"It's not easy to explain. Two people, ten years, feelings change—is this important? I mean, if you're really interested, I'll do my best, but it's a long time ago and I can't see that it makes much difference."

"Not if you don't want."

"It would be just my side of it anyway. Something like this, there's always two sides. At least two. You asked her, you'd get a whole different story. I bet she doesn't sit around dwelling on it, either."

"Don't be sure," she said.

If she asks about your wife, she is yours, Bembo had told me a couple of days before, while Franklin drove. She will hold out as long as she can, because she won't want to admit that it matters to her. But if she truly cares, she will have to ask.

The fan began to tick again. When it moved I glimpsed the speculative edges of her mouth.

"You know in the Philippines we have no divorce."

"That's not the worst idea I ever heard."

"Therefore a woman has no second chances. Even if it were legally possible, once a Filipina gives her heart, it's gone forever."

"Filipino men don't get second chances, either."

"Men," she said, "will always make arrangements to suit themselves."

It was a perfect opening for rancor, but she didn't let it in. She sounded wry, almost teasing.

"It's awful to go through," I said. "Even if there's nothing left in the marriage, it's still like cutting off your own fingers. When there's kids involved, it gets worse. If I ever get married again it will be for good."

Her eyes hadn't left me. They were big, soft eyes, delicate but deep.

I said, "I understand more now. If I was married I'd be devoted to my marriage. If I had kids I'd be devoted to the kids. The next one would last."

"You're sure."

"If it went down, it wouldn't be for lack of trying. It wouldn't be me who ended it. I can say that."

I could feel hours and days departing with the sureness of a big bird rowing the air. The seamy weight of the last few nights had nothing to do with Vangie. The days were Vangie's, and I hadn't had enough of her—hadn't done what I intended, and was running out of time. I could see myself returning alone to the house, the emptiness embracing me like a wattled hag pulling a child to her bosom.

"You say the right things, anyway," she said. Somehow still keeping it light. She had that touch.

"Let's not kid ourselves," I said. "We've been doing a lot of dancing, a lot of round-and-round, that's fine. I'd rather do that with you than with anybody else I ever met. But what we're talking about is the two of us together. That's what it's been about all the time, and maybe we ought to face it straight for a little while."

Once more the fan stopped in front of her face.

She said, "What?"

"We both know. I'm out of here in a few days and I don't want to leave without you. I want you with me when I go."

"Jack, don't."

"I want you walking into America with me. I want you to hold my hand and walk into the house with me, and I want it to be our house. I want you there forever. Do you know how happy that would make me? Do you know what that would do for me?"

"Please don't."

"Maybe it's not feasible, the two of us leaving together, not this time. But if we had an understanding. If you told me you'd be there, that would be good enough. I know if you said it, it'd happen."

"No." With gentle feeling.

"I want to change your life and I want you to change mine. I can be a good husband. I'm a good man. I've made mistakes but I can pull it off this time."

The fan had come down now. Her face was fluid. Hopeful, tortured, happy, fearful.

"This is only the second time I ever asked anybody this. I know I'll never ask anybody else. Vangie, will you marry me?"

"No," she said.

"I need you. You'd always have that to fall back on, the way I need you. It would be your security."

She said, "No."

"I want you to think about it."

"No."

"Why not?"

She smoothed the housedress over her thighs. I had

learned that it was one of the ways she bought time to compose herself.

She said, "I told you at the beginning. Nothing will happen between us. I told you."

"We haven't had a lot of time together. I realize that. You must have a lot of questions about me. I wish we could do this right, spend all the time we need to find out about each other. But it isn't going to happen that way. If this is going to happen, we'll have to take some things on faith."

"Time isn't the problem."

"No?"

"I already know you, Jack."

"Yeah? And what do you think?"

She didn't say anything. All the hope and happiness had left her face. What was left looked like anguish.

"What's the problem?" I said.

She shook her head. A slow, mournful tolling.

"Is it me?" I said. "You don't trust me, is that it?"

She kept shaking her head.

"Is it something else? What should I do? You can tell me. Whatever it is, you can tell me. I wish you'd tell me, I want you so bad, just tell me."

She put up a hand to stop me, and I did stop. But she kept shaking her head, tight-lipped, bleak, as if she had nothing to give me, not even answers.

In the afternoons, Bembo and Franklin would come to the hut after they drove up. That day it was only Bembo, and he was late.

He said, "The car is a casualty."

"It isn't here?"

"In Hermosa. We experienced problems on the way down this morning. Franklin assured me it was nothing. This afternoon it gave up the ghost when we tried to climb the long hill out of town."

"How'd you get here?"

"The jeepney. Franklin is with the car in Hermosa, attempting repairs."

I stepped down out of the doorway.

"That's just great," I said. "We'll have to take the jeepney out of here."

He showed me the little pursed-mouth hesitation that he'd use when he wanted to say no without using the word: he hated to say no.

"You don't want to take the jeepney?" I said.

"This late in the afternoon, so close to darkness . . . they don't run very often when the sun goes down. Hardly at all. With good reason."

"We can't stay here."

"The bungalow," he said.

Vangie had come out to the door. In his grand way he said hello, and he told her about the car.

"You shouldn't try the jeepney this late," she said.

"My opinion exactly, miss."

"Someone will give you a place for the night, if you don't mind a grass mat."

"We have arrangements already," he said. He threw out an arm in a theatrical sweep toward the bungalow. "The alabaster palace."

Something tightened in her, I could tell.

"It's all right," I said. "We have permission."

She got Alex to show us a way through the fields. Something still nagged in her, it seemed to me. I could almost see her pushing it aside.

She looked tender and melancholy when we said good-bye. I thought of the leaving I would take in a few days, when it wouldn't be just for hours, and it chilled me. I said good-bye and turned away fast.

Alex brought us out the back side of the barrio, into a field of cane. We walked into it, single file, between rows. The stalks were tall. The leafy tops arched into a bower overhead, slashing across sun and sky.

A few minutes through the cane, we were at the foot of a forested incline that we began to climb, using a trail that ran through the trees, beside a dry gully. Maybe a quarter of a mile farther, the trees ended and we came out at the foot of the bungalow. A line of stone steps climbed up the little knoll, to the front door.

Hector greeted us there like an innkeeper. He showed us to a room down the hall; it was big and bright, with a screened window that in a few minutes would have a sunset view. Down below the cutters were at work in a field, the edge of the cane standing like a wall, flaking off as the bright knives swung.

Hector shut the window and turned on the air-conditioning.

Vilma brought towels and soap, a razor and toothbrushes, and terry-cloth robes. The shower had walls of native stone. The fixtures were American, and the hot water worked—clouds of steam rolled out when Bembo showered.

He emerged looking like a scrawny wet rat, lost in the terry-cloth. The air was cooling already, pumping out of grates in the floor; he pulled the robe tighter around his shoulders.

The floors were the same polished slab as the *sala*. The bed was queen-sized, the dresser and table slick white wicker.

The generator droned beneath our feet.

"Rich men," he said.

After dinner we sat at the patio. Bats chased bugs, the night grew solid. Hector brought up a guitar and a two-liter bottle with a Shell Oil label. Tuba, he said; leaning hard on the second syllable.

Now you're getting into the real Philippines, Bembo said.

It was tart and astringent, with a lurking sweetness.

Tuba was supposed to be coconut beer, but it didn't taste like coconut. It didn't taste like anything I recognized, except maybe the undertones of motor oil. I drank one glass and Hector poured me another. He said a few words to Bembo, and Bembo said, "He tells you to be careful. It will knock you on your ass if you're not used to it."

The high was sneaky. Hector began to play the guitar and sing Ilonggo ballads. Before I could fight it, the tuba had slipped my legs out from under me, and the music was tugging off my shoes, and I was asprawl on a featherbed of strong drink and sultry night and weepy song.

Hector filled my glass. I said to Bembo, "Back home I never drink this much."

"Back home you have no excuse to drink this much."

I said, "That reminds me. I've been thinking that you ought to visit the States. You've earned a vacation."

"Regrettably, the fare to the States is beyond my means."

"The company can handle it. You're a valued employee."

"I am a minor contractor, seldom-used and low-paid. Even if money were not a consideration, your government requires a visitors' visa. Only the well-heeled or the well-connected qualify. I am neither."

"You have connections now. We'll make a little end run around the embassy. The company has juice. They'll handle it. They'll pop for the ticket, too, when I tell them all you've done for me. If they won't, I will. When you get there you can stay with me."

"Don't make promises," he said, and we both let it drop.

We drank. Bembo matched me glass for glass. I had seen him drunk twice, and both times I'd been startled at that lupine surliness that seemed to come from nowhere, so unlike him. I should have noticed it coming on again; at least, I'd have been expecting it.

Hector began another ballad and Bembo said, "This

one is Cebuano, but it's still beautiful. Most Ilonggos understand Cebuano—they speak it on the other side of the mountains."

"What's it called?"

"This song?" he said. *"Usahay.* Sometimes."

He was translating.

"Sometimes I dream. I dream that we've fallen in love. Sometimes I'm troubled. Why am I alone in this life? Why does heaven jest with me?"

When it was finished he said, "I used to court my wife with *Usahay.*"

"I didn't know you were married."

"There are many things you don't know about me. But that's all right. She's dead twenty-two years. We had no children."

"An Ilongga?"

"Yes an Ilongga, naturally an Ilongga, what else? I was thirty years old before I ever slept a night off this island. As it happens, she was from Hermosa town. I would come down at night to visit her. Sometimes it was right after a job. One night her mother gave me hell because blood dripped off my cane knife and stained the floor."

"The resistance, I've been meaning to ask you about that."

"Pfft. Nothing. Especially at that age—nothing. Isn't it odd, the way old men with so little life in them will cling so hard to it? While young ones with so much are so ready to throw it away?"

"You must have some memories."

"We lived in the sticks and killed Japanese. They bled and died like anybody else. That's all. We were led by an American: there's a detail for you. He was a Navy ensign from the base in Cebu. An ensign. His boat had been torpedoed out in the straits, and he ended up with us.

"We had Filipino officers, regular army, captains, even a major. But on the radio MacArthur's headquarters would talk only to the American ensign. MacArthur had the guns we needed. Excuse me, for a long time it was the promise of guns. Therefore the American ensign commanded us on our own territory. Shit. He couldn't have led ducks to a pond."

"I guess that's war."

"That's war all right."

I was on a woozy plateau; I didn't want to fight anybody.

I said, "That song, it must have worked for you, huh? I'm thinking, maybe I ought to give it a try."

He cocked an eye at me.

"Are we having difficulties with the reluctant Vangie?"

"I don't understand what's going on. I know she likes me. You'd have to pay attention to see it, but I know. Everything goes great right up to the moment of truth. And she says no."

"Don't tell me!"

"Not just no, but flat-out, forget-it, no."

"Brava for the Ilongga," he said.

"Thank you."

"In America, the girls just fall over when a desirable man walks by?"

"It happens now and then, something like that."

"Not with Filipinas. They don't give themselves away. You know, a man here might court a girl for months without even bothering to ask the question. He knows it won't do him any good. You're here for a few days, you expect her to swoon so you can take her home like a trinket? Your souvenir of the trip?"

To Hector, in English, he said, "The 'Cano has balls. Not much sense, but plenty of balls."

Hector held his guitar and nodded without comprehension.

"I appreciate your support," I said.

"You don't need my support. You'll get what you want. Let the girl have her moment of self-respect. Let her pretend that she held out for a couple of days. Can't you give her that?"

"I don't know what you mean."

"It's done. It's all over." He was yelling. "Don't you know? It was all over the second you decided you wanted her. Think about it! You show up here with your pink skin, your pockets full of dollars, that glow, that goddamn prosperous glow. And an immigrant visa, the ticket to the land of milk and honey—every American bachelor over here has a green card to give away. Half of the people in this country would kill the other half to get an immigrant visa, and you have one to bestow on some lucky girl."

He stopped to drink. He was calmer when he put the glass down.

"You've got it all. The skin, the dollars, the green card. My support, you must be joking. You've seen Lanao. You tell a barrio girl you want to take her away from that shit-hole, she's going. Believe me. If you want to bring her home with you, she's going."

"I don't see it happening. But if she does, it won't be for money or a visa. She's not that kind."

"Vangie's a treasure, don't get me wrong. She's a true Filipina, the best. And you're a nice guy. However, that is irrelevant. If you want her she's yours. It's a foregone conclusion."

He turned to Hector and said, "She truly is precious. He doesn't have any idea what he's getting. Isn't that the way? The 'Canos take our very best, they flash their dollars and they've got it. Most of the time they don't even bother to say thank you."

I was turning it over in my mind. I was thinking that I didn't care why she went with me, as long as she did. In time I'd make it right. I was wondering if it might be true, hoping it was, when I heard what he had said.

I told him, "Someday I'd like to know what you've got against Americans."

"You think you would like to know."

"I'm sitting here. I'm listening."

"Listen all you want. It won't do you any good. What I feel is not in words, it is here"—he slapped his chest—"and the problem with you people is that you are crippled here, where it counts. You say the right things, you go through the motions, but in here, you are stunted."

"Okay, that's one."

"Don't do that! It isn't just one on a list! The heart is everything! What are you if you don't have it there? *We* have it, Hector and I, and Vangie, and the squatters, and even soldiers, and even guerrillas, we fuck up too often, granted, but not because our hearts are withered."

He leaned over the table. He looked straight at me. When he spoke again, his voice was dead calm.

"Let's be fair. Your way is more efficient. Look at results—there's no arguing with results. Americans live in comfort. Americans walk on the moon, Americans win gold medals and drive big cars. You have hospitals and clean streets . . . you people can really do it. And we're proud of you for it! We are! It's like watching our cousins make a success.

"That's it—you are family. For us there is nothing like family, and nobody like Americans. We can't get enough of you. We try to talk the way you talk. We want to live the way you live. If it says Made in U.S.A., we must have it. We are obsessed with you. You dominate us without even trying, and it is killing us. Still we love you. You sons of bitches, we love you."

Beside him, Hector was full of grave dignity; he did understand, after all.

"We love you," Bembo said, "and you hardly know that we exist. Can you imagine how that hurts? But we still love you. After the war, you rebuilt your enemies while you gave us next to nothing. It does you no honor to scorn loyal friends that way, but you don't seem to understand honor the way we do, so what can we expect? We still love you."

He stopped and lit a cigarette in his careful, unhurried way; certain that I had no reply. He took a couple of drags before he spoke.

"You don't mind if I get personal? Speaking frankly, when I met you I wanted you to be a jerk. It would have been much easier to take. But you treated me with decency, and I was pathetically grateful. To be treated with decency by an American. You had me. I would do anything for you now. It's obscene.

"Every kindness you show me is a knife in my back. You just make it harder. I know I will never see you again. I will never hear from you. You are an American, after all, you are busy winning gold medals and flying in space. I will never hear from you again but I will think of you too often. I will remember our exploits with too much fondness. I will be like a jilted girl waiting for a long-gone Lothario. Already I hate myself for it. But that's how it is when you live in the heart the way we do. We don't discard our loves. They are too precious to us. We hold on to them long after they've stopped being useful."

I was about to speak. He stopped me with a raised hand, the butt of the cigarette pointed at my face.

He said, "Don't say a word. I don't require assurance. I don't want to hear it."

He spoke a few words of Ilonggo, and Hector chorded the guitar and began to sing. Bembo filled our glasses and we sat listening to the songs, drinking until the tuba was finished, and then we went in.

We took turns using the bathroom. I finished first and got into bed, and he came out a few minutes later, wearing boxer shorts big as bloomers. His bony little frame made no disturbance when he lay down on the other side of the mattress.

He lit a cigarette and drew on it as he stared up at the ceiling.

He said, "If you marry her here, you can't just bring her home with you. I looked into it today. Your Immigration

Service won't allow it anymore. You file a petition from the States. The paperwork takes three or four months, and she must wait here until it is processed. The alternative is to help her get a tourist visa. You know someone at the embassy. With a tourist visa, she can fly tomorrow. Get her over there, then marry her. You can be together while you file for her green card. They frown on it, but it's legal. That's how I would approach it if I were you."

I said, "You really think Vangie will come with me?"

"I don't know why not. You must be the answer to her prayers."

"I need her, too."

"You are smart to realize it."

"I'm sorry you don't want to visit me back home."

He was watching his smoke rise.

"What I said was, don't make promises."

"I can promise to do my best. Does this mean that you'd like to make the trip?"

He said, "What do you think?"

· 20 ·

The next morning was Saturday. Bembo and I walked together to the barrio, retracing the route that Alex had showed us: the trail down the forested hillside, down to the cane field, then between the cane rows until the field ended behind the barrio. Bembo stayed a couple of hours, trying not to get in the way, looking restless. Franklin still hadn't returned by then, so Bembo decided that the car must still be under repair in Palo. He left to catch a jeepney into the town, and promised to return with Franklin that afternoon, to pick me up.

For most of the day it was airy and easy between Vangie and me. People were around, and that was a distraction;

I didn't mind. In the afternoon, though, we found ourselves alone together. Somehow—I don't remember—one of us mentioned Tuesday morning. My flight out of Bacolod was Tuesday morning.

She said, "When you get home, will you think about me?"

"Does it matter?"

"That's cruel." I saw that she was hurt.

"I'll think about you," I said. "I'll never forget you. How could I?"

She liked that.

"If you were with me," I said, "you wouldn't have to ask."

"No," she said. Adamant. "Don't. Not again."

"You mean it."

"I meant it from the start. I told you."

"I'm not going to make you get into it again," I said. "But what I would like to know—you don't have to answer me, but I would like to know—if there was no chance, why did you let me?" Before she could say a word, I said, "I know you told me. But you didn't stop me. You could have stopped me but you didn't."

Anybody else would have pretended not to know what I meant, or would have embarrassed us both with artificial apology. But Vangie was never coy when it mattered, and she was incapable of artifice.

"It was selfish," she said. "I shouldn't have. I was wrong." She said it with such quietness; but it was a quiet like the stillness before a storm, the kind that makes you pay attention.

It made me want her even more. Whatever she did seemed to make me want her more.

"Don't worry about it," I said. "I'm a big boy. But why?"

Her hands twisted in her lap.

"To imagine it," she said. "To think how it would be. It made me happy."

*　*　*

A little while later I left her. It was all too much, my desire set against the steady progress of time, Tuesday morning onrushing.

I told her I wasn't feeling well, that I was going up to the bungalow to rest; I asked her to send Bembo and Franklin when they came.

I took the trail through the cane. Before I reached the forest, the boy named Alex came running up behind me, calling Hey Joe. He had a note from Bembo, sent up by jeepney. Automobile still under repair; will return tomorrow.

I wasn't anxious to stay. But I didn't know how to find Bembo in Hermosa, and I didn't want to try getting to Bacolod on my own—the jeepney routes baffled me. My clothes were rank, but Vilma took them while I was in the shower, and in a couple of minutes she had them washed, spread out to dry on the bougainvillea.

I showered Filipino style, sluicing out of a bucket. When I was finished I didn't bother to use a towel, just closed the door and opened the window, lay down naked and wet and sleepy, letting the dampness evaporate, cooling me as I slept. An afternoon nap, naked and wet, is one of the tropics' carnal delights.

The room was chilly when I woke up. The generator was running and the floor register was churning out cool air. I put on a robe and went out. Nobody was in the house, but on the patio Luis Correon sat alone, drinking scotch.

He caught me looking, waved me over. I came out and went to the table. A bodyguard with a shotgun stood in the shade of a big mango tree; another leaned against a corner of the bungalow.

"You're here!" he said.

"My car broke down—"

"I know, I talked to Hector. Great. You'll be around for my little blowout tonight. Saturday night, you know."

"If you have plans, I'll get out."

"The hell you will, you'll enjoy my hospitality."

I wondered where I stood with him, how much he knew about what I'd been doing. Whatever he knew, it didn't seem to bother him.

"I appreciate it," I said.

"Hector and Vilma, they're taking good care of you?"

"Terrific."

"That's about how it went last night."

"Now you've seen my farm." He had a cunning look. "You want to give me a hard time about it?"

"I wouldn't do that."

"A gracious guest. But you've got your thoughts on the matter."

From the table I could see the barrio, the Solanos' hut. I could see the copse where we had opened the grave.

"It's a hard life," I said.

"Life is hard. You and me, we're privileged exceptions. Down there, that's how the majority of the planet lives. Americans don't get their noses rubbed in it. But it's a fact."

Vilma came out with my clothes. I excused myself and went in, and when I came out again, Luis had gone to his room, next to mine.

I didn't see him again until after the sun was down. In that time Hector put out bottles of Black Label and a tub of iced beer in the *sala*. Vilma set platters of food on a table. Julio Ferrar drove up with Baby Correon; their bodyguards mingled with Luis's outside. Right behind them was a Toyota Land Cruiser, Luis's driver bringing four young women in gay dresses.

They came in with loud whispers among themselves, flocking and giggling. I recognized two of them from the disco at the Green Fields; their eyes skimmed around the place to Ferrar and Baby and me, to the furniture, the food.

When they appeared, Correon came out. He wore a fresh white shirt with the cuffs turned up, and pleated black slacks that hid his paunch. His hair was combed straight back. He greeted Ferrar and Baby from across the *sala*. He gave the girls the sort of up-and-down examination you might give to a fresh paint job on a fence, and he said, "Very good as always, I approve, but don't be greedy. We have a guest—Julio, you remember Jack from the States—so I want you to *share*."

He was standing beside me. He called over to the girls. One of them detached herself from the others and came to us. She seemed shy but she didn't hesitate.

"I'm giving you a good one," Correon said to me.

He spoke to her in Ilonggo; first in the tone of a question, which she answered, then as instruction.

"Her name is Lina," Correon said. "I told her, she's yours tonight, she shouldn't leave your side, and above all she shouldn't let those lechers touch her." He was enjoying himself. Louder, mock-gruff, he said to Ferrar and Baby, "You'll have to make do with three between you. It's more than you can handle anyway." Back to me he said, "She claims she's never had an American before. Don't disappoint her."

I said, "She's yours—I wouldn't want my host to go without."

"Don't worry about me. I'm taken care of."

That was when another set of headlights rose up the knoll and crunched the gravel outside. The front door opened. Nonoy Paloma came in. He held it open. And Vangie walked in after him.

That night, when I had time to think about it, I marveled at what guts it must have taken to enter the way she did: head up, wrapping herself in level disinterest as she stopped a couple of steps inside. What nerve, what enormous discipline. Because she knew I was there, knew I'd be watching.

Only much later have I realized that it wasn't a question of guts at all, or nerve, or discipline. She had no choice.

"Here she is," Luis said.

She wore the red dress from the first time I'd met her; but with a wide patent-leather belt that raised the hemline and gave it some form. Her heels seemed a little higher, and I didn't have to guess whether she was wearing makeup.

Luis spoke a few words in Ilonggo, and she answered, and he went across the room to her. He had been beside me, so his path followed the line of sight between me and her. I watched her as he approached, and though her eyes seemed to be on him, I knew that at least part of her gaze was mine, and that some message for me was encrypted in the edges of her bland expression.

I knew it was there but I couldn't read it.

He reached for her hands. She put them out for him to hold, and he took them and leaned in and kissed her on the lips. He had an arm around her when he faced us.

"You know Julio . . . this is Jack," he said. "Jack is from the States. He's been in the barrio."

"I've seen him," she said. "Hello, Baby," she said. And to me, "Hello."

"Don't get any ideas," Luis said. He wagged a playful finger at me. "This is private stock."

I endured the next couple of hours. Shock carried me part of the way. And I could occupy myself with the stultifying mystery of it; I had questions to pose, conversations to replay while I stood with a glass in my hand and looked at the two of them together; Luis touching, hovering, proprietary.

I got close to her once. She was alone at the buffet table, putting food on her plate. I got up and stood beside her, filling my own plate. She wouldn't look at me, though, and I didn't know what to say.

It wasn't a rowdy party. ("Luis's blowouts are much more fun when *she*'s not here," Ferrar said to me at one point. "Too bad for you. Bad timing.") It wasn't much of a party at all. We drank and ate. Baby picked up a microphone and crooned some Elvis Presley with a sing-along tape. There were moments when I forced myself to stop watching Vangie, and moments when I couldn't bear to watch.

It ended fast. Baby and Ferrar arm-wrestled for the third girl, and while they struggled, Luis walked Vangie down the hall. She went along with him; all her modesty going down the hall with him, all her reserve and her beauty and her self-possession going, with a crushing readiness that made me wonder how often, for how long. She didn't look back. Luis did, though. He stopped and leered over his shoulder at me and said, "Remember we're neighbors; don't be too loud, but if you have to be loud, don't be long."

I watched the door shut behind them. Ferrar and Baby gathered up the others and took them to their rooms, across the hall from Luis's and mine.

I was alone on a couch with Lina. I sat, immobile. I thought of Vangie and Luis behind the door. Lina was uncertain but patient. She had taken Luis literally: hadn't left my side. Three of the bodyguards came in for food, saw us there, and scurried. I imagined them out there in the darkness, lurking like hungry dogs.

"You are American," Lina said. Her first words to me.

"Yes."

"Very nice, the States."

"Yes."

She held my hand and stood.

"We go," she said, and I let her pull me up.

The click of my door sounded loud when I closed it. Lina went back to lock it. I sat on the edge of the bed, and when I didn't move, she turned out the lights and stood by the closet to undress. She hung her clothes up carefully. She opened the window and closed the air grate in the floor. I realized that she had been here before. Maybe with Luis, I thought.

She went to shower, came back damp, in a towel. When I went in I could hear water running next door. I tried to imagine them on the other side of the wall. But their intimacy, the shapes it might take, was beyond me.

When I came back, Lina was lying on the sheet, naked in moonlight. She had rich skin that was even darker against the white cotton. She was small, slim.

She watched me as I came to the bed. The moon was bright enough that I could see her eyes, but there wasn't much to see. She was neutral. I don't mean jaded or bored or abject or even empty. She was just there, waiting.

I took off my towel and crouched next to her on the sheet. She didn't move. I slid one hand along her body, over the flat of her stomach and the sharpness of her hips and the wispy crown of her mons.

It was just automatic. I felt no desire. I kept trying to see Luis with Vangie in moonlight and shadow, then Luis with Lina. I was trying to see myself with Vangie. None of it worked.

I moved over her in the offhand way you might cover a boiling pot or tie your shoes, when it is done before you think of doing it. She felt fragile under me. She put her hands on my shoulders, not in affection but to keep me politely at a distance. When I took her she turned her face away. I did too, and we each of us fled alone to private shames and sorrows.

· 21 ·

The bungalow woke up early. I pretended not to, and burrowed my head into the pillow while Lina showered and dressed. She closed the door carefully, to keep the bolt from snapping.

By then the others were outside. I could tell by voices and footsteps. One of the voices was Vangie's. Cars' engines spun and started, one by one. Car doors banged shut. Tires ground gravel down the knoll. I could hear them all the way to the road. I waited, waited, for more footsteps or voices or engines. I had nothing else to do. The quiet persisted, and finally I got up and put on my pants.

I went out and walked through the *sala*. The guards had eaten most of the food and drunk all the beer. Their plates were stacked on the floor, bottles collected in a corner like debris in a backwater.

The day looked pristine. The stone of the front step was warm under my feet. I stood there and closed my eyes and turned my face up to the sun. I stood in the hot light and let it scrub me.

A noise made me turn around. It was Vilma, in through the back door, padding into the *sala* to gather dirty dishes. I said good morning, her head bobbed and she went on.

I stood there soaking in the sun. I remembered how the fog chills San Francisco, what a miracle the sun could be there, even the skimpy drained sun of winter. I knew that I would miss the sunlight in this place, its extravagant warmth; the sunlight and warmth, if nothing else.

A ripple of movement distracted me. A woman was coming up the trail from the barrio, emerging from the woods at the foot of the knoll. She got closer, and I saw that it was Vangie.

I watched her take the steps up the knoll, head up and shoulders back, climbing to where I stood. She stopped a couple of paces from me. She was in her housedress again, once more the provincial maiden.

She said, "I have to talk to you."

"No you don't. We don't have to put ourselves through this again."

"Don't judge me," she said.

Who am I to judge? is what went through my mind. But I couldn't find the words. My hands just moved vaguely and dropped to my sides.

"Not until you know what's involved," she said.

"I can guess. It's an old story."

She shook her head decisively.

I said, "Hey, I've seen this place. I don't blame you for trying to keep your head above water."

Vilma came through the *sala*, stopped abruptly. Vangie said a couple of words to her, and Vilma went away.

To me Vangie said, "It isn't a matter of choice."

"You don't have to go into it. What's the point?"

She was just a couple of steps away. It was a chasm.

"Try to understand. I don't want you to be angry."

"Angry, I've got no right." My hands were trembling; my hands were always steady. I made fists to stop the shaking. I said, "The only complaint I've got, you should have told me. You could have done that. I mean, I see now, it all makes sense. I'm an understanding person, you could have told me." The words chattered out, spontaneous, like the trembling of my hand. "It would have been better to know, to get the picture, some idea of it, before things got out of control. I wish you had done that. I wish you could have trusted me. You would have showed me some respect if you had trusted me that way. Before feelings got hurt."

"Jack," she said, and she moved close to me. Closer

than we had ever been. Like a mother to a child, she touched her hand to my face.

I have to say it again: she wasn't like other people. I can imagine a whole possible world of guile, a universe of manipulation, in those two steps and that touch. But Vangie was without guile, and I knew it.

It surprised me. That I still knew.

Her face was uplifted toward me, the way I had been lifting mine to the sun a few moments before. I reached and got the hand at my cheek. It tightened around my fingers, and I brought it to my lips and kissed it.

It had a scent. Not hers, I thought. Must be Correon. She hadn't showered. Correon, some vagrant trace of him. I didn't care.

Her other hand came up, and I held that and kissed it too. Her eyes searched me. I took her head in my hands, her hair through my fingers, and brought her face up to me. I kissed her very lightly above the eyes. Harder on the mouth, and it parted.

I searched for the spot along her neck, where my eyes never got enough, and I kissed it. Luis's smell was there too. I inhaled it and kissed it. A wracked noise caught in her throat. I took my lips away, to let her speak if she wanted to speak. But she didn't say anything. Her mouth opened again when I kissed her, and I held her, and she held me. She kept holding me tight while I took her in my arms and brought her down the hall.

"He always paid attention to me," she said. "Recognition. Even when I was a child. He'd have a peso or two for me. He would call me by name. You don't know what that means, to have the big boss call you by name."

She lay in the bed, in and out of the rumpled sheet, her black hair spread against the pillow. I was beside her, holding her hand. While she talked, her fingers would twine around mine, independent of her words, seeking and locking.

"I knew he liked me. My father always had work. If there was just a single crew drawing wages, my father would be on it. Nothing was ever said, but we knew it was because the big boss liked me. He sponsored me through high school. My parents could never have afforded it. Tuition, books . . . the jeepney was two pesos each way to Hermosa, every day. My parents couldn't afford even that.

"I knew it meant a debt, what he would expect. Nobody told me, but I knew. Sooner or later. I was surprised that he waited as long as he did.

"The day after my graduation he sent me a gift. A watch. My Lord, nobody in my family, nobody in the barrio, ever owned a watch. The driver who delivered it said he'd be back at the same time tomorrow to pick me up. Very casual. My mother cried. But that's all. We'd had plenty of time to get used to the idea.

"I wore my school uniform. It was the best dress I had. The car brought me here, and we had dinner. Luis can be a gentleman. He thought the uniform was amusing. He apologized for overlooking me, and the next day the driver brought me dresses and stockings and shoes. I don't want you to think it was a terrible trauma. It wasn't. We grow up fast here."

She said this as if it were a recitation. In the wake of passion her dry calm was jarring. I tried to find some bitterness in it, some catch of hatred or resentment; anything but this terrible resilience.

I said, "That's monstrous, all of it."

"No, I was flattered. A hacendero doesn't have to go to all that trouble to get a girl on his farm. He can take what he wants. That's accepted. It's always been that way."

"He's been using you ever since."

"Don't pity me, Jack. I won't have it. In the barrio they don't pity me. I'm envied. It reflects well on me, that he treats me this way. He paid for my college. It ran ten thousand pesos a year. How did you think I managed that? When my father died it could have been the end of us, my mother and me, two women alone. My salary at the school is eight hundred a month. After my expenses I might have a hundred and fifty left. *Pesos.* But my mother has never gone hungry. Whenever she's sick she's taken care of.

"Look. Three years ago sugar prices dropped. Nobody was planting. There wasn't any profit in it. If the planters don't plant, the workers don't draw wages. People were starving to death on the farms. But my mother ate.

"What is that worth? At first he wanted me at least once or twice a week, here or in Bacolod. Now it isn't so often. Once a month, sometimes less, I can't predict. He sends for me and I come. I know he has others, but he always did. I would never refuse him. It's good to be liked by someone with power." Her voice began a descent, darkening in timbre. "He treats me well. He's the only man who ever touched me. Until you. It could be much worse. I'll be sorry when he stops sending for me."

"You don't mean to tell me you're going to stay."

Her face was inconclusive.

"It's a dead end. There's no way you can be happy. Living this way."

"It's more than I ever expected."

"You'd better raise your expectations. I'm not leaving you here. Not after this. You're coming home with me."

"Don't say it. Not now." She touched my face. I could feel the tenderness start to return.

"We can afford to feed your mother and send her to the doctor. We'll get her something better than a grass hut in the barrio. Come home with me, you'll find a job that pays a damn sight more than forty bucks a month."

She held me. Both tenderness and heat returning.

"Not now," she said.

* * *

Later she sat up in bed and cradled my head in her lap. She stroked my face and traced a line of soft kisses along my brow. It should have been splendid languor, but I kept thinking about Tuesday morning. Forty-eight hours, I'd be in Manila, ready to fly home, and I wanted her with me when I did.

She wouldn't talk about plans.

I said, "Are you afraid of him?"

"I've never been happier than right now. Don't spoil this."

"Is that it? You don't want to leave because you're worried about what he might do?"

"I've thought about it."

"He sees you once a month, I can't believe he would care. Not that he wouldn't be losing the best day of his month. But I don't think he realizes that. Once a month. It can't be that important to him."

"He doesn't think like most people."

"If he ever found out about us . . ."

She laughed an empty, graveyard-at-night laugh.

"He's in Bacolod," she said. "Every Sunday at this time. Noon mass at the cathedral, with his wife and his son, he never misses it."

"Vilma and Hector."

"Vilma and Hector are from the barrio, and in the barrio we stick together, remember? Nobody will tell him. Nobody told you about him and me, the same reason. They're on my side. They want me to have a chance."

"But if he did find out. What would he do?"

She twisted my hair into a ringlet around one finger, and she bent down again and kissed me full on the mouth.

"I don't know," she said. And, "I believe he would kill us both."

* * *

· 197 ·

The light through the bedroom window kept deepening and softening. Vangie said she had to go home soon. I still hadn't seen anything of Bembo and Franklin, and I knew that I couldn't stay there alone; when she was gone, the room would be a cavern.

Take the jeepney, she said. Down the highway to Hermosa, Hermosa to Palo. In Palo you might find one direct to Bacolod. Otherwise go to Bago, then Bago to Bacolod.

Easy, she said.

I said good-bye to her inside the front door.

"I'm coming back tomorrow," I said.

"I'll try to meet you here."

"Not here. You've got other things to do. I want you to pack your stuff and tell everybody good-bye. You're getting out of here with me tomorrow. Tuesday we fly to Manila together."

She didn't say anything, but abruptly kissed me and held me, released me, turned and went straight down the hill to the ditch and the trail and the trees.

I went the other way, following the driveway around the back of the knoll and out to the highway. I flagged the first one, and they found room for me somehow among the fourteen other passengers, their boxes and bags and packages. In Hermosa, and again in Palo, all routes converged on the town square. Jeepneys stacked up in echelon against the curb, and drivers stood on the sidewalk shouting destinations like barkers on a carnival midway.

I kept looking for the Cortina coming the other way, but I never saw it. In Palo I got the direct ride. The route went past the Green Fields, and I walked into the hotel around sunset.

There was a white envelope in my box. The clerk said, "Sir, you wanted the boy?"

On the other side of the lobby a boy, no more than ten, stood behind a potted ficus. A wooden box hung from his shoulder by a strap. Eddie the bellman was already descending on him, from behind. I followed them both out the front door and got to him when Eddie let go.

I held out the envelope and said, "You brought this for me today."

I could see the calculation go across his face. It settled into a dumb look and he said, "No sir, not me."

"It's no problem. I just want to talk."

He watched my hand go into my pocket, come out with a red bill. Fifty. He took it with reverence, folded it until it was the size of my thumbnail, and stuck it into a slit along the sole of one rubber sandal.

"Maybe that's the one I bring."

"This one and some others."

"Maybe." Guarded. "I'm not sure."

"I just want to know who gave it to you."

"A man. The same man each time. That's all you want to know?"

"I want to know who he is."

By now it was mostly a matter of curiosity. Vangie and Tuesday morning had pushed the rest aside.

But nobody wants to miss a punch line.

"Ah, sir, I don't know his name, no kidding, I don't. I see him in Green Fields sometimes, but I don't know his name."

"If I had a name, that would be worth at least a hundred."

He was instantly tortured.

"A hundred . . . if I knew . . . no kidding, I don't know who he is." He brightened. "But I can find out."

"You do that," I said. "That's a hundred."

"Plus expenses."

"Get me his name, we'll talk about expenses."

I went up to the room. Eddie was right behind me, with ice water. I drank some, and put the envelope in my back pocket before I dialed Bertina and Rogelio.

A woman's voice answered, and I said, "Bertie."

She said, "I am not Bertie."

I had trouble hearing her. Behind the fuzz in the line was a noise like wailing.

I said, "I'm looking for Bembo Rojas. Is he there?"

She didn't answer. Except for the howling, the next sound I heard was Rogelio's voice.

"Who is this?" he said.

"This is Jack. I'm looking for Bembo."

"My God, it's you. Where are you?" He didn't wait for me to answer. He said, "We were about to send Franklin to fetch you. You don't know, do you?"

But I heard the keening of a grief-struck woman. Who had to be Bertie.

I knew, all right. I put the phone down before I could hear him say it.

From the next morning's *Star:*

TWO SLAIN IN AMBUSH

Unidentified gunmen killed two individuals in broad daylight yesterday as they walked along Gatuslao Street near the north city boundary. Witnesses said that Virgilio Rojas and Maricel Soto were set upon by two shooters who jumped from a sedan parked along the street. Rojas attempted to defend himself with a knife but was swiftly cut down by bullets.

Both were shot several times. Police recovered shell casings from .45 caliber and 9mm automatic pistols.

Rojas, 64, was a resident of Manila. Miss Soto, 18, was employed as a hospitality girl at a nearby discopub. The two victims had just left her rooming house, a few doors away.

Police speculate that the two may have been victims of a new holdupper gang. However, the assailants did not remove Rojas's wallet, containing several hundred pesos.

· 22 ·

The funeral parlor is one American institution that Filipinos have never embraced. They abhor the idea that a beloved, newly jolted into eternity, should lie alone in a strange gloomy place.

If there is family nearby, an undertaker will surrender the prepared corpse within a few hours, to stay in the *sala* until burial. There will always be light, at least one candle on the coffin; at least one of the living will always keep vigil, though most often the room will be bright and crowded. The vigil can last for more than a week, until relatives and friends have been summoned from remote provinces, and after a few days it may become as much a ritual of joyful reunion as of mourning. A flat coffin lid becomes a handy place to rest a bottle of beer.

Or so I'm told. When I got to Rogelio and Bertie's house the undertaker had delivered Bembo's body within the hour. There was no joy, no drinking. About a dozen people stood in the room and around the casket, most of them looking stunned. I recognized Franklin and Rogelio, and Bertie, who sat weeping in a corner, consoled by two women I didn't know. Rogelio met me at the door and told me how Bembo had died, no surprise.

The casket was on a bier. Behind it were three electric

candelabra on brass stands. A taper burned on the glass plate above his face.

I've learned, there's no predicting how you'll feel at that first glimpse of someone you love, suddenly ensconced in satin and rendered as a waxworks figure. When I looked down at Bembo I wanted to tell him about Vangie and me. I wanted to find his fedora and put it on his head. I wanted to ask him what I should do next.

"One of the bullets struck him in the right cheek," Rogelio said beside me. "You see, the *funeraria* did a wonderful job. You can't see the wound at all."

"A wonderful job," I said. But they probably get a lot of practice, I thought.

I took him aside.

"I have to know everything," I said. "I'm very sorry about it. I loved him. You probably think this is my fault, and you're probably right. You might think this isn't the time or the place, and you're probably right about that, too. But I have to know how it happened."

"I don't know much. Yesterday a message came for him. A boy from the neighborhood delivered it."

"Like this," I said. I still had the sealed envelope in my hip pocket.

"Yes. That's it. I saw it last night. But he didn't open it until this morning, when he showed up from Hermosa."

Franklin had come over. He said, "As of this morning, I was still repairing the automobile. Bembo found me. He didn't want to wait. He decided he will ride the jeepney to Bacolod."

Rogelio said, "I wasn't here when he came in. According to my wife, Bembo was agitated when he read the message. A few minutes later he took a telephone call. Then he was even more agitated. He told Bertie that he was leaving for a while. She said lunch was almost ready, why didn't he stay, but he said no, he had an obligation. An hour later he was dead."

I said, "The message . . ."

He was digging a piece of paper out of his pocket. It had been crumpled and smoothed.

Maricel Soto
2220 Gatuslao Street
Witness

"I Mourn the Demise of Justice"

"Who?" he said.

"A self-righteous bastard who loves to play games."

"Why?"

I shook my head and said, "The call, I don't suppose he said who it was."

Bertie blurted from beside the coffin: "I know the voice from before. I don't know the name, but I know the voice. He called you here. Remember? Perfect English."

I saw myself going to the telephone. It was breakfast time. On the other end of the line was Nonoy Paloma.

Faithful retainer.

"You must consider leaving Negros," Rogelio said. "There is grave danger for you."

For me, I thought, and for everyone around me.

"I can fly tomorrow."

"Last flight to Manila, ten-twenty," Rogelio said. "Plenty of time."

Tonight, he meant.

"I have to go to Lanao first." I was looking straight at Franklin.

"Not much time for that," Rogelio said.

"To go to Lanao, we must hurry," Franklin said. "We must leave right away."

"You'll take me?"

"No problem."

"They may be watching for me. They've got more reason to kill me than they did Bembo, and he's dead. I want you to know that."

"I understand."

"Are you sure?"

"No problem."

Rogelio came out with us. He'd get out at the airport and buy my ticket, make sure I had a seat.

Two tickets, I told him.

After some grinding, the Cortina started.

"We'll make it to Lanao and back?" I said.

"No problem."

The Green Fields had been safe for me less than an hour before; I decided I could return. I had my passport, but nearly a thousand dollars in cash was in the hotel lock box. Franklin and Rogelio waited outside. I went to the cashier's desk and checked out fast. Eddie the bellman was at the front door. I gave him my room key and told him he could have what was there. It was considerable: a camera, a pocket tape recorder, luggage, besides clothes and shoes. But I was counting minutes, and I wanted to be gone.

"Truly?" Eddie said.

"Yes. All yours." I gave him the key.

"I will send those things."

"Forget it."

I said it over my shoulder; I was already headed for the door. He said, "Oh! Sir! Don't leave this."

I stopped, feeling irritated: business was finished. I turned. The clerk at the front desk was holding out a plain white envelope.

I had to go to my pocket to be sure that I hadn't dropped the first one. It was still there.

"Within the last ten minutes," the clerk said.

I took it without thanks and left and got into the car. Franklin pulled away and I sat there, staring down at it in my hands. Furious. I kept staring at it as Franklin pushed through traffic. Finally I put it in my pocket with the other one when we jolted into the airport.

My wristwatch said 7:02. I gave Rogelio a fistful of pesos.

The coast road heads south from the airport. While Franklin drove I kept looking behind us. Several sets of headlights stuck with us as we overtook slower traffic. But when we turned off the highway, outside Bago, everybody else kept going south. We were alone, rapping toward Hermosa and the hills. My watch said seven-fifteen.

We plowed past the tall stands of cane, and in the settlements we routed dogs and chickens from the roadside. The car kept chugging; the engine had a steady, throaty sound. Between Palo and Hermosa we met an improvised checkpoint, a couple of dozen soldiers and a row of boulders that they'd placed across the pavement. The passport and the papers blew us through; the soldiers rolled away one of the boulders and we were gone.

The Cortina strained on the long uphill stretch outside Hermosa. I told myself that it always strained going up hills. Then we topped out the rise, and it sounded throatier again. We plunged on. The road was empty. After we left Hermosa we didn't see another vehicle.

In the dark I missed the little cues that I had picked up on the daytime trips. But Franklin knew. He braked to turn, and we were headed down the spur road to the barrio before I recognized it.

He parked in the clay courtyard and left the engine running. My watch said 8:29.

Day or night, the barrio was a maze. The path to Vangie's was a series of juts and angles and narrow paths that I never followed twice the same. It didn't seem to matter, though. I always came out right as long as I kept heading for the far back corner of the settlement. That's what I did this time, and it worked again. I turned a corner and found myself in front of the hut. I recognized it from the potted vines that grew in the windows and a thin blue curtain drawn across the doorway.

Inside was dark. I went up the steps, rapped on the post and said my name. A match flared in the back room, and the light burgeoned. Vangie sounded uncertain as she said come in.

She was holding a bottle lamp that threw a sooty orange flame. The sleeping mats were already out on the floor; her mother was still pushing the net away. They wore house-dresses to sleep.

"You didn't go?" she said.

"Down and back."

"You shouldn't be driving around at this hour. Why?"

"It's important. Come here, sit with me."

I put two stools together in the front room, waited for her to take one, and sat on the other. When I reached, she gave me one of her hands. I held it, small and warm, between mine. It brought me back to the afternoon, the bed.

Her mother watched us with what I thought was mixed fear and hope.

"I'm going," I said. "Tonight. The plane leaves in two hours and I have to be on it."

A betrayed look came over her. She snatched it back.

"I'm glad you told me," she said. "That's decent of you. But you'd better go. You don't have much time."

"Somebody wants to kill me," I said. "They killed Bembo and I'm pretty sure they're after me too. I want you to come with me. It's my life at stake." I meant murder but I could have been talking about her and us.

I told her about Bembo, in a few words. Shot on a sidewalk.

"Bembo," she said. Her head shook once, with sadness, for him. Again, firmly, for me. She said, "I can't go with you. Tonight? I can't, Jack. Impossible."

"I know it's asking a lot. But that's circumstances. I love

you. I need you—do you know how much I need you? We leave here together, it's our start."

Now it was her hands holding mine. Tight and secure.

"I need time," she said.

"Time"—I gestured to the door, the darkness, feeling desperate—"I've got minutes, is what I've got."

"You have as much time as we both need. Go home, think about it. We'll both think. Write me some letters. Filipinas go crazy for love letters."

"I've thought about that. It scares the hell out of me. That distance. Not just the miles. You can't know how far I had to come to get here, how far apart we were. We'll never get over it again. I'll write you letters, fine, and you'll write to me. We'll think about each other, and we'll think we should do something about it. It won't happen, though. Not to be a pessimist about it, I'm trying to be plucky as all get-out, but I'm afraid if I walk out of here alone, it's the last I see of you. With all the best intentions, that's how it'll turn out."

Three or four times she started to speak—as if trying words in her mind, finding them inadequate—and then seemed to settle within. She said, "How long will you be in Manila?"

"Only as long as it takes me to get a flight."

"Can you wait two days . . . no, three?"

"Wait? For what?"

"For me," she said. "I have to get my mother out of here. Bring her to Bacolod, so that he can't find her at once. He may be upset when he hears that I'm gone. After a while he'll calm down, but she shouldn't be here when he finds out. I don't want to have to worry about her. I'll be so far away, after all."

"You're coming with me?"

"Isn't that you want?"

I said, "Let me get the picture. Three days, you meet me in Manila, we go home together, you marry me, we're never apart again, is that the size of it?"

She nodded, happy, pleased with herself.

It should have filled me with happiness. It did, almost. But in a small part of me I felt a chill, a shadow passing over my soul. I tried to force it out. I didn't want to ruin joy with misgivings.

"Three days," I said, "I can handle three days."

"I'll need a visa. You know that. You said you can arrange the visa."

"Hey, I've got the visa handled. First you need a passport, though, that's something I can't do for you."

She squeezed my hand, got up without a word and went into the other room, came back a moment later with a greenish-brown passport, like the one I had taken from Precy Allen half an eternity ago, which had catapulted me on this trajectory.

Wry, abashed, she said, "He brought me to Hong Kong for a weekend, three years ago." She gave it to me. "What else do you need?"

"Just your promise. That you'll be there, three days, and from then on it's you and me."

"You have it," she said. And she shrank my fear down to almost—almost—nothing.

I got up. I could feel the minutes disappearing like firecrackers on a string. Over to the door was just a couple of steps, and she followed me over, and I stopped at the threshold. I gave her the rest of the pesos in my pocket. There had to be at least five thousand.

"You'll need it for the ticket," I said, "and for your mother, her room, all the rest, from now on we make sure she lives right—we can afford it."

"Yes."

"This is Sunday," I said. "Monday, Tuesday—can you be there Wednesday? Wednesday afternoon?"

She said, "There's a flight at about a quarter past two every day. I know it, it shakes the schoolhouse when it goes over. To Manila it's about an hour. So at around a quarter after three, Manila, Wednesday . . ."

I had an image of myself standing at the airport gate. But Vangie wasn't in it. I was waiting at the gate, just waiting, disappointed, crushed.

"I'll be at the Silahis hotel, if you have any problems, you want to talk."

"I doubt it," she said. "I won't be near a phone until I get to Bacolod."

"This is happening fast," I said. "I realize that. If there's any reason you might change your mind, just say so. Now's the time. I could take it if you told me now. But finding another way, I don't know, that would be too much. You sure you want this?"

She said, "I've wanted this, I've wanted you, since before I ever met you."

She let me take her lightly in my arms, and I kissed her with more longing and tenderness and need than I ever knew was in me.

She stepped back as the old woman came up to me. Rosita's frail hands came up and grasped my collar.

"Take care my daughter," she said before she released me.

"Now go," Vangie said, and I went.

I told Franklin all about it on the way down. The Cortina kept running, and he drove it hard. The soldiers were gone, the boulders were out of the road. By my watch we had four minutes when we got to the airport.

It isn't a big airport, and Franklin took me straight to the terminal doors, the Philippine Airlines counter on the other side. Rogelio was there with the tickets and the boarding passes.

The jetliner was out on the ramp, engines alive and shrill. The only other planes were military, two Huey helicopters and a T-28 propeller fighter with rockets slung under its wings, guarded by sentries. Two ground handlers had begun to roll the stairway away from the jetliner's fuselage; when we hurried out, the soldiers yelled at the handlers and the handlers pushed the stairway back. I was hardly in my seat before the plane began to move.

I thought of the envelopes. I took them out. Here, now, with Vangie's promise in my head and the plane rocking down the taxiway, they didn't seem so threatening.

One at a time I opened them.

The first:

Dolores Rosario
419-B Jison St., Tondo, Manila
Victim and Witness

Azucar Room, Green Fields
7 P.M. Thursday

"Who Speaks for Those Without a
Voice?"
"Who Stands Up for Those Without
Standing?"

The second envelope was fresher, less time in the pocket:

YOUR LIFE IS IN DANGER—LEAVE THIS PLACE AT ONCE
FORGIVE ME. YOU WERE MY HOPE. WHO ELSE BUT YOU?

The engines bansheed, the plane swung onto the runway. It rolled, sped, lifted. We climbed. Out my window were the lights of Bacolod, not very bright. I couldn't see much in the darkness, but I imagined rusting corrugated roofs, barefoot kids and squatters and teenage whores, killers and the dead.

The plane banked and climbed. The city lights halted abruptly at the water's edge; in only a few seconds they were out of sight. I felt like a thief fleeing in the night. Like the fleeing thief that I was.

· 23 ·

I got a room at the Silahis, and the next morning I slept late. I ordered breakfast and called Dalzell's number at the embassy; the woman who answered the phone told me he wasn't in yet. Nearly ten o'clock.

I said, "Are they by any chance playing ball in the States?"

"That isn't a bad guess," she said.

I took a taxi up the boulevard to the go-go palace off Del Pilar. I walked again out of the heat into the cold air, again past the upturned chairs to the horseshoe bar where ten or twelve Americans watched the TV on the wall. It struck me, how little time had passed since the other morning here; and in that time, how much I had seen and felt, how much I had done.

I sat on the stool beside Dalzell. He didn't turn around at first, and when he did he just said, "Hey, how you doin'? Back from the wars, huh?"

"Made it."

Thousands of miles away the basketball zipped, zipped, arched and flipped the net.

"Lakers," he said. "Awesome. You get business wrapped up?"

"As well as I could under the circumstances." I had already decided that I wouldn't go into it. I figured he didn't care. If it got too complicated, nobody cared. I said, "This isn't America. You've got to adjust your standards."

"That's the spirit."

"Cut your expectations in half, and then settle for half of that. Less about twenty percent for shrinkage."

"You'd fit right in over here."

I said, "I need a favor."

Dryly he said: "And would this involve an individual of the female persuasion?"

"How did you know?"

"It's a safe guess. A guy comes over here, he sees the women, a couple of things can happen. He falls in love or he diddles till his dick drops off. Or both. If he's in love, he wants to bring her home. If it's the other one, he wants to find an American doctor."

"Yeah, well, I'm in love."

"Did you marry her?"

"Not yet."

"Good move. Tell you what, Jack, here's what you do. Go home, file a fiancée visa petition with INS. It'll take them three or four months to put it through, give you a chance to mull it over. Maybe it's the climate, but these things do look different when the frost's on the pumpkin."

"I'm not worried about that."

"Many a guy is grateful he had a cooling-off period. I could name names."

"I just want to get her out of here."

"You're looking for a visitor's visa." He rubbed his temples. I remembered an assistant district attorney who used to do that when he wanted you to know that he was feeling put-upon. "Obviously she doesn't have a chance of getting one on her own."

"She's a schoolteacher."

"I think Eisenhower was president the last time an unmarried female schoolteacher got a visitor's visa in Manila. What do you think? We just throw these things around like trick-or-treat candy?"

"Something like that."

"We get 'em lined up every morning, you saw it. They

wait for hours in the sun and the rain, and we turn most of 'em down. Why should we treat you any different?"

I leaned closer; it was noisy in Los Angeles.

"Because that's them, and this is you and me."

He was beginning to grin.

"You really would fit in over here."

"I know how piss-ant systems work."

"She has her passport?"

I took it out and put it in front of him. He put it in his pocket without looking at it.

"I hope you know what you're doing," he said.

"How long does it take?"

"Rubber stamp, that's it. Once I get back to work. You at the same hotel? Tell you what, I'll get it back to you this afternoon."

"I appreciate this."

"We have to look out for each other, strangers in a strange land."

"Strange is one word for it."

"Jack," he said, "I assume if you're taking this little dolly home with you, you won't be going back to Negros."

His breeziness had a firm undercurrent.

"What's the difference?" I said.

"Come on, man, don't yank my chain. I'm doing you a favor so you can go home happy. You want to screw around over here, you don't need that visa."

"I have no reason in the world to go back to Negros. I'm headed the other way, sooner the better."

"I'm glad," he said. "That crap is all theirs. They're good at it. It's not for you and me."

REBS, VIGILANTES TANGLE ANEW

Information has reached Bacolod of another major encounter between the Sac-

ramentong Dugo vigilante group and an
NPA guerrilla unit. The vigilantes are said
to have staged a desperate attack on a guerrilla base camp in the mountains of central
Negros, inflicting considerable casualties as
they overran the guerrilla band commanded
by Remigio Ortiz, "Kumander Rocky."

· 24 ·

The passport came back that afternoon, with the visa
stamped in. After that it was just waiting, getting by, the
old drill of being alone. That I knew. That I could do.

On Tuesday I went with a tour group to Corregidor,
out in the mouth of the bay. It was a lonely windswept
hump of cratered earth topped by broken concrete buildings. The point of Bataan peninsula was about a quarter of
a mile away; the tour guide talked about soldiers living for
weeks in tunnels, deaths in the thousands.

The trip was four hours each way on a ferry, which
killed the day painlessly. The sun was setting behind us
when we docked. That left just one more evening alone,
one more night. I had dinner in my room and watched the
news. In Laguna province the army had unearthed sixty
graves containing the bodies of "zombies"—suspected
collaborators—killed in the latest NPA purge. The customs chief in Manila promised a full investigation into the
overnight disappearance of twenty-five cargo containers
of impounded goods. A renegade colonel who had led the
last two coup attempts had been spotted in Manila's fi-
nancial district, where he was thought to have been meeting with sympathetic business leaders.

Wednesday I stayed in my room past lunchtime; I
called Philippine Airlines and found that the flight left

Bacolod at 2:20, arrived at 3:25. I teased myself with images of her progress through the morning. Now she would be waking. Now dressing. Now saying good-bye to her mother. Now buying her ticket, plenty of time to spare.

I stopped to buy roses on the way to the airport, still got there early. The domestic airport, across the field from the international terminal, is about the size of a forties-era supermarket. The arrival area and the baggage claim are in an annex, partitioned from the rest of the building. Disembarking passengers cross the airstrip pavement, entering the annex by a single large door at the rear. The only exit is another door out onto the sidewalk with its hyperactive menagerie of drivers and porters and vendors. An airport cop guards the exit. I gave him twenty pesos and he literally looked the other way while I slipped inside. It had the ambience of a warehouse. Grimy yellow walls, bare concrete floor, a few benches; steaming hot.

I walked to the open door at the back. From a bench there I could see the apron with several planes parked. I sat on the bench with the flowers beside me. It was two-twenty. Her flight would be lifting off.

Three or four times planes came and parked, disgorged passengers and took on others, and left. There were no announcements, no video screens to tally the flights. At first I ignored the planes and the lines of passengers that came across the pavement, into the annex. Still too early. But at about a quarter after three a plane trundled up and stopped, the stairway rolled out and the people came off. This time I met the first of them at the door.

"Bacolod?"

"Tacloban."

At 3:20: "Bacolod?"

"Davao."

At 3:25: "Bacolod?"

"Cebu."

At 3:35, to a young woman in a linen suit, a Vuitton purse: "Bacolod?"

"Yes, Bacolod."

I went out to the edge of the tarmac. With the flowers in my hands I watched the people trooping miserably across the pavement, through the waves of rising heat. My heart bobbed like a buoy in chop. I was nervous; or if not nervous, at least heightened. I told myself that it was pardonable. Life's launchings aren't usually so definite. Most often we don't recognize them until they're behind us. But this was different, I thought; the moment she stepped up in front of me, our futures would shift and correct. We would never be the same.

I watched. The stream through the door thickened and stayed thick for a couple of minutes, and then got thinner as I watched. Across the apron I could count a few stragglers: a family with several kids that a nanny herded along, a teenage girl holding the elbow of a very old woman in a black dress and a mantilla.

A figure appeared at the open hatch, at the head of the stairway. A woman stepped out. A stewardess. She looked around and retreated from the heat and the light.

I didn't know how I could have missed Vangie coming in. But I walked around the annex anyway, looking again. I didn't see her.

I told myself, if she got past me she might have gone straight out into the sidewalk, thinking I'd be there—she might've. I went out, looked hard, but she wasn't there. I told myself that I must have missed her in the crowd inside—I must've. The cop wanted twenty pesos again. Inside again I coursed back and forth, wall to wall, looking.

She wasn't there. This time I was sure. The annex was one big room, open. Not the kind of place that would hide someone who wanted to be found.

She missed the plane, I thought. Pressed for time. Her taxi broke down. I imagined her sitting in the Bacolod terminal at that instant, waiting for the next flight, guessing my dismay, amused.

At the ticket counter I found that the next plane was due at six; the next after that was the night flight that arrived half an hour before midnight. The ride from hotel to airport had been a grinding thirty minutes, and would be worse at rush hour. I decided to stay. Across the street was a coffee shop. I bought two newspapers and read and waited. The count of zombies' graves in Laguna had risen to two hundred. The customs chief denied allegations of corruption in his department.

At a quarter to six the rosebuds were drooping on their stems. I left them in the coffee shop and went across the road to the terminal. The guard took my twenty pesos. In the gloaming outside the back door I breathed jet fumes and watched three planes pull up during the next half hour.

"Bacolod?"

"Baguio."

"Bacolod?"

"Zamboanga."

"Bacolod?"

"Yes, from Bacolod."

I stood close enough that I could see every face as they passed; could have counted them. I didn't see her. Even so, I went back in and looked them all over again and went out on the sidewalk to look around there.

At the hotel there was no message. If she had gotten to Bacolod she could have found a phone, I thought. Therefore she did not get to Bacolod. I waited in the room, and around half past ten I took a cab to the airport. By eleven I was standing by the back door with a sense of weary duty. Only one plane came in.

"Bacolod?"

"Yes, Bacolod."

She wasn't there.

The next morning's flights came in at eight and a little before twelve. She wasn't there. I went to the ticket office near the departure gates. I grabbed a ticket agent and gave her my story in three or four sentences. I must have looked sincere, must have looked sincerely miserable, because the agent went right to her video screen.

"I see nothing for her yesterday. No. No. Nothing for today. Nothing in the evening. Nothing tonight."

"Tomorrow," I said.

"No. No. No. Nothing tomorrow. But she might purchase at the airport."

I took a cab back to the Silahis, got my passport and papers and five hundred dollars and all my pesos and went back to the airport. Without any expectations, I waited out on the apron for the evening arrival. The agent had mentioned that a single plane flies the route, shuttling back and forth all day with about an hour's layover at each end. So when I saw that she wasn't there, I had time.

I went around to the ticket counter in the terminal. It was Friday, a little after six. I said, "I want to go to Bacolod."

· 25 ·

Bacolod has a minor version of the melee outside Manila's air terminals. It too has hustling porters and aggressive taxi drivers, but fewer than in Manila, and not so frantic. Maybe a dozen drivers were outside the airport, pouncing on fares, when I said loudly, "I want to go to Hermosa."

Most of them stopped and looked.

"Hermosa is very far," one of them said.

"Hermosa town?" said another. He was in his twenties. He wore a Dodgers cap.

"Rural Hermosa. A barrio called Lanao."

No, no, they all murmured. Sorry sir, no.

All but the one under the cap. He was handsome, with

a hungry face. He had a personal gravity that told me he was not a trivial man.

"Tomorrow I will take you," he said. "Tomorrow morning early."

"I want to go tonight." He didn't say no. I pulled him off to the side, away from the others. I said, "This is important to me."

"It is a dangerous trip. Hermosa is a critical area. Daytime, maybe not so bad, night, very dangerous."

"I was just up there, two nights ago. You see, I got back okay."

"Is the barrio on a hacienda? Permission is required to visit a hacienda."

"I have permission. I have all the documents you'd need."

He took them under a bulb that burned at the entrance of the terminal. He looked at them closely.

"I'll give you a hundred dollars." He wouldn't earn that in a week.

"U.S. dollars," he said. "Not Australian."

"U.S."

He went back to the papers.

"I bring you to the barrio and leave you?"

"I don't know if I'll be staying. You might have to wait half an hour."

He returned the papers to me and said, "If it is worth one hundred, it is worth one hundred and fifty."

He was right. I said, "I'm ready to go. Where is your taxi?"

"No no. My taxi is junk. We will use the car of my brother. He has a Mitsubishi, only two years old."

"Where is your brother's car?"

"Very close," he said. "My brother is a driver-for-hire at the Green Fields hotel."

It was a few minutes after eight, Thursday.

I don't know whether I remembered the note, the time

and place. At that moment I had plenty to think about; but then the note, and all that it represented, had never been totally out of mind, either.

I could have stayed at the airport while he went for the car. But for reasons that might have been obscure even then, I said, "Come on. Let's go."

His name was Ray Nobles. His cab listed to one side and sipped its gasoline from a plastic bottle in the passenger footwell. He pulled in the driveway of the Green Fields. Thursday night, the parking lot was full. He stopped under the portico, by the front door. The drivers-for-hire usually waited there. Tonight there were just two. Ray spoke to them and I tried to stay out of the light.

"My brother is gone for a short time," Ray said to me. "Soon."

And a kid's voice said, "Joe! Hey Joe! He is here!"

It was the shoe-shine boy, waving his arms as he ran to me, pointing into the hotel.

"We cannot take this car," Ray said. "Do you want to wait?"

"He is here, Joe," the kid said. "One hundred peso, Joe."

"You saw him? Where?"

"He is here with the many hacenderos."

"He's a planter?"

"I don't think so. He is a companion of the hacenderos."

"Show me."

"One hundred peso, Joe."

I told Ray, We'll wait. The boy and I went into the hotel. He pointed to the closed twin doors of the Azucar Room.

"In here."

The signboard in the lobby said:

Planters' Ballroom
Jereza/Espina reception 7 P.M.

"Joe. One hundred peso, Joe."

In a back corner of the lobby was a service bar for the coffee shop and the restaurant. It adjoined an anteroom that had a couple of tables and a booth. It was empty now. The action was in the disco, which was already shaking the walls.

In the little bar I'd be inconspicuous. I could see most of the lobby and the doors of the Azucar.

"Watch for him," I said. "When you see him, I want you to go up to him. Ask him to come back here."

I went to the front desk. Two clerks. One of them said, "Mr. Hart. Back again."

"But don't tell anyone. It's supposed to be a surprise. I'm curious about the group in the Azucar Room. Socorro Foundation."

"Regular customers. They meet with some of our local planters."

"Are they a company?"

"Agricultural assistance, I think."

"No," said the second clerk. "Overseas investors. That's what I heard."

I told Ray Nobles where I would be, and I buried myself in the booth. Behind me a busy bartender filled orders.

I watched the lobby and the doors of the Azucar. I listened to the clink of ice in glasses, the snap and hiss of caps coming off beer bottles, the voices in Ilonggo of waiters bringing orders. I was thirsty. After a few minutes I stood to ask the bartender for some water.

From the other side of the bar the bellman, Eddie, said, "Mr. Hart, sir."

"Eddie."

"Oh my God, sir, the recorder, those clothes, so much . . . tomorrow I'll bring you that recorder."

"No, it's yours."

"Your camera, I sold that already. The clothes were too large for me, but I have a second cousin, Buboy, almost as big as you. He is very happy to have them."

"I'm glad."

The bartender had put a bottle of Black Label and several glasses and a bucket of ice on Eddie's tray.

"Pardon me," Eddie said. "I must go now. Tonight we're busy." He made a round-'em-up motion that took in the disco, the restaurant, and the two meeting rooms. "Wait for me, huh? I will be like MacArthur. I shall return."

He carried the tray across the lobby and entered an unmarked door in the corner. It was the same side of the lobby as the Azucar. That's where he's going, I thought. Black Label on the rocks for the hacenderos.

His tray was empty when he came back through the door. He tossed off a series of orders to the bartender and came over to me.

"You're covering the Azucar," I said.

"Yes, dinner at seven, now a meeting."

"What do they talk about?"

"I bring in the trays, I don't listen," he said. It sounded pat, though, and a little mischief crept into his face. "Well, I listen once in a while. They talk about money . . . weapons . . . patriotic volunteers." His grin became cheeky. "Gold, guns and goons. An American, too."

"They talk about Americans?"

The bartender had filled his tray again.

"No, an American in there with them. He runs the show."

He stepped over and picked up the tray.

"You want to see?" he said. "You can see."

"I don't think that's a friendly place for me."

"No, easy."

His hands were full. He beckoned with his chin and his pursed mouth.

I followed him across the lobby and held the same door open for him. It put us in a service corridor, hot, full of kitchen smells. We went down the corridor to another door that I opened. I went in after him.

It was a large, dark room; but narrow. Eddie crossed it and stopped at the far wall. He put the tray down on a table and motioned me forward.

On the other side of the wall an American said, "These are the figures for the four-week period that ended last Saturday."

I walked over to Eddie—slowly, quietly. I saw that the wall where he stood was actually a heavy drape that divided a single larger room. We were in the Azucar.

"Now the same sector, average figures for the identical period over the last five years."

Eddie parted the drape a couple of inches. "Yes?" he whispered. He let the panel drop, picked up the tray again and slipped through.

I went to the edge of the panel that he had parted. I held it open, maybe an inch.

The other half of the room was dim, too. Most of the light was from a slide projector that threw a bright rectangle on a screen to my left. Some dining tables had been arranged in the shape of an elongated U. Thirty or forty men sat at the tables. The projector was on a stand in the cup of the U, with the screen down at the open end. Currents of cigarette smoke dodged lazily through the projector's beam.

Penney was standing at the projector. The voice was his.

"I want you to note estimated tonnage lost to arson," he was saying. "Down forty-two percent over the baseline figure. You can work out the pesos better than I can. Actual incidents of arson committed by the guerrillas or their sympathizers, down fifty-eight percent. And we're only in the first quarter of the unit's operation. The full impact won't be felt for months yet."

"Sixty rifles only," said a skeptical voice.

"Sixty excellent rifles," Penney said—the AK's, I thought—"and now pistols, and more than a hundred motivated volunteers, expertly trained and overseen."

"Thank you," said Danny Boy Orlando, in a way that got a laugh. He was at the table that formed the base of the U. Luis Correon was beside him, laughing as hard as the others.

"But I don't want to dwell on figures," Penney said. "The real value isn't something that numbers can express. It's about you and how your people think of you. Respect—don't take respect for granted." He sounded like a car salesman. "Prestige," he said. "Be the first in your province." They laughed again. I've never been to a lodge meeting, but this was how I've always imagined them.

"Seriously," Penney said, "this is a question of your heritage. This is who you are. Your fathers and grandfathers walked this land like kings. These days most planters can't even walk the streets unless they pay blackmail to communists."

"Don Luis," said Julio Ferrar.

"That shit is about to end," Correon said. "I had my reasons."

Eddie had been stopping at different tables, putting down bottles and drinks, picking up empty bottles and glasses, nodding at orders. He came around to the drape again, and when he came through I started to follow him out.

"That's fine for Luis," I heard someone say. "Luis has the guns."

"I'm glad you brought that up," Penney said. I stayed at the door to listen. "As of today we happen to have available two lots of new F.N. carbines, a hundred units per lot. These are Belgian-made rifles that fire the .30 caliber NATO round. I'm sure you'll all agree that it's superior to the M-16 cartridge under most conditions encountered here."

"Shit, an F.N., that's expensive." It was Ferrar, I think.

"If you want to boogie you have to pay the piano player," Penney said.

I closed the door on their laughter and went back to the booth. I kept seeing Luis beside Danny Boy, and I felt the tangle of acts and events that snaked back to the afternoon when Collins and I had sat in Gilsa's office. I thought of how little we had known then. Our ignorance.

I sat and waited, I wanted to be home again. I wanted to be ignorant once more.

Ray Nobles came over twice to tell me soon, soon. The shoe-shine boy loitered near the front of the lobby, watching the double doors of the Azucar. And then the doors did open. A couple of men strolled out, chatting. Then a group of five, and four more after them.

Penney was with the next bunch, five or six that turned toward the back of the lobby. I sank myself back in the booth. Luis came out, with Danny Boy and Ferrar; they walked up toward the front desk, where there were racks of cigarettes and candy and magazines, out of my sight.

Nonoy Paloma walked out of the room alone—I hadn't noticed him.

The shoe-shine boy, slouching by the front door, straightened and began to walk across the lobby. He walked straight up to Nonoy and said something to him and touched him on the wrist. They came over to me.

The little bar was dark. Nonoy didn't see me until he was inside and right in front of me.

"Jack," he said. "This is dangerous. You should not be here."

"You," I said.

"Yes." He sounded ashamed. Before I could ask, he said, "Things were going on, I wanted someone to know, an outsider."

"You had Bembo killed."

"No!" Emphatically. Then less sure: "It was my fault. I called. I told him where to go. But I didn't intend . . . I didn't think they'd suspect . . . the girl was ready to talk. Maricel. You were at the hacienda, and I thought someone ought to hear it."

Out in the lobby Luis called, " 'Noy!"

"Hear what?" I said.

"You should have it all by now. If you don't, it doesn't matter. You can't do anything. You never could. I'm sorry. I thought it should be known."

"What do the girls have to do with it?"

" 'Noy!"

"I have to go. You, you have to get out of here. This is crazy. I never should have involved you."

"Why me?"

As if the answer were perfectly clear, he said, "You're an American."

"You could have just told me."

"I did my best."

"Your best wasn't very good."

" *'Noy!*"

He gave a hunted look out into the lobby and said, "If you really care to know, you have everything you need."

I said, "It's pathetic, in fact."

Sharply, in deep pain, he said, "What do you want from me? He's my father. Do you understand? I'm a barrio boy, and Luis is my father."

He went away fast. I was glad.

I gave the boy his money and moved to the back of the little bar. Nobody came in until Ray Nobles, fifteen or twenty minutes later.

"My brother is here," he said. "You want to go?"

"I want to go," I said.

· 26 ·

Rudy Nobles had the same keen face as his brother. He looked a couple of years older than Ray; he drove. Before we left he asked me why I was going to Lanao, and I told him I was trying to find a woman. After that none of us had much to say, but as we turned off the coast highway he did tell me: "If we run into the army, show those papers. If it's the NPA, try to hide the papers. Tell them it's because of a girl, it will make sense. Otherwise it doesn't make sense. And tell them, 'I am not an enemy of the people.' That helps."

"Just to say it? Anyone could say it."

"A true enemy of the people would never say it. It would choke him."

Except in the towns and the roadside settlements, though, we didn't see anyone. Once we were in the hills I had to pay attention so that we didn't miss the turn to Lanao. There had been rain here. Puddles sat in the road's depressions, and the air was soupy. We drove up the spur and parked, and once more I wound and poked my way among the huts, the clay sticky on the soles of my shoes.

The hut was dark. I knocked and spoke my name, and hers. Through the sheer fabric I watched the lamp glow float across the room. A hand pulled the curtain aside. An old woman's hand.

"I want Vangie," I said.

"Vangie is no here." She said it with pity. For me. The last time anyone looked at me with pity, I was bleeding on the floor.

"Where is she? I want to talk to her."

"Wait," she said. She drew me inside and went out. I

sat on the stool, alone in the darkness, until the light floated back, Rosita with another woman.

"The mother of Vangie has not much English," the woman said. "She ask me to tell you that Vangie is okay, she is well, but Vangie cannot leave with you to the States. Vangie's message to you is that you must go home now."

"Why?"

"It is impossible." Translating.

"Vangie wanted to go with me."

Directly, the woman said: "Yes of course she want."

"Where is she now? I should be hearing this from her."

"It is better you do not disturb Vangie." Translating again. "The situation of Vangie is the same now since before you come here."

"Correon?" I said. "She's with him?"

"Vangie belong to Correon," the woman said.

"Nobody belongs to anybody else."

"Vangie belong to Correon."

In the silence outside, in the direction of the courtyard, a automobile engine turned over and revved. I listened to the sound. The revs picked up. The Nobles' car was moving. I went out on the top step. The car was moving fast along the spur. In the space between two huts I saw its headlights rake the papaya trees.

I hadn't paid them. I wondered what would make them drive away from a hundred fifty dollars. Death, was all I could think of.

Somewhere in the barrio a woman began to shout, a frightened jabbering.

I heard a rustle, a pounding of feet.

A young man stepped around the corner of the hut. He looked as if he belonged to the barrio. Gym shorts, rubber sandals, a T-shirt. He was in front of me before I could react. When he saw me, he raised a pistol and pointed it at my face.

I raised my hands. He wasn't army.

"I'm here to see a girl," I said. "I'm not an enemy of the people."

Another young man came around the corner of the hut. He was carrying a rifle. I saw the curved clip, the wood stock. It was an AK.

The first one grabbed me by the wrist and yanked me down the steps. They exchanged a couple of sharp bursts of words. Something shone around the neck of the second one: a silver crucifix that hung from a leather thong. There was more to the shine: a tiny glass vial, liquid-filled, with a cap of silver filigree. At his hip a knife handle grew out of a long, broad, wooden scabbard.

He turned me around. The muzzle of the rifle bumped me hard in the back, and bumped me a second time. He wanted me to walk. I walked. The one with the pistol jumped up into Rosita's hut, and in a few seconds jumped down and went into the hut next door.

From the shoves and bumps in my back, I guessed that the one with the rifle wanted me to go toward the courtyard. I did, and he stopped pushing. Up and down the irregular rows of huts I could see more vigilantes going in and out of doorways, sometimes coming out alone, other times dragging out men and herding them toward the front of the barrio. About half a dozen other riflemen were waiting in the courtyard. They lined up the ones they had taken from the huts. They held their guns on the line, and they made me join it.

The line expanded for a few minutes until it contained fifty or sixty men, all about the same age, early thirties. The bustle in the barrio simmered down. More vigilantes came out to the courtyard as they finished searching the huts; they must have gone through every one.

One vigilante walked out to face us in the line. He was a short, round figure, who strode with a stumpy swagger. If vigilantes had officers, he was one. A name wriggled out of my memory. From the *Star*: a certain Baldomero Capas.

He wore camouflage pants and a black T-shirt. His hair was long, shaggy, filthy, and he needed a shave.

He swaggered to the far end of the line. He aimed the flashlight into the face of the first man, took him by the chin and swung his head to the side, to see him in profile. He said a word and the man backed out from the line, then turned and walked quickly toward the barrio, then ran.

The next in line. The next. Next. Blinking in the light, standing for examination, running away when they were released. He went down the line and examined each one and sent each one away.

When he finished the last one he said, "Hijo de puta."

He came over to me. He put his belly up against me and peered at me with a dire scowl that might have been comical at another time and place.

The rifleman who had taken me said a few words. His officer said, "So you're not an enemy of the people. The people must be happy to hear that."

"I'm an American," I said. "Look, my passport."

He let me take it out of my pocket. I gave it to him, and he put it under a flashlight.

"See, and a safe-conduct pass from the general, and a note from Luis Correon."

He examined it all. The papers seemed to fascinate him.

"You're looking for someone," I said.

"Remy Ortiz. NPA. Kumander Rocky."

"In Lanao?"

"That is the report."

"Well, you can see, I'm not quite him."

One of the riflemen knotted a length of hemp from around his waist. He stepped behind me, grabbed my right arm and pinned it back. Another rifleman grabbed the left, and they tied the rope around my wrists.

"My passport, I'm an American," I said.

"Shut up," said Baldomero Capas. With contemptuous care he slid the passport and papers into my shirt pocket.

They walked out of the barrio and marched me with them. We headed east, into a cane field, toward the mountains. The stalks weren't as high here as on the other side, and I bent to keep them out of my eyes. We left the field, crossed a freshet, and entered another field. That one stopped at the foot of a bluff hillside, and when we got to the top, the mountains were directly ahead of us, dipping in and out of clouds that obscured a rising moon.

Twice we climbed high scrub-covered ridges, twice dropped down into valleys where terraced paddies mirrored the moon. There was no more cane. In the second valley, we didn't climb straight out, but followed a stream that rose gradually, the valley pinching in around us, flocked in high, dense trees that formed a canopy overhead, real jungle.

We came out on a clearing fringed by cogon grass. Beyond the clearing was a stand of rattan and more jungle, billowing foliage. We were almost across before I saw that we weren't walking into just grass and trees. An unkempt flourish of brush became a thatched shelter. A lodge of bamboo materialized out of the rattan. Boys with rifles stepped out of the cogon's pale stalks and white tufts. I glimpsed barbed wire strung on posts. Sentries, a lookout tower of coco logs, slit trenches.

They took me through a break in the wire, to a dugout with a canvas roof. They pushed me inside without loosening the rope at my wrists.

Inside, darkness was heavy. The floor was mud. The walls were rough-sawn planks up to ground level, topped with courses of sandbags.

I picked myself out of the mud. I saw that I wasn't alone. Another man crouched in one corner. I went to the opposite corner, but before I could sit he said, "Don't be uppity. We've got enough problems."

His English was fluid and unaccented. I went over and sat a few feet away from him. He was thirty or so, as close as I could tell. There was little light, but there hadn't been much light for the last hour or more.

"American," he said.

"That's right."

"Not the American who's been coming to Lanao."

"That's me."

"Luis's hospitality isn't what it used to be."

I didn't know him, and from the upturned lines around his face, he seemed amused that I didn't know.

Even in full light I might not have recognized him. In all the world he was the last man I expected to see.

"Your night isn't a total loss," he said. He waited a couple of beats. "I'm Lito Sanchez."

When he said it I knew. He was Lito, and he was there, grinning at me, and the grin infuriated me. It was as if my troubles were embodied, having a good laugh at my expense.

I said, "You little twerp, if I could put my hands on you, you'd be a dead man."

"Precy'd get her money, anyway."

"Laugh," I said. "People are dead because of you."

"I know." He got serious. "When I saw what was happening, I wanted to stop it. But by then there was no stopping it. There were other lives involved, too." When he stopped talking I could hear the plink of water into a puddle, somewhere in the dugout.

He said, "Believe it or not, I had my reasons."

· 27 ·

The son of a bitch has had his hooks in me since the day I was born (Lito said, with a con man's easy command of the vernacular). That's the way it is on a hacienda. You own nothing, not even yourself.

You may think you do. You think you have a life, even if it's not much, it's yours. But there's the *amo*, that's the big boss, the owner of the hacienda, and what you think is yours is really his. All of it. If he sees something of yours that he likes, you can kiss it good-bye. I don't care what it is. Your water jug, your dog, your daughter. If he wants it, it's his.

He doesn't necessarily even have to like it. Sometimes he'll take it just for the hell of it.

I'm telling you this so you'll understand the mentality of somebody who was brought up on a hacienda. The *amo*, the hacendero, he's God. The *amo* giveth, the *amo* taketh away. Mostly he takes. You do not question the *amo*. What he wants, you give him.

In my case, what he wanted was me. I look at myself, I can't blame him. Not to brag, but let's be realistic. I've got brains, I've got balls, and I've got nothing to lose. It's an unbeatable combination. Fucking Luis is not stupid. He knows a good thing when he sees it.

What got me noticed, I was eighteen years old, cutting cane, living in the barrio. My *cabo*, that's like a crew boss, an assistant foreman, had a brother that was a peeper. He'd hide in the bushes by the creek when the girls were out taking a bath. One day Precy comes home crying. She was alone at the creek, and she saw the guy doing his thing, you know, choking his chicken, shuffling his cards. She was all upset. These barrio girls, they're sensitive.

Normally, a case like that, you expect the father to make things right. But my father had the farmhand's attitude, meek, don't rock the boat. A *cabo* is a powerful guy, and furthermore this one and his brother were cousins of the overseer. My father told Precy, don't go to the creek alone anymore. Not a word to the *cabo* or the brother.

To me that wasn't good enough. I sweetened the edge on my cane knife. I waited till the middle of the night. I went to the *cabo*'s house, I found the brother, I put that knife to his throat. Believe me—there's nothing will wake you up ruder than sharp steel on your neck. I told him, you're still around by sundown, I'll eat your eggs for dinner.

He was out of there. But first he told his brother. The brother told the overseer, and the overseer must have mentioned it to Luis. Next thing I know, I'm sitting in Luis's office. I'd seen him once or twice before, but never this close. Never to speak to, definitely. And he's saying to me, "You threatened the brother of your *cabo*." I say, "That's right, I got nothing against my *cabo*, but his brother is a fucking pervert." I say, "You want perverts on your farm? It's your farm, it's up to you, but if you ask me, this makes you look bad, perverts on your farm." Talking all kinds of trash, you understand, because I was scared. I already knew, the scareder you are, the crazier you should act.

I'm not saying that Luis bought the act. But he liked it. He told me I didn't belong in the fields. He was right about that—you don't want troublemakers on the farm. He made me a bodyguard. Really, I was on a crew of four or five guys that more or less took care of details, you see, all the jobs that people with juice and money always need doing. Deliver this, pick up this, meet so-and-so. I don't mean going to market, either. The kind of thing where you carry a gun, use your head, and don't ask questions.

The rough shit didn't get bad for a couple of years. It'd be, Hey boys, they caught another union organizer on the farm, why don't you escort him off the property. And if you want to kick the crap out of him while you're at it—hey, all the better. I didn't think much of it. We weren't touching anybody I knew. It was strangers, outsiders.

I was good at it. Not just the rough shit. All of it. Luis trusted me. He had something tricky, he'd call me. I'd get it done. Me, I'm living high. My father is busting his ass for fifteen pesos a day, I'm making one fifty, two hundred. Big money for a kid from the countryside.

One night, I'm visiting my family, Remy Ortiz walks in. My best friend from the barrio. By now he's with the Nice People, I haven't seen him in over a year. And he's got a gun. He says, I was sent here to tell you, what you're doing is wrong, and if it doesn't stop, I have to make you stop. He meant the rough shit. He says I shouldn't be doing dirty work for a criminal boss. Luis.

I had no idea it mattered to them, what happened on the farm. I wasn't seeing the big picture yet.

But a word to the wise. I got the hell out of Dodge. I had a little bit of money, I went to Manila and bought a share in a taxi. All the time, Luis stayed in touch. He's always got this or that he needs doing in Manila. Not rough, necessarily, but where you have to trust the guy who's doing it for you. It was money for me. I didn't mind. Even if I'd wanted to say no, I never would have. He was still my *amo*.

I met my wife in the taxi. An airport fare to the Hilton. We got married in city hall, Manila, we went back to the States together, I got my green card, I got divorced. I stayed. I didn't hang around with homesick Filipinos, either. No way. I dived in with both feet. I learned to walk the walk and talk the talk. I was an American!

Inside of a year I was speaking English like I'd been weaned on it. I loved the food, I loved the life. America is so easy. But even in America, Luis kept in touch. Through my family, you see. He wants this and that. Ship him a color TV and a microwave. Parts for his Jeep. One time I went to a gamecock farm in Alabama, picked out a dozen fighting roosters, air-freighted them over.

In '84 he came and set up a bank account. He made me a co-signer, so I could draw on it when I had to pay for this stuff. He wanted something, he'd transfer the money there, I'd take it out. By now I had my own little sidelines working. Luis was starting to be a pain. Besides, I'd had a chance to think things over. I'm realizing, the situation on the hacienda, he's getting rich while people like my father are working themselves to death.

But what could I do? He had my family. It was weird, walking around in the States, knowing that some son of a bitch had owned me since day one. Here I was in the Land of the Free, thousands of miles away from him, and he still had a piece of my ass.

Then my father did die, just plain worn out, fifty-two years old. The more I thought about it the more pissed I got.

I went over for the funeral. Luis told me, buy a couple of pistols and bring 'em over. He said not to worry about customs, he had it fixed. He did. A little later, the same thing, only it's not two pistols, it's ten, and ten shotguns, and a couple of Uzis. He was selling some and keeping a few for himself. These planters love their guns.

That was the year sugar prices went through the floor. I came over, I went to the hacienda, people were starving to death. Not my family, I saw to that, but our friends, neighbors. It was never that bad before. Babies with swollen bellies, the whole sick scene. Luis had to cut way back. Instead of a new Mercedes that year, he only bought a Cadillac. I was at the point, whenever I was around him I'd have to take a shower after I got home. It was like swimming in a cesspool. But I still didn't know what to do about him. Even after I bought the house for my mother, he could still get to her. And there's all the brothers and sisters, the aunts and uncles and such.

If I was alone in life, it'd be different. I'd have told him to screw himself a long time ago. But those people are in me, they *are* me, and as long as he's got them, he's got Lito.

Three months ago, he calls, he wants me to buy guns. Fucking assault rifles. It's all set up, where I'm supposed to go, what I'm supposed to do. He wired sixty thousand to the account. That's how confident he felt, to put that kind of money in my hands. He knows I'm not going anywhere.

I thought he was bringing the guns in to sell. Everybody from the farm is writing, telling me that Luis has seen the light, no more rough shit, he's treating them decent, he's actually paying off the NPA. Luis is bitching to me, how much it's costing him to stay straight with the Nice People. It didn't sound like Luis. But who am I to say?

I did what he said. He could have done it himself, but I don't think he wanted his name connected with it. All right, I've done my job, I figure I'm free and clear. Then he tells me, I should come over ahead of the guns. He needs me here. I should plan to stay two, three years. I'm going to be working for him again. Not asking me. Telling me, I'm going to be working for him again. He says like before, only more so.

Then I know, Luis may be paying, but he's still fighting. I didn't want to get involved in it. I also knew, as long as I was alive, I'd be doing exactly what he told me. That's when it came to me, what I had to pull off. If Luis wasn't going to let me go till the day I died, I'd have to die.

It wouldn't be the first time, right? Not that he'd be as easy as an insurance company.

If I had to die I might as well do it right. I cashed out everything over there, I took out the policy, I brought over a new car and a couple of pistols. One of 'em I sold. The other one I was going to keep. But Luis's boy saw it, Baby, and he loved it. He took it. Promised to pay me, but I knew he never would. The son of a bitch just stole it.

Luis told me what he had in mind for me. There was

this bunch of crazies living up in the hills, the Holy Bloods, fighting the NPA with nothing but knives. He said they deserved to get the odds evened up some. Bullshit. He wanted them to take charge of his haciendas. The NPA are telling him how to run his farms, how to treat his people, and he's not going to let that happen. Under no circumstances.

Other planters raise their private armies, they tell the world about it. A guy hires three or four security guards, all of a sudden he's calling himself a warlord, he's begging the Sparrows to put him on their hit list. Luis is much too slick for that. He keeps quiet, he still pays his NPA dues, he stays off the Top Forty.

Me, I was supposed to join a new goon squad that he was forming up. Heavyweight stuff this time. He mentioned names that I knew from before. I told him I wanted to spend a couple days looking up old friends. No problem. He never worried about me—he always had me, any time he wanted.

I looked up old friends, all right. A few years, Remy has turned into Kumander Rocky. A goddamn folk hero. Give me a break. We got together. I told him what I needed, what was going on, but I don't think he believed me. Then the guns started to show up. The S.D. gets sixty new AK's, Yugo-made, they're kicking ass all over the place. Including the hacienda, *my barrio*.

Now Remy is ready to help. They have a shootout with the S.D., they recover a body. Remy's boys carry it into the cane outside Lanao. I show up with rum, get half the barrio drunk, I know everybody's going to be sleeping real hard. I have the empty hut all picked out. They haul in the body, we torch the hut, I head up to the hills with Remy and his bunch.

I'm dead. Everybody knows I'm dead. Best of all, Luis knows I'm dead. I'm so dead, I can't believe there's any problem with the insurance. It's the last thing I'm worried about. But the first insurance guy shows up from the

States. I didn't even know about him until he was dead. Then you. Jesus. And more people dying.

It was supposed to be a bonus, fifty thousand, icing on the cake. I told Precy before I left the States, anything happens to me, I want you to use the money to get Mama and the family out of the province. Everybody, right through second cousins. Buy a couple big houses, maybe in Cebu. A few hectares, two or three little businesses to keep money coming in. It would be enough, fifty thousand. Over here fifty thousand dollars is a fucking miracle. It will buy you anything. Including freedom.

He said he'd been captured in the NPA camp when it was overrun. One of the vigilantes was from Lanao, recognized him, and knew that Luis would want him.

"A good thing, too," he said. "Otherwise I'd be in little pieces now. It might still happen, but, hey, small favors."

"Nobody knew you were alive?"

"The Nice People, that's all."

"And Nonoy."

"Never. He'd be the last I'd tell."

I told him about the note that said LITO LIVES. To understand that he had to hear the rest, so I told him about the names, the girls, Father Dado and Collins, through to Bembo. I talked a long time, a ghastly recounting in the damp darkness.

He took it with an equanimity that shocked me at the time. I suppose I understand now. Those were my deaths. I had claimed them for myself, felt the hurt, nursed the anger. But when deaths pile on deaths, miseries upon miseries, who can assign any of them a particular outrage, bestow on any one a special grief? Who is entitled?

And when I had finished, and it still seemed incomplete, I told him about Vangie and me, up to Rosita telling me to go away. He listened hard without interrupting.

"The girls," he said when I was finished, "the names, I

don't know. Why he would want the priest killed, I have no idea. It could just be personal. Hacenderos take small matters very seriously. I think it must warp 'em, to have things their own way all the time, all their lives. That's how it's been for Luis. You can't psych him out. He's got his own way of looking at things.

"I can tell you, Nonoy didn't know I was alive. He wasn't even guessing. That was just his way of getting you to stay around. You were his wild card, man, you were his great white hope. He didn't want to lose you."

"But he couldn't tell me?"

"That's exactly it, he couldn't. If he was my father, I'd be ashamed, too, I wouldn't be able to tell anybody. And with him it's even more complicated. Luis isn't just his daddy; he's Nonoy's *amo*, too.

"Think about it, what it must be like. He's got Correon blood in him, so Luis hauls him out of the barrio and dresses him up. But he's got the barrio too. Every time he comes up there, he knows it's in him, but he's not part of it any more. On the other hand Luis doesn't treat him like a son. So he's everywhere, he's nowhere, he's got two families, he has no family. For sure, I wouldn't want to be sleeping in his skin. You have to understand his position. Like you have to understand Vangie's position, if she tells you to take a hike."

"Vangie and I have plans." The present tense sounded empty.

"No doubt you did. I'm sure she'd be with you if she could. But if Luis found out about you two, and he tells her she's not going anyplace, and she knows that he's got her mother—I mean he has *got* her mother—then plans mean nothing. She's not even gonna fight it."

"What?" I said. "I just go home, forget it? Nothing's changed?"

"That's the hardest thing for Americans to understand. That some things can't be changed. Actually in your case the situation isn't necessarily so bad."

"How is that?"

"Your only problem is to get rid of Luis. And it happens, the way he's been acting, people are lining up for the chance."

· 28 ·

Next day the sun unloaded on the canvas. The wet floor cooked with an odor of compost. A guard stood outside, a silhouette on the fabric. Lito and I sat pouring sweat, inhaling the miasma, motionless except to shift our cramped arms.

We spent the whole day this way, then another night. In the afternoon of the second day—Saturday—the rain came again, a few minutes of thunderstorm that soaked but did not cool.

The camp seemed sluggish until evening, when we heard more movement, shouts that sounded like orders, the click and snap of magazines and firing bolts, the squeak of cartridge belts. They were leaving the camp; from the sound of it, by squads, about ten at a time.

Not long afterward our guard and another rifleman came down. They had been in twice during the day, to loosen the ropes and hold rifles on us while we drank water and ate some rice and voided into a bucket. Now they came and pulled us to our feet.

"We're out of here," Lito said.

They sent us up the steps.

"I want you to know," he said when we were outside, "when you get to the States, you should do what you have to do about the insurance."

"I will."

"So. What are you going to do?"

· 241 ·

"I don't know," I said. Wondering if I would get the chance.

"Remember, I could just as well be dead. It might be more convenient to *think* of me as dead."

He was laughing when he said it.

The guards brought us over to where eight more riflemen were standing, waiting, beneath the guard tower. With five of them in front of us and five behind, we walked out of the camp, through the cogon and down the widening valley.

The air was torpid. The moon was fat, fuzzy behind clouds. In low spots the mud sucked at my shoes. On the steep slopes I grabbed brush and trees to keep from slipping, but fell anyway, and before we had gone far my clothes were soaked and smeared.

After about an hour the clouds slid free. We were going in the same direction we had come the night before; not the same trail, but from the top of a ridge I could recognize a valley below, and another ridge embracing it on that side. I could see trees and a few huts and the silver rectangles of the paddies. We dropped down through the forest, down two hillsides into rolling cane. Through fields, through fields, the cane leaves making ticks and swishes until we briefly broke out into the clear. That's when I heard the low coursing sound of the generator at the hacienda bungalow.

It was Saturday night. I knew where we were going.

Another wide field. The cane here was nearly as tall as a house. The generator's drumming seemed to center itself directly in front of us, when gunfire grumbled distantly to our left.

"Curba," one of the riflemen said behind us.

"Curba, that's a sitio," Lito said. "Like Lanao, but smaller, couple of miles away."

"Part of the hacienda?"

"It sure is."

The grumbling stopped. Almost at once a couple of

short bursts pricked the silence on our right, much closer. Lanao.

We emerged from the end of the long row. Above us were stars and black sky again. The bungalow sat on the hill. There were riflemen at the foot of the knoll, others behind clumps of bamboo. Orlando was waiting at the first of the stone steps that notched up the incline.

He went to Lito first.

He said, "Compadre. Very stupid," and cuffed Lito on the side of the face with a soft swat that was not soft enough to be friendly. He said a few words, and two of the riflemen held Lito by the elbows and took him around the knoll, in the direction of the caretakers' cottage. The door was closed. Lamps burned behind the curtains.

Orlando was unsnapping a pocket knife when he came to me. He walked around to my back. He didn't touch me except to hold my arms as he slipped the blade between my wrists and yanked it upward. The ropes fell apart.

He said, "Next time, my friend," and gestured up the hill.

As I climbed, the rifles sounded again in Curba, an irritated mutter that quickly died. I stopped at the top of the knoll and looked back. A ruddy glow bulged above the horizon, out where the first shots had come.

The Mercedes and the white sedan I had seen behind Danny Boy's were parked beside the bungalow. A flag-stone walk brought us around to the front, where four bodyguards lounged. One of them was a kid cradling a shotgun. A tall kid with gaunt cheeks and a dirty bandage on his right arm. He smirked when he saw me. One hand came up to his forehead, and he made a motion like tipping his hat. Though he wore no hat. I was past him, opening the door, when I understood. The hat was Bembo's straw fedora.

The riflemen stayed outside while I went in, out of the night and into the incandescent glare, the eerie chill. The buffet table was laden. Penney stood at the table, holding a plate. So did Dalzell. His presence seemed natural. More than natural: inevitable. I imagined Vangie's passport in his hands. Making sure that friends stay friends.

Vilma and Hector carried in the tub of iced beer. I wondered who was in the cottage. They went out, and it was just three Americans in the room.

Dalzell pulled a bottle out of the tub, popped the top and crossed the room to bring it to me.

"You smell like a dead rat," he said. When I didn't take the bottle, he drank from it.

"You knew her," I said.

"Once I saw the picture, uh-huh. I met her once or twice right in this very place."

"You told Correon."

"I shit you not, Jack, this job's nothing but a juggling act. Try to give to one without taking away from the other. I had to cover myself."

"Anyway, it's all over," Penney said.

"What does that mean?"

"You're going home," said Dalzell. "Embassy plane's at the airport. We got you booked on United out of Manila, first flight tomorrow morning."

I said, "I want to talk to Vangie."

Penney piped, "No can do. I'm afraid she's a write-off."

"Why make it hard on everybody?" Dalzell said.

I went to a chair across the room and let myself down in it. I didn't want to speak right away. I had to get something solid under me.

"Don't fight it," said Penney. "This is a done deal."

"What's going to happen to her?"

"I didn't ask."

"He doesn't even want her."

Dalzell said, "I didn't think he would—he's got a million of 'em. Really, when I told him, it was just a courtesy call. When he found out she was splitting, though, she started to look real good to him again. Ain't that the way?"

I held the arms of the chair.

"I'm not leaving until I see her. You can't make me go."

"You got to be joking," Dalzell said. "This isn't a question of can we make you, it's what happens if you don't. You have a guy extremely pissed off at you, he isn't somebody you want to be on the bad side of. As a personal favor to Rick here and me, he's letting go of you. He doesn't owe us any favors, believe me, it's all the other way around. A personal favor, though, he's letting you go. That's as of this minute. Subject to change."

I said, "Do you realize what he's into? His people killed Collins."

"Not according to the reports," Penney said.

"The reports are a bad joke. Correon owns Orlando, and Orlando is running a bunch of killers. They murdered Collins and they murdered a priest. They tried to blame Collins on the Sparrows." I kept going, running out of breath. "With the priest they tried to make him out to be a communist, but he wasn't even close. He died because he found out something about girls, prostitutes, four of them that disappeared from a club in Bacolod."

"Fascinating," Dalzell said.

"Ask him," I said, gesturing to Penney. "He knows, he's in on it."

"Fuck you," Penney said.

"Furthermore, you two and Luis and his scum have got a war going over here."

"This is right by the numbers," Penney said quickly, with some heat. "It's absolutely legal. Socorro is a private enterprise. We don't wage war. Advice and assistance, that's all. That's not breaking anybody's laws."

Dalzell was much calmer, almost bemused.

"C'mon, don't get righteous on me," he said.

Penney said, "I'll do anything to keep our boys from getting in a real war over here. But maybe you're not enough of an American to see it that way."

"No, Jack's okay," Dalzell said, easy and smug. "He's

just lovesick. He has his nose stuck in a sweet little honey pot, and it's got him all turned around. It happens to the best of us."

I held the chair and tasted a black, impotent fury. I couldn't move. I couldn't think of moving. I saw that Penney was distracted, alert to something outside: gunfire, rattling again in Lanao.

"The hacienda is a nest," Penney said when I noticed it. "Commie Central. The G's have been using it for one big safe house. Harvest's almost over, Luis can do some housecleaning."

"Can we go now, Jack?" Dalzell said. "Please?"

"I want to talk to Vangie."

"God *damn*," Penney said.

Footsteps came down the hall, into the *sala*. Baby and Nonoy. Baby put his clutch bag down on the buffet table and began to fill a plate.

"You'd better get him out of here," he said.

"We're trying," Penney said.

"Yes, Jack, right away," Nonoy said. His voice had an urgent quaver. He was wound tight.

Baby took his plate over to a window across the room. He said, "He should see this. Maybe it'll light a fire under him."

I went with Dalzell and Penney. Nonoy came too— reluctantly, I thought—and we looked out together, down to the bottom of the hill.

Correon was leaving the caretakers' cottage. He had a pistol in his hand. Lito Sanchez was standing in the open area between the cottage and the foot of the hill. The two vigilante guards stood nearby. Correon walked up to him and spoke. Lito spoke. A broad grin grew on his face; I recognized it.

Correon clubbed the grin with his pistol. The force drove Lito to one knee.

Lito stood again. The grin was still there. Correon began shouting; ranting. His arms waved as he shouted, and the gun waved, too. He walked twice around Lito, still shouting. Lito wouldn't look at him, and his amusement wouldn't go away.

It seemed to infuriate Correon. He stopped pacing. He shouted even louder. His head bobbed as he spat what had to be curses. Lito wouldn't look at him. Correon pulled the slide of the pistol and snapped it back. That loads the chamber and cocks the trigger. It makes a loud, purposeful noise that will get anybody's attention. Lito didn't flinch.

I heard Nonoy's breath catch beside me as Correon put the muzzle against Lito's head. Lito's grin was determined. Correon took the gun away and stepped back. I thought he was finished. Abruptly he stepped up again and put the gun to Lito's head and fired. Lito jerked and collapsed.

Nonoy grunted, like taking a punch in the stomach.

That's when the shooting started, in the field behind the bungalow. Maybe they were expecting the signal of a single shot, and Luis's seemed right. They opened with the popping of two or three rifles at first, a series of quick reports, automatic fire. This was out in front of us as we watched, not in Lanao but much closer, on the other side of the bungalow. Quickly the two or three guns became eight and ten and more.

"Armalites," said Baby. "NPA."

We crouched at the window, Dalzell saying shit, shit, shit. I looked over the sill. The two guards had flattened on the ground; one of them steadied his gun on Lito's chest. Correon was walking quickly to the shelter of the cottage. The two riflemen cut loose long strings of fire.

Beyond where Lito sprawled was a band of landscaped grass and shrubs. Beyond that was a stubble field eighty to a hundred yards wide, a minor patch where an enterprising overseer had shoehorned a few extra rows of cane. At the other side of the stubble was cogon and brush and bamboo and scrubby trees, the riot of growth that explodes on any untended ground in Negros. The guerrillas were attacking from there: I could see the bursts of orange flame out beyond the stubble, star-shaped flashes that winked and were gone. I got a quick vision of guerrillas trickling down out of the hills, drawn to the generator's Saturday-night drumming, come down to kill.

Bullets thumped the turf halfway up the knoll.

Four more vigilantes, then three more, ran from around the back side. They took cover where they could find it, and began firing over the stubble. Correon left the cottage and started around the side of the knoll. I watched him until he was out of sight. When I looked again, one of the vigilantes was on his back, mouth agape, staring at the sky with eyes that didn't blink.

The door opened. Orlando said, "Time to go."

"Yeah, I think I've seen enough for one night," Dalzell said. He stood up to leave, and a bullet shattered the window above Baby, spraying glass across the *sala*.

"The lights," Orlando said. "Stay down, are you crazy?" He reached around to hit the switch, and the *sala* went black.

We moved low in the darkness, scuffling blind. The buffet table got bumped hard. Platters crashed to the floor. Dalzell and Penney were out first, and I followed them into the moonlight. Baby got to the door and said, "Shit, my gun," and duckwalked in again.

Nonoy came out. He sat with his back against the door post. His tension had resolved itself into something else: he seemed almost distant. There might have been no gunfire, no guerrillas. I watched him for a few seconds before he noticed me. He said, "Don't worry. Soon this will all be over."

It sounded absurd at the time. I wondered if he was quietly losing his grasp.

Orlando was at the Mercedes, shouting into the radio mike. The firing was louder, hammering of AK's and hard pops of M-16's; the pops were closer than they had been, more insistent. The blister of light pulsed in the sky above

Curba, and over toward Lanao I could see flames through the trees.

"My gun." Baby was inside, groping on the floor where the food had spilled. "What happened to my fucking gun?"

Correon came up the back side of the knoll. He stopped at the Mercedes and spoke to Orlando, and while the radio squawked he pointed up the long driveway that tracked to the road. More vigilantes—I could make out the AK's—were emerging from the field east of the drive.

Dalzell said, "Why don't we just haul our asses out of here?"

But as the new squad came into view, more orange stars winked from behind the mango trees that lined the drive. Some of the vigilantes dived, some fell.

"That was battalion headquarters," Correon said loudly. "Help is on the way. Fifteen minutes."

"So it'll be thirty anyway," Penney said.

"What if it is? Thirty minutes is nothing."

"We have the high ground," Orlando said.

"I'm thinking that we might make for the trees," Dalzell said. He was looking at the forest where the gully ran through, the path to Lanao. "Jack and Rick and me. They don't especially care about us."

"Fine," Correon said. He was miffed.

"Unless you think we can help you here."

"I wouldn't presume. 'Noy, go hide our friends. I'm sorry, I can't give you any guns. We need all our weapons here."

"Oh that's all right," Dalzell said.

"I'd rather stay," Nonoy said.

"Go. Stay with them until it's over. It would be a shame if they got lost."

"I can help here."

"I said go."

When we left them, Correon was yelling at the vigilantes in the road, and Orlando had taken the bodyguards around the other side.

We went down the knoll, to the path and into the trees. Right away the frenzy became more distant; the tall growth smothered sound. It cut off moonlight, too, but it was a comforting cloak, to be out of sight of the fighting. Every step carried us away from it.

Nonoy was agile on the path. He had grown up here, I reminded myself. He stopped twice to let us catch up. The second time he halted at the edge of the forest, where the gully met the cane field: I remembered the tunnel through the stalks. But in the last week the cane had been cut. The field was stubble, all the way to the back corner of Lanao.

Nonoy was looking that way when we caught up to him. Several huts were burning; the fire turned his face vermilion.

"Too far," he said. He turned at once and led us back up the path, a short distance to a spot where the gully was deep and narrow. A natural trench. We slid down inside and found ourselves standing neck high in it. We were hidden from the tumult, safe from anything but a fateful wild bullet. A few minutes later a squad of vigilantes came up the path from Lanao, ran past and up to the bungalow without realizing we were there.

Dalzell and Penney sat glum at the bottom of the gully. Nonoy hiked himself up the side and rested his arms at the lip; I joined him up there. Brush grew between the gully and the trail, a screen that didn't block our view entirely. I could still see up and down the path, but the path was empty. The forest was empty, except for the noise from outside. The firing had stopped in Lanao and over in Curba. Up toward the knoll it had an acrimonious rhythm, rising and cascading, a tempest that couldn't sustain itself. Inevitably it would dwindle to a gun or two, or to nothing. There would be silence; once the noise lapsed so long, I thought it might be finished. But each time it picked up again, bitter as before.

Nonoy turned inward once more, and I did, too. The forest was a private place. I thought of Vangie and felt my longing. I thought of deaths and betrayals and unkept promises and humiliations. I felt them deeply; later I would be astonished at how clear and whole my emotions were, not just that night but all those bright days and murky nights. So unlike me. They were never more clear and whole than in the minutes when I lay along the side of the gully. I can be snappish, but I need time to work up a good head of anger. In the forest I had time. I had never hated, never had reason to hate; but in the forest I found reason. All this, with the muted sounds of violence in my ears, murderous and suggestive.

Thirty minutes, Penney had said. Maybe—hard to tell. But however long it was in coming, it came sudden and shocking. First it was helicopters, two of them, racketing in from the east. One launched a parachute flare from high above the bungalow. The forest became a black and white mosaic, shadow and light swaying as the flare rocked slowly to earth. The second chopper swung in low over-head, shaking the trees and raining brass shells from the machine gun that fired out of one hatch. It had hardly passed when a T-28 attack plane ripped overhead, bellow-ing, guns clattering, so low it shook trees and earth.

Through breaks in the forest canopy I watched the helicopters rake slowly back and forth over the battlefield, lacing down tracer streams. The T-28 flew a pendulum path, swooping low to fire, climbing and turning and swooping low again: the sweeping of a scythe. On the ground the firing was scant and suddenly irrelevant.

Dalzell and Penney were up at the edge of the ditch now, whooping and shouting.

"This is the World Series, man, this is goddamn Indy and the Derby." Dalzell was shaking my shoulders, yelling into my face. "This is the freaking Super Bowl, baby, and we've got sideline passes."

One of the choppers broke off and climbed over the

trees. It released a flare, a sound like putting out a match in a glass of water. The chopper sauntered and released another flare, almost over our heads. Then a red one, as it hovered at the edge of the forest. The helicopter began to descend.

"Pickup time," Dalzell said. "Curb service, can you beat it?"

I heard voices on the path, up near the top. Voices I knew.

Dalzell and Penney didn't notice; they were climbing out with all their noise.

"Let's go," Penney said.

Nonoy had noticed. Through all the shaking and the roaring, his face hadn't cracked. His face . . .

"In a minute," I said. "I want to watch."

"You want to *watch?*"

"It isn't over yet."

"You watch. We're skedaddling," Dalzell said. They were walking through the brush. It was above their knees. "The chopper won't wait."

"It'll wait. Luis isn't there yet."

"That's all right. First one in gets the seat by the window."

"I'll be there."

"You got guts, Jack, I have to hand it to you." He was yelling at me from the path. Penney was beside him. "No kidding, I never saw anything like it."

They ran. The chopper was settling into the field; I could tell from the noise and the dust. Four men had appeared up the path. The second flare wiped them with light and shadow through the trees. It was Baby, Luis, Orlando with an AK, and the gaunt-faced killer carrying a shotgun. They were walking single file in that order, coming our way, briskly but by no means in a panic. The chopper would wait.

Nonoy was looking up at them. Staring. He didn't seem

to know I was there. He pulled himself out of the ditch and crouched in the brush.

He reached under his shirt, his loose cotton *barong*, and pulled out Baby's .45. It was the gun I had held and fired at Correon's backyard range.

The brush hid Nonoy. I was in the gully, almost completely out of sight. The four of them came walking, tramping. Nonoy's hand kneaded the .45. They were walking toward us, yards distant, feet distant; walking; passing.

Nonoy stood.

He didn't bring the gun up; kept it at his side. I watched this over the tops of the brush, in the swinging light of the flare. The four of them had passed us already, but Nonoy's rising stopped them and swung their heads around. The kid with the shotgun, at the end of the line, was now closest to him.

Luis said, " 'Noy."

Nonoy began to raise the gun, much too slowly. He got it up and held it at the end of his rigid arm, as if it were a viper. He had probably never held a gun. He swung the gun past three of them, and it seemed to settle on Baby.

Luis said, " 'Noy."

Baby said, "Shit," and bolted down the path. The pistol in Nonoy's hands swung to follow him, and Baby ran, and Nonoy kept pointing the pistol but didn't fire.

His face was contorted. He was in agony.

Luis raised his own gun, and it roared. Nonoy flew off his feet and did a dead man's pratfall back into the gully, splayed out beside me.

Baby kept running down the path.

Nobody had seen me yet through the brush. Luis said a word, and gaunt-face came toward the gully. He came closer, using his shotgun to part the undergrowth. He bent and picked up Nonoy's pistol where it had fallen, and put it in his pocket and kept coming. With a look of mild curiosity and contempt, he stepped to the edge of the gully—the shotgun nearly brushing my head—and looked down to see the body. And grunted with surprise when he stared down into my face.

I grabbed the shotgun, pulled hard. His grunt drew out, he fought for his balance. With one hand I held the barrel out away from me, and hooked the other around his ankles, and I brought him down.

He toppled headfirst into the gully, and we both fell on the body. I reached for the pistol, on his right side, and he punched and kicked. The shotgun roared once into the air, and we kept grappling, and the pistol flopped out of his pocket. Onto Nonoy's chest, sticky with warm blood.

Heavy strides were breaking the brush, coming on, closer. Orlando. I grabbed the pistol. Gaunt-face kneed me and lunged for the pistol.

I squeezed the trigger. Nothing. I thumbed the safety—still on—*Nonoy poor fool*—squeezed—the gun roared and jumped—and gaunt-face's limbs shot out in convulsion, and he fell back.

"You fucker," Orlando said at the edge of the gully.

I turned my head to look at him. I could see him, above me and to my right. The AK was already pointed down into the gully, and though I started to bring the pistol around, it was with painful slowness, painful deadly slowness, and while I swung the pistol up and around he had only to tip the rifle down a few degrees more, and he did, and I was looking up into the muzzle, a couple of feet away.

His eyes met mine. A rifle hammered, a burst, and Orlando seemed to dive into the gully, a sudden and curious dive, headlong, the AK leaving his hands and sailing. His face was the first part of him to thud into the earth. He lay prostrate. Even in the night I could see dark rosettes of blood blooming on his shirt.

I peeked over the edge of the gully, and what I saw made me push over the edge and stand, to see it better.

The boy Alex crouched about fifty yards up the trail,

holding an M-16 rifle that was nearly as long as he was tall. It was trained on Luis Correon, holding his pistol. The barrio boy and his *amo* both glanced over once at me, then looked back at each other.

Baby was running down the path without looking back, lumbering toward the noise of the helicopter.

Correon spoke a word. What he said I'll never know, and anyway it was probably less important than the way he said it, with a sneer. And maybe that didn't matter, either; maybe nothing he might have said, no way of saying it, could have saved him.

Anyway, he spoke a sneering word, and Alex touched off a burst that nearly cut him in half, starting at his groin and stitching upward through his face as he flew backward.

Baby kept running without looking back. Alex leveled the rifle down the trail, but the trail dipped and bore Baby out of sight.

Alex lowered the rifle and walked down the trail to Correon. He stood over the body and stared down at it for a few seconds. He was not angry, not repelled by the gore; curious, mostly, I thought. A few seconds was all he needed. As if the body wasn't even there, he picked up the pistol and stuck it in his pants. His legs made quick little steps over to the gully, where he climbed down, slung the AK, held the shotgun. He put his hand out for the .45. I let him have it.

Down the trail, out of sight, Dalzell and Penney were shouting my name.

"Come dis way," Alex said.

He climbed up the back side of the gully and pushed into the trees. I followed him. Carrying half his weight in guns, he ducked and slipped through undergrowth that stood above his shoulders. I barely managed to follow.

The firing had stopped everywhere. I didn't hear the plane anymore. One helicopter was still on the ground; the other seemed to be loitering above the knoll.

We had gone a couple of hundred yards off the trail when Alex stopped beside a matted tangle of vines draped over a fallen coco log. He pushed the vines aside. He brushed dirt and lifted the top of a crate that had been buried flush with the ground. Expertly he dropped the magazines out of each gun and emptied each chamber. He laid the guns and the ammunition in the crate, replaced the top, covered it with dirt, and put the mat of vines back where it had been.

He took me out of the forest and into a cane field. We cut across the grain of the rows, then followed one row until it ended.

We emerged near the end of the long driveway. The bungalow was to our right, chalky under the moon. Dolorous moans wafted across the clearing. Between the cane field and the knoll I counted nine fallen figures, a couple of them writhing, the others still. Vigilantes and communists, I couldn't tell the difference. We walked down the driveway, away from the bodies and the moaning. We walked out into the road, into one of the most amazing sights I have ever beheld.

The road was full of people. Lanao was in flames, and the people were pouring out of it, hundreds of them, bringing what they could in rice sacks and boxes and in their arms. What struck me wasn't so much their numbers as their compliance with disaster. They walked slowly, wearily, mostly with eyes downcast, as if shamed by what had befallen them. As if they had done this before and expected to do it again. They were silent; there were many children, but not a cry or whimper. I could hear the scuff of rubber sandals, the snort of a pig being led on a rope. I could hear a young woman's voice softly inquiring: "Rosita? Rosita Flores? Rosita?"

It was Vangie. She was standing by the side of the road, looking like the daughter of the barrio that she was. Hector and Vilma were with her. She gave Alex a hug that he endured with a look of distaste. Your parents are up the road, she said. With me her control was impeccable. Under the scrutiny of her neighbors, and conscious as ever of propriety, she gave me only the tips of her fingers to hold. I held them for a long time. I was holding them when her mother shuffled along, carrying the Santo Niño and her housedresses in a string bag.

We joined the exodus down to Hermosa. In Hermosa the town council had set aside a couple of vacant lots for use by evacuees from the rural barrios and sitios. In Hermosa they were accustomed to this kind of thing.

We got there around dawn. The money that I was going to give to the Nobles brothers I gave to Rosita instead. Vangie said it would be much more than enough for a furnished room in town, and that a furnished room in town was much more than she expected.

Go, go, the old lady told us.

From Palo we caught the express jeepney straight into Bacolod. We were on *Princess of Negros* when she sailed that noon.

· 29 ·

I expected Vangie to loathe the duplex with its fog and bland mornings. To my astonishment she nestled in. I still have moments of joyous surprise when I find her sitting with me at dinner or beside me in bed; none is so shocking, though, as the sight of her walking the beach in a heavy wool jacket, out with gulls and seals and hissing wind. I think the grayness appeals to her.

We were married in our living room, a month and a day after we arrived from Manila. Not long afterward, she returned from one of her sandy treks and announced that she wanted a graduate degree. She is pregnant now with our first child, and in graduate school. I'm still with the company. When I went back to work I told Gilsa that I couldn't add much to the P.C. investigation of Collins's murder. I also filed a report that the death certificate supporting Precy Allen's claim was genuine. *In the opinion of this investigator . . .* It seemed fair, and far less complicated that way. I told Gilsa, Truth's the truth. He wasn't happy to have spent three weeks and five thousand dollars to hear that, but I was back in his graces soon enough. I am good at my job.

I have never told Vangie what happened along the forest path. Correon's death, attributed to the NPA, was in the Manila papers the day we docked. She may have read it, perhaps not. In any case she has never mentioned him, and neither have I. She did tell me that she had been in the caretakers' house that night, and witnessed Lito's execution. Otherwise, we have never discussed the cruel hours between our kiss at the threshold of the hut and our reunion on the Hermosa road.

Acquaintances ask: Has she adjusted? The easiest answer is that Vangie would never languish anywhere. She is happy, and she belongs. She has learned to drive the freeways. She reads food labels and has been properly indoctrinated in the hazards of cholesterol and saturated fats. At movies she laughs in all the right places. She fits as if she were born here. Actually the fit is even closer than that—she has a newcomer's relish for our comforts and opportunities.

Yet there are moments when I know that she is not one of us, and never will be.

I have to go back to my last full day in the Philippines, the day the ship docked in Manila. We had taken the ferry because nobody would look for us there. For the same reason, we checked into a cheap pension on Mabini Street. I still had a lock box at the Silahis, though; I wanted to empty it and arrange our flights. It was early afternoon. We needed clothes. Vangie left to shop while

I went on my errands. I knew she wouldn't be back for two or three hours.

I finished at the Silahis in five minutes; the travel agent was almost that fast in snapping up seats on a flight the next morning.

The agency was in the ground floor of an office building on the boulevard. I came out knowing that I had our future in my shirt pocket. Knowing that in a day I was gone and might never be back.

The building had a doorman. I stood with him in the heavy heat, looking out at the bay and the beggars along the breakwater. The pension on Mabini Street was two blocks away.

I said to the doormen, "Do you know a place called Tondo?"

"Yes sir, Tondo Manila. Near by the North Harbor."

So we had gone through it when we left the docks. A cramped, shabby district.

"Right across the river."

"Yes sir, other side of the Pasig River."

Twenty pesos, a few minutes.

"Taxi, sir?" Looking for the tip. I said yes, and he whistled one into the curb.

Earlier we had only skirted the edges of Tondo. The 400 block of Jison was in its squalid bowels, an amorphous clutter of shops and shacks. Burning garbage fumed in a heap at the intersection; kids poked sticks at a dog's rigid corpse. Four nineteen was a beauty salon. A sunless alley-way, barely wider than my shoulders, led to the back. I heard Sinatra, faintly. Chicago, Chicago.

A closed door, four steps down. On the door, scratched into the paint: KNOCK TO ENTRANCE.

I went down and knocked. Somebody opened it, and Sinatra got louder as I stepped in. A mattress lay in the middle of a basement room. A man and a woman were humping on the mattress, to an audience of about a dozen men who gawked from chairs against the walls.

Around the back of the door a woman said, "Forty pesos, sir."

"I'm looking for Dolores Rosario."

She said, "I am she."

She was about Vangie's age, and she was gorgeous. A cascade of long black curls, the big eyes of a fawn, perfect skin, perfect teeth. Under a thin bathrobe she was naked and womanly-slim. It was the kind of beauty that doesn't have to try.

"A man named Nonoy Paloma sent me to see you."

"Nonoy is my friend."

"I think we're supposed to talk about something that happened at a place called Danny Boy's."

With hope and caution she said, "You know about this?"

"Some of it. I think girls have been dying."

She said, "Girls? More than one?"

"Lorna Rodriguez. Alma Solano. Tetchie Salvador. Vivian Maamo. I think. Does this mean anything to you?"

Each one seemed to strike her harder. She put her hands to her face.

"The monster," she said.

"Correon."

She nodded dumbly.

She let me take her gently by the elbow, to two empty chairs in a corner. Courtliness didn't seem out of place. She was no slattern.

I moved the chairs to put the mattress behind us.

We sat, and she said, "I know only Lorna. Four years ago already. I am living in Hinigaran, in the south of Negros. My husband dies, my child is hungry, I go to Bacolod—"

I said, "You went to work at Danny Boy's. You needed the money. You met Correon."

"Yes. He is a friend of Orlando. They are partners, I think. He doesn't come to the club. Orlando sends girls to him at a special house in the countryside. Nonoy brings

the girls to him. I and Lorna go there sometimes. All right?
That's life. He likes us together. He wants us to do things.
He does things to us—"

"Correon."

"He is sadist." She shifted the accent; I didn't understand right away. "One night it's different. He is angry.
Not a game. Very angry. I am tie with a rope. All right?
Lorna is tie. To me he is cruel. But I don't fight. I'm still
alive. He wants somebody to fight, I think. Lorna fights.
He kills Lorna with his hands. I'm watching. I see it. *I am
there.*"

She was daring me to challenge her.

"Some men come for Lorna—I don't know who they
are. Nonoy brings me to a doctor. He says because of what
I have seen I must leave Negros. He gives me money. He
feels bad. I know, Nonoy always likes me. He writes me
letters, even up until now. I don't know anything about
three more girls. Nonoy promise me, it will never happen
again. Suppose to be, the father is very displease."

"The father—"

"Luis. The father of Baby."

For an instant I was back in the gully beside the forest
path. Nonoy swinging the pistol past gaunt-face, past Orlando and Luis, to cover Baby.

"Baby killed her?"

"Yes. Baby. Of course Baby. He is sadist. The monster."

I collapsed inside. I guess it showed: she held my hand
in maternal comfort.

"Don't feel bad. That's life. My boy is five years old. A
beautiful boy."

Someone called her name.

She said, "Sorry. My turn." The mattress was empty.
"You go now, huh? Good-bye."

I went to the door, but I didn't leave right away. I
watched her stand at the mattress. Along one wall four
men had begun a puerile joshing among themselves. One

of them got pushed out toward the center of the room. He approached the mattress in a burlesqued swagger.

With enormous dignity she awaited him. I was aware again of her loveliness. It amazed me. The existence of it. Here.

A market exists for beauty. To be base but realistic. Prices are bid, goods are shown and find their niche; rare goods bring high sums and are consumed in stylish places. By the logic of the marketplace she didn't belong in this toilet, at forty pesos. If anyone did.

She looked directly at me as she opened the robe.

Her stomach was a mass of welts, horrible scars mottled dark and light. They wrenched the eye from her beauty. Once she exposed her midriff, she might as well have been a hag; it didn't matter any longer.

The man was affronted. He called out roughly. She didn't answer him. He took off his shirt and snapped it at the scars. His friends found this hilarious, and he began to circle the mattress, waving the shirt. She turned to keep him in front of her. In turning, her back came into my view. It was a vivid road map of mutilation. Grooved depressions scored her muscles, some straight across, others slashing at a diagonal from shoulder down into buttock. What had created them, I couldn't imagine. She had no skin: only tissue that had hardened into slick lumps.

As I was saying: Vangie. She is happy here, she is thriving, but she is not like us. She has too much in her. Most often I am aware of it when she has gotten some news from home: a letter, or the occasional Bacolod dateline on a newspaper squib. The news is almost always bad, and it always affects her. I know; she would never insult me with false good cheer.

Our private life is rich and quiet. I approach her when she is hurt. I am privileged to touch her bruises and to behold their depth. I embrace her in the night. We do not speak. I stroke her with utmost gentleness. I am reminded of grooved scars, lumpy tissue. I become aware of her pain, like an entity between us. I embrace her in the darkness, and we do not speak, but the suffering of Sugarland is a roar in our heads.

ABOUT THE AUTHOR

Phillip Finch has been a reporter for the Washington *Daily News* and the San Francisco *Examiner*. He now lives in Howard, Kansas, and is the author of nine books, including *The Reckoning*, *In a Place Dar and Secret*, and *Trespass*.